DARK DIGITAL SKY

DARK DIGITAL SKY

DARK PANTHEON SERIES BOOK 1

CARAC ALLISON

A Crime Planet Press Book
Crime Planet Press is the publishing arm of the Ethan Ellenberg
Literary Agency

ISBN-13: 978-1-68068-000-3

Chapter One

DONOR

"California Cryo Futures was different," he tells me.

"You knew that because you had donated at other sperm banks?" I work him along.

"I took the tests to donate at other places. And I was cleared to do just that at all of them. But California Cryo Futures offered more money if I signed a document guaranteeing exclusivity."

"You signed the papers. You got the money."

"Yes," he answers. "I don't know what the laws were then but I think they were working around them. I don't believe what I signed would have held up in . . . Legally."

"Did Cryo Futures pay you in cash?"

"They paid me by check for everything. It was a straight fee for my eventual donations. But for the last part of the screening process and while I was providing samples, I was hired on as a consultant."

"Did they explain how the anonymity worked?"

"There were details in the papers that I signed. They gave me a copy but I don't have it anymore."

I exhale and make this a break.

Sugarfish is a sushi restaurant in the Financial District. A sign just in the entrance politely asks patrons to take their shoes off. I made the reservation. It's close to my client's main office but not pricey enough that he'll have to keep waving to Hollywood colleagues. I arrived first and waited for him. There are no tables here. Sitting on the floor is required but we haven't had to cross our legs. They have comfortable holes for our lower limbs to dangle under the table.

We ordered black cod with miso, blue crab hand roll, salmon nigiri, seared ono.

"How many donations did you make?"

"There were three private donation contracts."

"Three pregnancies."

"I assume yes but. That's part of what I want you to investigate."

"We're getting there Mr. Robertson," I assure him.

"Sorry."

I look away and give the restaurant a scan. "Why do you think they wanted you as a donor?"

"I have a very high IQ." He states this.

"Just that?"

"Good health in the family. No mental illness."

"Do you really have a high IQ? Or did you cheat the tests?"

"Why would you ask me that?"

"I know how you made your fortune Mr. Robertson. You've been investigated by the Securities and Exchange Commission. The IRS."

"I make television and movies."

"Let's be honest with each other. You don't make anything. You steal hundreds of millions by selling the certain profits of uncertain media futures. By finding new ways that the art of character and conflict can sell the conformity and happiness of dish soap. By reducing scripts and actors and the visions of directors to assets on spreadsheets."

He glares at me. "Are you new to America?"

"It seems to me that successfully cheating an intelligence test requires intelligence. So it's not actually cheating. It's just recalibrating."

"I like that reasoning. But I didn't cheat. I scored a high IQ because I have an IQ."

"That's super. Test validity always warms my heart."

"I wasn't the Hollywood Hyena then Mr. Chalk."

"Just Chalk. Do you prefer just Hyena?"

"The Cryo Futures money was what I used to start my first company."

"That was your Faustian deal. You sold your essence and the money they gave you enabled you to become the great and powerful Hollywood Hyena. Now you want to go right back and get the kids too." I'm challenging him, trying to bring him out more. I like to know who really is hiring me and what the real reason is. I rarely figure it out at the first meeting.

"Your real name is Chaucer?"

"My father was an English Professor. I'm not. Call me Chalk."

"I've been married three times Chalk. My first wife was with me when I started to make the big money. We tried everything to conceive. I left her for a younger woman but again no luck. By my third wife I was fucking every woman I could and I never used protection. I started getting STDs. Now I have HIV."

This is not known information. He's extending me a little trust before he makes the pitch.

"I want you to find out how many children I have out there. And then I want you to find them."

"The answer could be none Mr. Robertson."

He slams the table with his palms. "You think I don't know that?!"

Heads turn, eyes search.

The Hollywood Hyena looks down and then up and wipes his weepy eyes.

"Before I agree to take this case, you have to be clear on how I work," I start. "There are five things to understand. First, I don't keep receipts. I don't waste my time or your interest drafting up stupid expense reports. I quote you a fee schedule and you pay it. If you want cheap, you dialed the wrong number. That's money.

Second, I routinely break the law to get the job done. I decide how far I go and I don't chat about it before or afterward. If I get caught nothing traces back to you and I don't know who you are. Third—notwithstanding what I just said—I do work with the LAPD and if I decide to give them a present of evidence, I will and that's my call not yours. Fourth, I will risk my ruggedly handsome face and if needed my life for you but I am not an assassin. You can't pay me enough to kill someone just on your say. Fifth and last, I've got a nice car but I am not batman. You can't pay me to kill but you can't stop me either. I don't capture the Joker just for him to escape from Arkham over and over. I debate my morals with good friends, great authors, the best shrink, and Jamesons Irish Whiskey."

"I don't know that those last two points apply to this case."

"Maybe not. But you get all five up front so you know."

"You're taking the case?"

"Yes. You already received the payment schedule. I will send you my bank account information. You set it up as a recurring transfer. And when we're done you stop it."

"Thank you."

We shake and he leaves first. I pay the bill and linger over my tea.

When I was a kid I read a lot of cyberpunk science fiction. The authors wrote about the entire planet becoming one massive sprawling city. No countries, no forests, just a global urban maze with cultures, criminals, cars all connected by streets and tunnels and glass and garbage. When that is a reality, when the population of this spinning marble is so great that everything is one grid, we will call our one city Los Angeles. Because Los Angeles is that city now: sprawling, glowing, endless. And when people around the world dream they dream of LA. It is Eliot's Unreal City, Lovecraft's Nameless City and it is my home.

Right now it is Autumn in LA.

My name is Chalk. And I have a new case.

Chapter Two

ORACLE

The first significant pay I got for PI work, I bought myself an almost new Porsche 911 Carrera S. Private detectives are supposed to drive bland cars while they're working. But in LA the iconic shape of the 911 fits in better than a Honda Civic. Whether it's a recently divorced wife's victory trophy, a screenwriter's carefully selected surrogate for a personality, an investment banker's death wish bonus or a blue blood's golf cart for the road, the shape blends in with those who have money and those who hope for money alike. I like to drive and the 911 has always been the test of a driver. Because if you're just good and know you're just good, the feedback will teach you how to carve canyon corners one white-knuckled gasp at a time. And if you're just good and think you're great it will kill you with an inside joke of physics called "snap-over-steer" that you get a millisecond before impact. With each new engineered generation the Germans say the danger of this is gone. But it's always still there at the extreme.

I've made the most of the space within the cockpit. I had them remove that silly chrono clock in the middle of the dash. In its place is an integrated radar detector/laser jammer head, no power cable dangling. Behind the steering wheel on the left, tucked up under the controls is a slim trunk tracking scanner with Bear Tracker tech. It's wired into the stereo so I can clearly hear emergency broadcasts over the roar of the flat six in the back. On a tray that slides out from under the glove box and tilts toward me is my ugly but valuable cell interceptor setup, cords to charge phones and other devices, and my MacBook Pro. When I turn slightly to the right I can type from the driver's seat.

In the glove box is the lock safe for a Glock that is not registered and has no serial number. It's standard FBI .40 issue. I carry extra clips with it and a silencer. I used an almost identical model for my first kill back when I was an agent. It didn't upset me the way it was supposed to. I went through the proper paper process, met with the assigned shrink, went for drinks with the guys, but I honestly wasn't bothered. I thought maybe I would have a delayed reaction but the angst, the regret, they just never came. Months afterward my anxiety worked on that—I felt guilty that it hadn't fucked me up. His name was Sakip and he was crazed on meth. My first bullet got him in the chest as he was coming around fast with a revolver. He dropped the gun, slowed. I shot him again in the head and he fell.

I've killed since. I will again.

In the back seat and the frunk are gym bags of other tools.

I email my client my banking information on the drive home.

My condo is just under 2,000 square feet. The space is all open concept. The living room and dining area stretch along floor to ceiling windows that open onto a curved balcony looking over the city and reflecting the screens of four televisions in a banked curve. There is a couch, chairs, a coffee table and an elliptical trainer angled from the wall. The kitchen is set apart by dark marble and chrome appliances.

I kick my shoes off.

Everything in my master bedroom is recessed behind black wood doors and black wood drawers: clothes, extra sheets, shoes. My bathroom is an altar to the many pills I take to manage my illness.

There are two other bedrooms.

One is my office: it's a small space dominated by a large straight desk. Every surface is covered by a desktop computer, a laptop, a monitor, cellphone or peripheral device. I have Windows machines, Macs, several of the wilder Linux strains, even an old box running BeOS. The room hums with fans and despite the best intentions of cable management products the walls and floor are a jungle of colored vines. Sleepy robot eyes flash red, green, amber, blue.

The other bedroom I have saved for my son. The walls are a collage of posters: movies I know he likes, movies I wish I could introduce him to, basketball stars. I often go into the room and make adjustments based on how old he is. The fantasy of how he will come to live with me always changes. He could run away from his mother and find me. He could send me a letter that is enough for me to hire a lawyer and start that fight again. Possibly it would just be for a weekend. I don't know. But the room is ready for him when he can come.

In the bathroom I stare back at myself.

I've never been good at wearing clothes. When I went to a public school I just couldn't get what was cool and what wasn't. Moving to a private school I liked the uniforms but I was never able to remember all the bits. I tried to cultivate a style in college and I guess I mostly pulled it off but I always felt like an imposter, like someone was going to come and point me out as a child or idiot in disguise. The G-man suit of the FBI presented a powerful archetype and I appreciated that. But I didn't want to continue with that look when I became a private investigator.

I decided on a standard appearance and I stick to it almost always. I wear black loafers—Gucci or Luis Vuitton because nothing can give you away faster than cheap shoes—dark designer jeans, black rock t-shirts and dark grey Nehru jackets. Nehru jackets button right up to the neck. A quick cover up of the underlying t-shirt makes me look respectable enough to step into a rich client's home. And if I want to go casual when asking questions I can unbutton the jacket or take it completely off. I don't know if the rock shirts make me hip exactly but the look is less intimidating than a suit. Today I'm wearing a *Sgt. Pepper's Lonely Hearts Club Band* circular logo in silver.

I change into my workout clothes.

I spend most of my working life in the 911 driving around LA. I'm not going to go home, pull on some runners, and see LA slower while panting. I can't swim. I disagree with pick-up basketball as a philosophical concept. I feel that rec softball leagues are most likely communist sleeper cells. I believe in-line skating invariably leads to spectacular death. I suspect that racket ball is entirely made up each time it is played.

So I get my sweat on with an elliptical trainer in the living room. And I watch horror movies while I do. It's just the one screen when I work out. I can't remember how I started with this combo but it works for me. The cardio elevates my heart rate for the coming scares and the screams and splatter keep the adrenaline flowing.

And I've always found good horror movies help me think about the deviant.

I use the remote to select my movie on the one TV, put my wireless headphones on and start my legs working in the skiing movement. I grip the handles that determine my heartbeat, adjust the volume and breathe long and deep.

When a Stranger Calls is a classic from 1979. A babysitter, alone after the children have been put to bed, answers the phone. A stranger asks her if she's checked the children. She thinks it's a joke but it's not and the calls continue. The babysitter gets the police on the same phone and the officer she gets says he will trace the call.

The phone call, a stranger's voice, that's where all the fear comes from. Just the suggestion that something is happening that we don't understand, that there is a person who knows something we don't about what is in the dark.

I shower after my workout, dry, pull on a Radiohead shirt with the smiling creep logo and shorts. I sit down in my office and start switching through the real and virtual computers I will need for this run.

California Cryo Futures was founded in 1978. It's central corporate presence is on La Grange. It has satellite offices in Westwood and Palo Alto. They don't contract their IT out. There is a server room at their La Grange headquarters. This preliminary profile is easily determined from their website, their online corporate phone directory and their public financial disclosures.

I use basic Linux commands for my first scans of their network. I then cycle through remote virtual machines I pay for in different countries around the world to aggressively probe. At this stage I'm trying to determine what kind of machines are in that server room, what operating systems they are utilizing and what services and protocols are running in the open.

The scan results scroll across the screens before me in jerks and bursts of text.

I breathe deeply.

Hacking is roleplaying.

I started playing roleplaying games before I was a teenager. We were visiting friends of the family the Christmas I was nine and my parents let me hang out with an older boy. He was reading a thin hardcover titled the *Advanced Dungeon and Dragon's Players Handbook.* The image on the front was a tableau of a large demon statue holding a metal bowl from which flames were rising. There were men about it, disfigured engineers, evil worshipers, thieves unseen. I was amazed. And then the older boy showed me the different sided dice to play this wondrous game: four, eight, ten, twelve and twenty.

I was always an imaginative kid. *Dungeons and Dragons* made it possible to share my imagination with my kind. Geeks united we conjured our characters with graph paper and pencils. We positioned painted lead figures on the kitchen table and they fought their way through ancient ruins, castles, labyrinths, temples, catacombs, tombs.

It was the structure of the rules that made this possible. We could debate how quickly a raging warrior succumbs to poison, the falling speed of a griffin turned to stone by magic, the response time of a major deity to a minor cleric's prayer, whether a vorpal blade will cut through a crystal neck guard.

As I got older I played other RPGs. There was *Earth Dawn, Palladium, Tunnels and Trolls*, all sword and sorcery games improving on *Dungeon and Dragons* mechanics but not quite capturing the same spirit. Then there was *Call of Cthulhu* where we were detectives and scholars who lost sanity points as we discovered the cosmic design behind the pantomime of reality. And there was *Shadowrun*, a cyberpunk game in which we became street samurai with vat-grown muscles and wired reflexes, street mages alive with magic that had returned to the earth in the great awakening. Big in *Shadowrun* was the matrix: the net accessed through neural interface technology.

Every smart hacker I've ever known played RPGs growing up. Defeating computer security is about learning the rules of the game and then trying to succeed within them. Forget courses. Forget certifications. We imagine, explore, level up, and roll the fucking dice.

I order pizza. I start drinking coke.

I stare at a star diagram I've created of California Cryo Futures' network. I've identified the web, print, and mail servers. I've reasoned that there are no honeypots or decoys. And I can see my target clearly: a Solaris box hosting Cryo's massive Oracle database.

Oracle does the best database security in the industry and has a strong corporate culture to back it up. They're adept at selling the features of their products and then delivering the proper training to help customers manage them successfully.

The patching level on the Solaris OS is current and tight.

I poke around for open paths or shares. There are none. No surprise there either.

I get my pizza from the front door and bring it back into the office.

It's three in the morning soon. I'm tired but I don't want to give up.

Time to bring another human into the game, roll different sided dice.

The online corporate phone directory tells me that California Cryo Futures has a Database Administrator and a Network Administrator. I can testify that the database setup is perfect. But the network deployment appears to be just good. The Cisco router is not patched to the latest level. There is an exploit for the version they are currently running posted online. Twenty minutes of work and I'm on the wire, able to monitor all the network traffic coming in or out.

IT administrators set-up notification triggers in their systems. They have routines parsing through logs, waiting for errors, pouncing on failures—all of these routines spawn emails. The California Cryo Futures DBA won't remember all the triggers he's set-up over his tenure in the position. But he will react to an email from the system whatever the time day or night.

I craft him a forlorn love email from his beloved Oracle database: an Instance Failure alluding to hardware betrayal, power loss, and a potential emergency shutdown. I send it with the necessary fake headers to seem legitimate. And I watch the wire.

It takes the DBA ten minutes to react. I watch him remote into the network and log directly into his box to find out that nothing is actually wrong. I can't see his password as he does this. But I am able to copy the jumbled password hash used for his authentication to a hard drive in my office.

The DBA will find the false alarm suspicious but at this time of night he'll be happy to just go back to sleep. Tomorrow he'll investigate and get more suspicious. But I'll have copied what I need by then. And nothing will trace back to me.

Cracking encryption is silly math. You determine the constants and the variables for the hash, the computing power available and start the software working. A good program will usually come up with one of three answers: this will be cracked in a few hours, a few months, or long after humans have died and the sun has exploded. The second is usually almost as useless as the third.

I start the crack, take my meds and go to sleep.

The Oracle administrator password is waiting for me when I get up. Yawning, I log into the database and start looking through California Cryo Futures' records. Everyone assumes that sperm banks are for women who have given up on finding a decent guy alive and in the wild. But couples with fertility problems also use sperm banks. And one group that is rarely discussed are dying men. The chemo and pain are enough stress without trying to conceive. So some men leave a supply of their genetic material for their wives to conceive as they are dying or even after they've gone.

As the legal documents he signed suggested, my client's sperm was used to achieve conception three times. There is nothing to suggest why his sperm was good then but useless after. But that's not part of my job. I have been hired to find his three children.

I'm going to run the mothers and their sons down one at a time. They're all sons.

Chapter Three

WRESTLER

The sexual advice in women's magazines is an enigma to me. Do women buy these glossy mags because they really want to read the article on Angelina Jolie's courage and the 100 oral sex tips disguise this? Or do they actually think the tips are going to be useful? Ambush him in a strange place, drop his pants while you chew a cold mango, take him into your mouth while humming his favorite song, corkscrew your tongue and mouth in opposite directions while keeping an eye contact with him that says he can watch the game later. . . . Seriously: it's hard to make a mistake with a blowjob but if you do fuck it up there will be abundant auditory clues.

Melissa Verduna has been writing for women's magazines for thirty years. She's never been married. She went to California Cryo Futures in the mid-nineties and selected my client's genetic promise from the catalogue of ghost fathers. She got an entire year of articles out of the experience of shopping and birthing. They're all available online. The whole thing was, apparently, very empowering.

Melissa named her boy Harlan.

The Hyena's first son is Harlan.

Harlan has run away to join the circus of professional wrestling.

Mizz Verduna is currently writing for *Beauty and Strength*. The business office is in Beverly Hills. Not knowing what hours she works, I park myself outside the office building that is home to her publication and two other monthlies targeted at men: *Muscles and Style* and *The Maximum You.*

I ran Melissa's name through the DMV. She drives a yellow Mini Cooper Cabriolet.

While I wait for her I pull my MacBook toward me to learn more about Harlan's wrestling career. He began hanging around Carnage Championship Wrestling sometime before he turned 18. It is a California promotion that travels within a five hour circle of Long Beach. Harlan's introductory grunts in the business came from erecting and tearing down the ring. There are pictures on his open social media.

The money for the wrestlers in Carnage Championship Wrestling was inconsistent and so the cards were constantly in flux. This would have provided Harlan with his earliest opportunities to take bumps. The name wrestlers would have called at the last minute with their excuses: they couldn't make it because they had to pick up a shift at work, because their ride had fallen through, because they had a new girlfriend who could do math. Harlan would have hung out in the change room nervously ready. The promoter would have told him who he was filling in for, when he would get to come out of the curtain, and crucially whether he was winning or losing.

Most aspiring wrestlers work on one persona from the very beginning. They think through their name, their appearance, their mannerisms and their backstory before they pull up the kneepads and get taped. Harlan approached it differently—as documented by the CCW website's photographic archive. The pictures show the muscled kid as a contrasting character each time he stepped between the ropes. Working within the great pro wrestling archetypes of baby face and heel he did mangled impressions. He shook and stomped like Hulk Hogan. He sprayed beer like Stone Cold. He painted his face like Raven. He arched his eyebrow like the Rock. It looks like he even brought a snake in one time as a homage to Jake himself.

No Mini Cabriolet yet.

I keep typing. I find a local wrestling blog that has a posted interview.

When Harlan felt prepared for professional training he packed for Orlando. I can't see how he would have saved any money from his work with Carnage Championship Wrestling. Mom likely wrote a check. Amidst the sweltering humidity and alligators he enrolled at the prestigious wrestling academy and occasional reality show NXT. The instructors loved his drive and ability but it didn't work out. He wasn't ready.

Not discouraged, Harlan came back to California and joined Awesome Wrestling Entertainment. This organization seems to be a step up from Carnage but it's still only a regional. Harlan came in as a name wrestler here. He was done with the kaleidoscope of characters. He arrived calling himself the Minister of Pain. He wore a priest's collar. He carried a hollowed out Bible within which he kept secret extras: powder, liquids, brass knuckles. He referenced scripture, denounced demonic possession and acclaimed angelic salvation. He got over right away and was soon at the top of the AWE card.

Harlan's brutal hardcore matches caught the attention of a WWE wrestler called Ricky Wrath. Ricky got Vince McMahon to sign Harlan and the young man is currently on the road with the Raw World Tour. Harlan has never appeared in a televised match. He seems to only fight the local shows they do during the week and those sparingly.

Still. He's in the majors quite young. And he owes that to Ricky Wrath.

I watch Melissa pull her Mini Cabriolet into her parking spot. I get out of the 911. I'm wearing an enigmatic Oasis shirt that has a dazed monkey with kaleidoscope eyes encircled by a weird musical machine.

"Ms. Verduna."

Big sunglasses, iPhone in a pretty case, Starbucks coffee, she stops. "Yes?"

"I think women who want to improve their sexual technique should watch porn. There are a hundred billion hours of how-to videos online. They're almost all free." I stop well before I reach her.

"Porn is made for men."

"But aren't your lists about what men want their women to do sexually? A 100 Ways to Please Your Man. Surprise Him in Bed Tonight. What He Wants But Won't Tell You. . . . My name's Chalk. I'm a private investigator."

She starts moving again. She mumbles backward: "I have a deadline."

"I'm really good at the start-stop game," I promise her.

"Please leave me alone."

"Your son broke a man's neck. He's paralyzed."

The clack of her heels stops. She looks at me.

I keep my features neutral.

"Not now that he's with the WWE," she tries to explain it to herself. "You must mean before."

"Will you talk to me about Harlan?"

"This is for an insurance investigation? Not criminal . . . no you're not . . . no of course not. This is for insurance."

I just stand. She's filling in the details of this lie quite nicely herself. They often do that.

"Come into my office."

I follow her into the building and past reception. Junior journalists approach her on the path to her editorial sanctum. Her desk has minimal technology: an iMac, a black phone, a mouse. The rest of the space is a cluttered Tetris game on pause, boxes and stacks of papers the shapes. She shuts the door behind us.

"The backyard wrestling and the amateur wrestling—he's done with all of that. He's a professional now. He's been trained. If this is about someone who was injured before and is just now coming forward . . ."

"Where is Harlan's father?" I ask.

"I don't see what that has to do with anything."

"Okay so you are not prepared to help your son." I move right for the door.

"Wait wait. He didn't have a father. He, I went to a sperm bank. I raised him. He didn't need a father."

"You see? That's the start-stop game. What I just did there."

"I . . ."

"What about growing up? Did he have a step-father?"

"Never for any length. I didn't lie to him. I told him how he was conceived as soon as he was old enough to understand."

"Did he seek out father figures growing up?"

"When he started going to the gym. He was twelve then. He, yes there was always . . . "

"When did he get to know Ricky Wrath?"

"I hate that man. I was never happy about Harlan wanting to be a wrestler. But at least it was something he worked hard at. It took discipline and drive. Before he met that sadistic little shit."

"Ricky Wrath got Harlan in with the WWE," I say. "That's what your son wanted."

"Ricky Wrath has gotten him into a lot of things." She takes her sunglasses off. "Steroids. More than that but he won't tell me. My son is in his twenties. Why does he need a father figure now? . . . You've said nothing about this broken neck."

"Did you ever watch his amateur wrestling? CCW? AWE?"

"I went a few times. No. Just twice."

"You saw the kind of dangerous moves he did. The extreme hardcore fights with the barbed wire and staple guns. You had to understand the risks that he would hurt himself or someone else."

"He got into all that hardcore stuff after CCW. I warned him. I asked him to stop. He didn't listen. He was obsessed with those Japanese hardcore tapes."

"Did you pay for his training in Florida Ms. Verduna?"

"Yes."

"Why? If you didn't want him to wrestle?"

"I wanted him to . . . continue being my son. I didn't want to alienate him. . . . Tell me who he's hurt. Please. I'm begging you now. Another young man? That's it, isn't it?" Her voice is smaller and ever smaller. "I wanted him to go into IT. Software. Video games. He had so many opportunities to work with computers growing up. Like it was his destiny. He kept winning computers in contests. And books. And there were offers to go to computer camp and and and . . . . and he didn't care. He just wanted to get big muscles and play out these violent adolescent fantasies."

She's shutting down on me emotionally.

I ask her straight up. "Is he your son now? Or have you lost him?"

"He's still my son," she affirms. "We don't talk as much as we used to do. But he's travelling all over the country. He calls. He still calls. He . . . He didn't break anyone's neck, did he?"

"No."

"You're not from . . . you tricked me." She slumps down in her office chair, her energy all gone. "It was just the two of us. Even when I was in a relationship it was always just the two of us." She's not talking to me anymore. She's remembering now. "I was a good mother to Harlan. I could still be if he wanted me to be."

I leave. She doesn't try to stop me.

Home among the blinking lights and the erratic percussion of my keystrokes.

I read more wrestling fan blogs. I message the men who maintain the two major non-affiliated pro-wrestling news sites. And then I find a gem on a torrent site: an unpublished tell-all book about the WWE which has a chapter devoted to Ricky Wrath.

Like many professional wrestlers Ricky's existence is a constant countdown before the next jump: hotel to car or bus to plane to hotel to gym to venue to hotel. He needs drugs to accelerate and brake and blur those jumps.

When Ricky joined the WWE the steroid tests were easy enough to beat. After he'd ricocheted around the country a few times, there was enough pressure in the media that new rules were brought in. These took more planning to cheat: greater attention to the timing of the cycles, greater consultation on the selection of masking agents.

Wrestling fans see a hundred times more matches than boxing and MMA devotees in a year. These fans only remember the spectacular jump off the ladder and the dangerous hit with the sledgehammer. Ricky was always up for the matches physically. Cocaine gave him the needed rush to be just the right reckless. But then he needed to come down. His body was throbbing and aching, his head was muddled and angry. Booze wasn't enough. He needed strong pain pills and Xanax and even weed. That would chill him out, kill him dead for the night until the alarm went off and he realized he was already late to get down to the car or bus.

In the unpublished book this is all written in the past, as Ricky Wrath's early years. But is it also the current reality? Is Harlan living this now as Ricky's surrogate son? Has the older man enslaved the younger in this lifestyle?

I read on in the manuscript.

Ricky got a reputation with the WWE writers for being open to almost any angle. His character got confused in the testosterone soap opera a few times. But he was always a regular on pay-per-views. When he had the joints of a seventy year old at thirty-five, he signed a huge contract. This meant somewhere in the country he had a big house with a fast car in the driveway and maybe he could visit it one day with his buddy Joe Walsh.

Most wrestlers lose their wife and kids several times over in a successful career. But Ricky never had a real relationship. Worried that his fellow Olympians might think him gay, he pushed himself on every female in the company. He mocked the women who slept with him and humiliated the women who wouldn't. He urinated on their clothes, told crude lies about them to others, tricked them into taking speed, jerked off in their food.

The bad luck came together in the one year. Wrestling in New Jersey, Ricky slipped while delivering a power-bomb to Viral. The shift of weight went wrong and Viral was paralyzed for life. No one blamed Ricky. It could have happened to any wrestler.

Then during a spot outside of the ring in a pay-per-view Ricky pushed Shawn John off a thirty-foot high scaffold. This had been planned. But Shawn John said Ricky threw him with too much force and the hurtling wrestler wasn't able to properly prepare for the coming impact. Shawn John damaged his spine and lost feeling throughout his body. It still could have happened to any wrestler. But it hadn't happened to any wrestler—it had happened to Ricky . . . again.

It was shortly after this streak of bad luck that Ricky discovered Harlan and convinced Vince McMahon to sign the Minister of Pain. One of the guys I'm intermittently chatting with on Pro Wrestling News confirms that Ricky controls Harlan's fights. And that Ricky stops him from interacting with the other wrestlers socially.

It's almost like he's punishing the kid for his own bad luck.

I visit the WWE website. The RAW World Tour is in Eugene Oregon tomorrow night. 850 miles from LA. That's 13 hours for mortal drivers, 10 for me if the radar detector is alert, my laser jammer plays strong D and I pay attention to the police scanner.

I grab my meds for the road trip.

Chapter Four

SCREENS

On the road to Eugene I make phone calls into the WWE office in Stamford CT. The first time I call I'm a graduate student doing a thesis on theatrical morality in American Wrestling. The second time I'm an angry pastor offended by The Minster of Pain's portrayal of clergy. For the third try I'm just a journalist fact checking. Each time I ask questions about Ricky Wrath and The Minister of Pain. I learn two things of value. The Minister of Pain is on the card to fight Ricky Wrath at tonight's show in the Mathew Knight Arena. And the wrestlers are all booked into the Hilton Eugene and Conference Center.

I call and buy the best ticket I can for tonight's Raw.

The Hilton is predictably fully booked. I ask to speak to the manager. I tell her that I am disabled and require an accessible room. She repeats that they are fully booked. I ask if she has booked the disabled room or rooms to non-disabled people. She pauses and then stutters. Five minutes later I've got a disabled room on the ground floor and somebody I don't know is going to get a voucher and an apology.

Still hours to go on the road. I use voice commands to search for articles on my client, the Hollywood Hyena. The MacBook reads the text back to me in Sean Connery's voice—an amusing little program that keeps me awake.

For the last two hours I listen to news on satellite radio. Robbers broke into a pharmaceutical warehouse owned by Abbott

Laboratories outside of LA. It was the distribution point for three pills: Lexapro, Prevacid and Vicodin. Lexapro is for depression, Prevacid is for stomach ulcers, and Vicodin is the most popular prescription pain medication in the United States. The thieves killed the security guards, climbed up to the roof and cut a hole. They dropped in, jacked a panel and rebooted the alarm system into a passive mode. Then they looped the cameras. They took forty million dollars in pills although there is no mention if that was the street value or the legitimate prescription value.

Strangely, they left six dead electronic screens behind: two new desktop monitors from Philips, two strong glass portals from 80s arcade machines, and two thick and obsolete computer eyes from jet fighters. Each visual surface had a letter or number circled on the top and a single line of the same message. Each was written in a different hand, all in red soap:

G: Graphics have made warriors terrorists.

D: Graphics have made warriors terrorists.

F: Graphics have made warriors terrorists.

1: Graphics have made warriors terrorists.

5: Graphics have made warriors terrorists.

3: Graphics have made warriors terrorists.

I arrive in Eugene stiff and hungry with an hour before the show. I give my name at the desk. The staff have clearly been briefed on my exchange with the manager. They're looking for my disability but no one has the courage to ask what it is.

I eat in the hotel restaurant. I recognize two retired wrestlers.

I shower and change and head to the arena. My seat is in section 112P.

WWE stars do a pay-per view every month and one or both of the two broadcast shows each week. Then there are three of these regional shows sprinkled in and around those commitments. These events are not broadcast so the storylines can be suspended. But the wrestling is still high-energy, high-impact.

While the wrestlers give their best in these regional shows, they generally shy away from the extreme matches. Because there has to be some extra sizzle to the TV shows and the pay-per-views. Because no matter how good your technique a chair to the back still fucking hurts.

Ricky has set up a Table and Chairs Match with Harlan tonight in Eugene.

It's strange that Ricky has been allowed to control Harlan like this.

But it's stranger still that their match this evening is an extreme one.

The show starts with fireworks. I feel like a loser sitting by myself.

We are treated to blustered threats, a tag team match, a fatal-four-way, action outside of the ring, an official knocked unconscious, twin sisters that seduce, a behemoth of a man going insane, a turn buckle used to draw blood. The last match is always a battle for the championship and tonight is no exception. But before the rumble for the strap, Ricky Wrath and The Minister of Pain enter the squared circle.

To win one man must drive the other through a table. That is the only rule. They swing at each other with chairs. Ricky Wrath runs up a ladder and flies at The Minister of Pain. Harlan slams Ricky's arm in the ladder.

Professional wrestlers are trained to improvise between major action points. The referee is the inside man even when there are no counts. The striped shirt is constantly checking the health of the fighters. He can speed the contest up, end it early, or just relay information between the men.

This referee is frightened. He's not in control of this. He doesn't know what's happening.

I look to the curtain through which the wrestlers have all made their entrances. Other faces on the roster are poking through to see what's happening—even though I can see they have a closed circuit camera feeding to monitors backstage.

This fight has gone entirely off script. Ricky and Harlan are trying to hurt each other.

A closed fist draws real blood. A chair shot brings a crack. Teeth gnash in a bite.

Every ref they have in the back rushes into the ring. And the theme music for John Cena hits. The company's leading man bluffs his way through a narrative explanation of what just happened that makes no sense at all. The refs pull the crazed combatants out of the ring, out of the lights, and away to the back.

I don't stay for the championship bout. I'll replay it later with action figures.

I go back to the hotel and walk around the perimeter until I'm sure I know where the WWE buses will pull up to the front. But Harlan doesn't come in a bus. He comes back walking. It looks like the battle continued backstage. His clothes are ripped and his hands and face are bloodied. He has a gym bag over his shoulder and he's carrying an iPhone. He has a jawbone Bluetooth earpiece in. He's on a call which he ends just as he comes within earshot of me.

I fall in behind him and trail him through the lobby, into the elevator and onto his floor. I walk past as he's opening the door to his room. He didn't even look at my face. I go to my room and get my MacBook. I return to Harlan's door. I can hear him inside, maybe packing, maybe just moving around angrily.

Like a lot of great technology ideas Bluetooth took a while to actually get great. I remember a wireless keyboard and mouse combo in an FBI conference room that never worked. I recall a hands-free car kit that required both hands to fix every time it lost the pairing. When Bluetooth became mainstream it was one more burden for me as a known IT guy to fix for friends and family. But now it's approaching perfection. My many devices are like teenage girls: constantly connected and ever aware of relationship strengths. What makes the unintended legacy of a Danish King work is that it's fast, it's smart and it scales well. It accomplishes all of this by creating a PAN: Personal Area Network.

Bluesnarfing is the technique of tricking a wireless device on a PAN to reveal information. Headphones, mice, keyboards and presentation remotes have little information of import. Yes the computers employing these peripherals have valuable information. But notebooks, desktops and servers are connected to bigger more easily exploited networks. Bluesnarfing is the best way to get information from a smartphone.

I'm sitting cross-legged in the hotel hallway. My MacBook sees three Bluetooth PANs within range: a dell notebook, a printer and Harlan's jawbone. The vulnerability that makes Bluesnarfing possible on an iPhone is concerned with the object exchange protocol. Like all persistent flaws it gets fixed and worked around again and fixed and worked around again. Running the latest exploit software, I am trying to convince Harlan's jawbone that my MacBook is another legitimate iPhone on the PAN.

Harlan's device is eager to give me OS info, texts, calendar details, a list of installed and running programs. What I want is the phone's electronic serial number and its mobile identification number. I will be able to get both of these from his iCloud backup. Harlan isn't actually using iCloud but I change that and set it to sync right away over the cellular signal.

The phone starts praying to Apple. And there are the numbers and letters I want. A quick copy and I have everything I need to have Harlan's phone cloned. I go to my room and send an encrypted email to Golden Earring.

Then I take my meds and wait for sleep.

I think Harlan fired his father figure tonight.

Could be he'll be happy to meet his real father.

CHAPTER FIVE

MEDS

I rise early in the morning and drift by Harlan's hotel door. I didn't realize last night that he was sharing the room with Ricky. A beaten and blurry Mr. Wrath tells me that Harlan was fired from the company and left last night so if I'm one of his gay friends come around to do gay shit I can just fuck off to gay land.

I have breakfast in the restaurant amidst the wrestlers. I overhear voices I know and strike up conversations with the unknown crew members who worked through the night to tear down and just want to get on the bus to time travel into the future. Some confirm that Harlan was fired. Others say he quit. Everyone says he was talking about going to wrestle in Japan. Everyone says he headed back to LA.

Which is my destination also. I miss the smog.

I'm wearing a Dead Kennedys' *Too Drunk To Fuck* shirt.

How I became an FBI agent is a story of my three fathers: my biological father who died and in dying helped me know my sickness; Dr. Fraser who took my dad's place and showed me that my brand of crazy can do great things; and Special Agent Barrett who trained me as a hunter.

Sadly, my ex-wife is also in the story.

In the late eighties I was a freshman studying computer science and psychology at the University of California. I was a mess that first year, depressed. My father died, peacefully, and with a book in his hand. I didn't cope with it well. Already so sad and lost, I crashed into a crippling depression. I tried to kill myself with an overdose of my mother's sleeping pills and a bottle of vodka. I fucked it up. I was transferred from emergency to the psych ward, the zoo of the disturbed. I was diagnosed as bipolar, put on drugs, and set up with the first of many shrinks I would come to distrust and disobey.

When I returned in second year, I applied myself to my studies and made up for the dropped and incomplete classes on my transcript. Wednesday mornings I was one of hundreds of students in Dr. Paul Fraser's Deviant Psychology class.

Dr. Fraser was an academic celebrity. He wrote popular books, appeared on talk shows, and was routinely consulted by the FBI. I suspect that he hated that large lecture full of criminology majors and kinesiology students taking a breadth requirement. But he went along with it as part of a deal with the University Administration that left him free to pursue his own interests.

For the final paper in his class, I contrasted Jim Jones and David Koresh. After reading it, Dr. Fraser wanted to find out who I was, he wanted to meet me. He said that more than just an amazing piece of academic writing, it was the keenest insight into cult psychology that he had ever encountered. I immediately liked the personality behind the book jacket photo.

I became Dr. Fraser's protégé. He had me over for dinner often. He helped me pick my courses. He began grooming me for graduate work and academic life after that. I wrote about cults, serial killers and the power of rituals.

I wanted to tell Dr. Fraser about the Bacchus killer. But even after years of studying psychology, I had little more than my instincts to describe what I'd experienced. And I was scared that my mentor would realize he had been wrong about me, that I was just a fool.

So I didn't say anything and I remained the good son.

A prestigious and rewarding University career lay ahead of me. It seemed almost too easy. And probably would have been. Except that one night in my fifth year the phone in my little apartment rang. I was preparing my application for the doctoral program. It was Dr. Fraser on the line. He asked me if I could come over. He said there would be a car outside my apartment in a few minutes. Before I could learn any more he hung up.

The car that came was a non-descript government Impala. I was on a good regime of medications then but at times when I was confused the paranoia could still claw through the chemicals. A tall man in a simple black suit confirmed my name and asked me to get in the back. He drove the familiar route to Dr. Fraser's, pushing the speed limit. There were another two identical cars in the drive. They all had government plates. The driver took me into the house.

Dr. Fraser's wife Mel was in the living room with a scotch. Her eyes were vacant.

I was ushered into Dr. Fraser's study. Paul was sitting at his large table with papers and photos spread out about him. He looked more like my dad in that moment than I had ever seen him. With him was a large strong man who was talking on a thick cellular phone. The man finished his conversation tersely, put the phone down and moved to shake my hand. He introduced himself as Special Agent Barrett from the Behavioral Unit at the FBI. I knew he consulted with Dr. Fraser on serial killers. Paul mentioned him often in his popular books. But usually those consultations were over the phone, by email, fax. Why had he come in person?

The answer was a cult. The photos on the table were of a secret compound, ritual torture, captives, dried blood, shining blades, mystery symbols. I sat down and started feeding my brain with what was there, thinking, imagining. Hours passed. By the time dawn had come, I had provided an insight that excited Special Agent Barrett. It hadn't occurred to Dr. Fraser but he immediately supported it. Barrett left for the airport, thanking me as he left.

I was wired the rest of the day. The feeling was like being manic but still in control. Life was surging through me, my blood was hot, my breath was deep. My mind was making connections at light speed.

A week later the story of the cult hit the news. Many had been killed but many more were saved. It dominated the media for several weeks, eclipsing a governor in a sex scandal, a Hollywood divorce, and dire economic numbers. My name was never mentioned but Dr. Fraser referenced me in the book he wrote and Special Agent Barrett sent me a handwritten note of thanks that I kept until the day I left the FBI in shame.

I started and finished the first year of a PhD but Dr. Fraser knew he had lost me.

I applied to the FBI. I was young, I had no law enforcement experience, but Special Agent Barrett took over from Dr. Fraser as my mentor and father. The day my improbable acceptance arrived in the mail, Special Agent Barrett called me and said if I put in two years as an agent he would get me transferred to Behavioral to hunt with him. True to his word I worked for 50 months on regular assignments and then I went to Virginia.

I met my wife in my first year as an agent. I was working in the new Cyber division. My timing was ideal there. Cyber wasn't a fully matured unit and they were taking a lot of agents whose IT resumes wouldn't get a second look today.

Maria was working with Crimes Against Children. She was providing investigative assistance to local law enforcement on linked child abuse cases. I became the techie for their task force. I helped them trace emails, restore deleted files on hard drives and fix the printer when it jammed.

It's hard to remember when it was good but it was good in the beginning. It started out as any other office romance, I guess, except our office investigated the sick and the dangerous. We made jokes about the senior agents. We flirted. When the task force case wrapped up as a success we ended up in bed.

We shared a background in psychology and a passion for books. She had a clear idea of the trajectory she wanted her career to take. And she was impressed with my connection to Barrett.

When I went to BSU, Maria began working more with kidnappings and missing persons. They were high profile cases and she got her picture in the media. She traveled. I traveled. We talked on the phone from similar hotel rooms in different parts of the country. She was worried that I was being unfaithful which I suspect now meant that she was cheating even back then. We thought marriage was the answer so we got married.

We thought a home was the answer so we bought a house.

Maria's career faltered. I remember her folded into my arms and crying until her face was sore and salty. She'd made a procedural error with evidence. A parental kidnapper got off and did it again and this time the kid died. They put her face in the paper then too.

She was still obsessing about that mistake when she announced she wanted to get pregnant. A family had always been just a future concern for us. Yet all of a sudden it was all Maria would talk about.

We thought a child was the answer so she got pregnant right away.

My son was born: this perfect little man whose eyes reflected mine. I would see gruesome pictures of victims bruised, bloodied, tortured. I would hear recorded screams and dying gasps. I would touch cold bodies. And my son rinsed it all away. I only needed to hold him, to hear his laugh.

Maria suffered bad post-partum depression. I knew what she was going through and I helped her as best I could. I called in sick, I took vacation time, I talked her to sleep. She got better but we were never the same.

She felt that her career plan needed to be revised drastically. She returned from her maternity leave early. She filled an open position working with fingerprints and criminal records. It meant less travel for her. I felt guilty about always being on the road with Barrett and I looked at transferring out of BSU so I could be home more often.

But Maria was working on a different plan.

Shortly after she started in her new position in the LA field office she began sleeping with her boss. She identified me as the major problem in her life. It was me who had messed up her grand plan, me who had always held her back. Everything would be good if she could just get rid of me. Which would have been fine, marriages end. Except an amicable parting was not enough for Maria. She needed to be fully vindicated by her lover, her colleagues, her friends and her Italian family who thought divorce was a fate worse than the death of a child.

The campaign to illuminate me as a monster began by revealing my bipolar diagnosis. I heard the rumor in the bureau from a friend. Maria claimed innocence when I asked her. The whispers continued. I was treated differently even in my own unit. Barrett began to doubt me—first privately and then openly.

I argued with everyone at work.

I argued with Maria at home.

I got angry and messed with my meds. I drank.

Maria secretly recorded our fights using FBI surveillance equipment. She amassed hours of me screaming and yelling at her. There was never any context but it was damning all the same. She goaded me into rage and saved the results for later use.

Maria had never kept a diary in her life but one materialized that her friend found. It categorized months of me directing mental and physical abuse at her. One day I woke up from a drunken blackout to hear the police downstairs. There were two officers, a man and a woman. The man took me outside while the female officer spoke to Maria. While I had been sleeping under the black dead blanket of the drunk, Maria had beaten herself and broken select pieces of furniture I guess she didn't want.

I spent a day in jail.

Barrett bailed me out. He hardly said anything to me.

Maria told me I had to leave.

I kissed my son goodbye and left, taking nothing, not even clothes.

I moved into an apartment and I got a divorce lawyer. I was drinking all day and recklessly mixing pills. The risks I was taking in the field were stupid and dangerous. I was headed for self-destruction without any help from my wife. But Maria had taken vows to be there for better and for worse and she did everything she could to make it worse.

With the help of her boyfriend boss she accused me of menacing her. She claimed I had a history of brandishing my gun and threatening her. She came out with the audio recordings. And she accused me of trying to kidnap my son. None of the staged evidence went forward for criminal prosecution because she knew it wouldn't stand up. But it was enough that by the time our divorce was heard by a judge any chance of seeing my son regularly was gone. And possibly is gone forever.

All those years that I was learning my craft with the FBI, I kept thinking about the Bacchus killer, kept secretly investigating. I'd made a few tentative connections to strange stories from other rock concerts. I thought I had enough to go to Barrett. I thought maybe my genius discovery would mend all the distrust. Barrett was just silent after I told him, embarrassed for us both. Worse than a fool, he saw me as an insane liability.

And that fit with what my wife was telling everyone.

My marriage and career ended within weeks of each other.

I remember selling my wedding ring. I took the cash, walked up the street to a liquor store and bought a case of Old Milwaukee. I put it in the car and drove to a higher end liquor store I knew. There I bought two bottles of Jameson Rarest Vintage Reserve. I made it home, sat down and started drinking with purpose. The whiskey had been aging in a port cask when I walked down the aisle at my wedding, when my son was born, when it went bad. The precious liquid waited for me all that time. The first taste was perfect. I poured three fingers in a glass, inhaled it with longing. After the third glass I started chasing the dull burn with beer. I drank through the afternoon and evening and into the night. I opened the second bottle by morning and was out of beer after a day. I took my pills and slept for hours.

I didn't stop but the drinking got better. Is better.

I took care of the shrink problem, mostly. And got on a proper regime of meds again.

I take three drugs on a daily basis now: Lithium, Celexa and Seroquel.

Lithium is the mandatory drug for membership in the bipolar club right back to the ancients. It's a magic salt that stabilizes mood. The dose has to be just right. Too little and it doesn't work, too much and it is poison. Lithium's toxic tantrums can bring on shaking, seizures, loss of memory and failure of co-ordination. But it's a drug that has always just worked for me. I've never had any real side effects, even the few times I've taken my dose twice by mistake. I take 1,200 mg nightly.

Celexa is my latest anti-depressant. I always seem to need one in the mix. Over the years I've taken Prozac, Luvox, Zoloft, Effexor, Paxil, Wellburtin, different doctors, different doses, different reasons for change. Celexa is working now but when it doesn't I'll want to try whatever's new.

Seroquel is my antipsychotic. I need it to lower the volume, the intensity. I've tried the others and this one is home for me. I take 300mg at night. Sometimes that needs to be adjusted. And sometimes I need to take it during the day as well.

I get back to LA in the afternoon.

Playa del Rey used to be a top surf hangout back in the Beach Boy days. Erosion has tamed the waves but still there are boards to be seen. I wish I surfed. No population of people is more consistently happy than surfers. It seems like hours of tedious paddling for a few seconds of excitement and maybe danger. But they're always smiling, especially the older ones, which is even more bizarre. The housing right behind the scene is known as The Jungle. There are lots of places in LA referred to as the jungle but it fits this area better than most. The apartments are close together and there is overgrowth and foliage everywhere.

I take my shoes and socks off and walk down to the beach. My contact is late.

Golden Earring is scruffy. He's never surfed. He likes to meet near the water so he can throw his cloned phones in the water if he feels the heat. It wouldn't protect him in any way but it makes him feel comfortable. And he's the only guy in LA I know who can clone a phone to order in less than 24 hours.

He hands me the smartphone. I like Androids for this work. I hand him the cash.

We part. I drive home.

The pharmaceutical warehouse robbery is still big on the satellite news stations. Different explanations of the message are being discussed. Some believe it is just an attempt to confuse a crime as a political statement. Normally you need a proper press secretary for that.

Graphics have made warriors terrorists.

Chapter Six

YAKUZA

Most cloned cell phones are just used as phones—to smuggle into prisons, to arrange drug and gun deals, to run up charges to phone sex operators. And that's how they get discovered.

I'm not going to make calls with Harlan's phone number.

I'm watching his text and voice activity. I'm looking up the numbers he communicates with. I can listen in when I need to but I don't want to do that indiscriminately. The phone companies are getting better at noticing that there are two live connections from one number in different parts of the city and I want to keep this clone alive as long as possible.

Professionally, I make great use of key loggers on computers and phones. I watch what people are typing. And here's the news from the front: Autocomplete is limiting discourse and killing the language. Smartphone users are delighted when their device anticipates what they're trying to say. Where are you? On my way home. I love you. I love you too. But this is not anticipation. This is limitation. The device is not figuring out what you want to communicate. It's telling you what you *can* communicate. I get that texting with one thumb while skateboarding through a hurricane makes it challenging to make insightful points about existence. But the technology that makes communication on that skateboard possible is always on. It defines all discourse transmitted through our handheld devices.

And it isn't much better on a full sized keyboard. People think they are thinking through Google. They think they're typing in questions and wants and fears into that box. But really they type a little and then let Google finish the thought. But Google doesn't finish the thought. It offers a list of thoughts to choose from. Bigger fucking screen, same fucking trick.

We are trading away quality in communication and thought for mere ubiquity.

Harlan's mother phones him three times throughout the day. He doesn't answer. She texts him to say she she's worried about him. She doesn't know that he's back in LA yet. He doesn't text her back. And he doesn't call her either.

A woman whose number is registered under the name Sheryl Sanchez texts him as luver boy. She doesn't know that he's back in LA yet. He doesn't text her back. And he doesn't call her either.

A woman whose number is listed as Marcia Cantrell phones but does not text.

Harlan responds to texts from a number with blocked information right away—first with a flurry of texts and then with a call. The texts he's receiving are in clipped and precise English. The two sides are arranging a meeting at a corporate building in El Segundo on Sepulveda Blvd.

I check the address online. The office building is new and not yet leasing.

The meeting is for 10 pm—two hours from now.

I tackle the blocked number. I can't get a name through the easy channels. But I determine that it's associated with an Apple account which gets me a username and email that I connect to Super Fire Pro Wrestling X Premium Japan.

The Japanese pay top dollar to fly over the giants of the WWE and TNA for single matches. Barely known wrestlers like Harlan go over there to be blown up and burned and cut to shreds. The Japanese love hardcore wrestling. They set fire to the ropes and rig explosives on the canvas. The wrestlers wield fluorescent light tubes like swords and they crash each other through panes of glass and onto nails.

The Minister of Pain seems right for the Japanese.

I make a sandwich in the kitchen and eat it as I rustle around my office. I pack a gym bag with a charged external battery for my MacBook, a concealable wireless camera/mic, a receiving firewire controller. The Glock and my picks are already in the 911.

I pull on the Sex Pistols shirt with the Queen's mouth and face blocked out.

The office building is a standard corporate tower. Build it tall, jam it with projectors and printers, cubicles and cowards, and the lease money will come in every month. This tower appears done. But there's no security. The front lobby is dark.

I decide not to bring the Glock in.

I park away and walk back with my bag and my long thin metal fingers.

The text said they were meeting in the conference room on the seventh floor.

The front glass door isn't locked. I move inside, scanning for cameras. The mounts are in place but the cold blinkless eyes are not there yet. There's a little construction clutter but otherwise it just needs a good clean. There's even sporadic furniture.

I take the stairs to the seventh floor. I move silently, listening. No one is here.

The conference room is furnished. There is a large table, there are chairs. There is an open presentation unit without a computer. I set my wireless camera up within this small metal closet, look-ing back at the table. I check its feed. I check my watch. I move out of the conference room and find an empty office near the stairs. I shut the door and set myself up on the floor. I run a mono earpiece from the receiving controller to my head and bring the screen up.

One ear listening to the wireless audio feed and the other ear anticipating movement from the stairs outside the office door, I type lightly on the MacBook's keys to find out what I can about Sheryl Sanchez and Marcia Cantrell.

Sheryl comes up in the tabloids and is mentioned in the divorces of two high profile basketball stars. She spent the last three years climbing the defined ranks of NBA groupies before leaving without the genetic prize.

She started as a Gutter Groupie. She hung around the hotels and arena gates hoping that her cleavage and makeup would be enough to illicit a quick invite to a limo or Bentley. Her time in either car would depend on her oral skills.

She moved up from that entry level to be a Working Girl. At this tier she hung around NBA parties and at the clubs and was just a single gal in the city. She danced and drank and winked. The end act was still the same but as a Working Girl she got a little conversation before the blow job and maybe some signed shoes after. The tender act might have even happened in a hotel room.

As a Working Girl she gathered intelligence on what the players liked, what kind of wives they had, and what the other Working Girls did for them. A tongue specialty got her promoted to Fly Girl by a first year point guard phoneme. The ceremony was private. She was then a known name among the players in the league, a shared number, the star of lurid stories told on planes and in locker rooms. It was finally at this level that she started getting the coyly anonymous gifts, offers to fly ahead and wait in the next city, jewelry, clothes, credit cards. She started interacting with bodyguards, drivers, agents, drug dealers as an equal.

It is exceedingly rare for a Fly Girl to ever become a photo approved girlfriend or wife. But after so many blowjobs, she was in the beds long enough to make vaginal sex happen a few times. NBA stars know more about birth control than they do about defenses and stats. But mistakes are made when eighty percent of your plasma is in your dick. Fly Girls get pregnant. And then they have something to bargain: child support for 18 years or an upfront hushed abortion settlement. She'd prayed for the money on her knees and earned it on her back but she never got it. The second divorce made her known to the wives as well and then that was it, that was all.

She took her rocking body to the wrestling ring and became Harlan's girl. She wants to be Beth to his Macho Man. But she wasn't on tour with him and Ricky Wrath. She doesn't know he's back in LA yet.

Marcia Cantrell can't be any kind of rival to Sheryl. She's the same age as Harlan's mother. She in fact appears to have been friends with Harlan's mother. She's a self-help author who has been interviewed by and written articles for glossies that Harlan's mother has been an editor on. They even look a little alike in their press photos.

I hear movement beyond the door and from the stairs. I stop typing.

On the screen I see three Japanese men enter the conference room. Even on the low quality display I can appreciate the superior quality of the older man's suit. He is the executive. The other two are his assistants. They are carrying briefcases. They stand and wait. They do not talk.

Harlan arrives on time. He has brought a briefcase as well. He is greeted with a bow and returns an identical one. Standing straight, the wrestler introduces himself to the Japanese executive formally. He extends his business card with both hands. And he then receives a business card in return. The principals sit down at the table.

I can't hear a goddamn thing. The mic is too weak and I placed it badly.

The discussion begins with exchanges of praise and respect. Harlan knows enough to not gesticulate with his hands. He also avoids relying on facial expressions to convey his tone. Moments pass in which neither man is speaking. This is normal to Japanese business etiquette.

A contract is produced and put on the table. Harlan and the executive both sign.

The business discussion concludes with small smiles of satisfaction from both parties. They take the business cards from where they had waited on the table, stand and then retake their exact standing positions from before. Harlan lowers his head and remains in this supplicate position as he asks for a permission. The Japanese businessman says yes. Harlan opens his briefcase. Inside is a rectangular gift box, beautifully lacquered wood with silk bows. However much the bottle of Saki inside cost the presentation of the gift was hundreds of dollars. It is offered and received again with two hands. It will not be opened here. That's why the presentation is so important.

It seems that Harlan just signed up with Super Fire Pro Wrestling X Premium Japan.

But why so secretive? Why here?

Both parties leave. I give them time to clear the building.

I collect my tech and make my way out and back to the 911. I sit in the dark watching the activity on the cloned phone. Harlan doesn't call his mother or Sheryl. But he is talking to the mysterious Marcia.

Well. If he's not going to talk to his girlfriend then I will.

I phone Sheryl from my phone and tell her I need to speak to her about Harlan's future in wrestling. She agrees to meet me at a restaurant/bar near her place called 8 Bit Bytes. I've never heard of it but the 911's GPS has. The German gears pull me there.

The restaurant is styled like an eight-bit videogame. The wait staff are dressed like classic blocky characters: Donkey Kong, Dig Dug, Mario, Pac Man Ghosts, Link. There are three levels to the place. I'm not sure what customers have to do to level up or why they would even want to. It's an interesting presentation but a horrible business idea. I've been a resident of this city long enough to recognize an eatery started by someone with money and no experience. Retirement check? Inheritance? Maybe daddy dollars.

Sheryl is waiting for me at a table. She's a little drunk and fixing that fast.

I order nachos and tell our waitress to keep her drinks coming.

"Tell me about Ricky Wrath."

She rolls her eyes. "Harlan wanted to wrestle in Japan. That's where he was going to go next. And I was going to go with him. Then Ricky saw him at a gig we did and went back to the dressing room. He said he liked his style and he loved the Minister of Pain character. It was a massive fucking deal. This big WWE star coming backstage at one of our shitty shows."

"Awesome Wrestling Entertainment?"

"Yeah I'd just started there. We'd just started working on our thing together."

"How is Ricky with Harlan?"

She drinks. "That guy is taking pills and doing lines and injecting every moment he's awake. He always wants to fight Harlan like for real. He tackles him down and pins him. Hits him. Harlan is his whipping boy. Like his own personal kid he can beat the shit out of and no one can do anything about it. Harlan is in with the WWE but so what if he's never on the screen? You know. Are you from TNA? Because if you want to offer Harlan a contract we go together."

I smirk. "Okay I'm from TNA. I wanted to talk to you before him."

"Because he's on the RAW tour," she explains it to herself. As they do.

"Right."

"I can be his manager in the ring and out of it. I can get him over. He's got the charisma and talents. And I've got the looks and the brains."

"I need to know he's not just going to make a name in TNA and go to Japan."

"Who would leave TNA for Japan?" She gets a new drink.

"Harlan sounds like he might."

"He won't. I won't let him."

"Tell me about his fascination with Japan though."

She drinks. "He's always showing me these tapes like actual old video cassette tapes of matches from Japan. He says it's a purer form of the art. He thinks the hardcore stuff is real . . . real . . ."

"Real what?" I lead her. I pick at my nachos.

"Real warrior shit."

I think on this. And then guide her back. "But the money isn't anywhere near as good."

"Thank you!" she exclaims. "The money is nowhere near as good. And believe me I will hammer that home when I speak to him about the contract you're offering us."

I correct her. "I'm not offering a contract yet."

She's embarrassed but drunk enough to not care. She drinks more and that helps.

"There isn't any more to the Japan connection?" I ask.

She decides to lie while guzzling. She looks away and back but not at me. "He has some Japanese friends."

Did I miss it in the meeting? "Do these friends have a lot of tattoos?"

Now she looks right at me. "Yes. But. Yes."

The expensive suit didn't look Yakuza. His assistants didn't look Yakuza. But the well-tailored cloth could have hidden the ink. And my video feed was far from an HD broadcast. It would explain why they were meeting on the seventh floor of an empty office building.

Sheryl can sense I'm getting ready to leave. Panicking, she grabs my arm. "He's not in with those people. He just he just—they expressed an interest in . . . Please mister tell me I didn't just fuck this up."

"The Minister of Pain fought Ricky Wrath in Eugene Oregon last night," I tell her. "And then Harlan quit or was fired from the WWE. It probably doesn't matter which from your perspective."

She shakes her head hard. "That motherfucker. He hasn't called me."

"Would he be in a position to go right to Japan and wrestle?"

"Yes. He never stopped talking to those guys."

"Those guys with a lot of tattoos?"

"Yes. Fuck him. Asshole said he'd said we'd do it together. Are you a cop?"

"I'm not a cop." I drop cash on the table.

"But you're not from TNA Wresting either. Liar. Fucking liar."

"I'm paying for your drinks."

She considers throwing her subsidized beverage at me but decides to down it instead.

"Do you know Marcia Cantrell?"

"His mother. No. I was supposed to meet her like five different times and each time she cancelled. He said. He was probably lying about that too."

"He told you Marcia Cantrell is his mother?"

"I know that's not a lie. He carries a picture of them together in his wallet."

"Do you know Melissa Verduna?"

"Is that his other woman? I fucking knew he had one. They always do. Any guy who's going to make it just puts his dick wherever he wants." She drunkenly throws her ice at me but I'm quick out of my seat and away.

It's late. I drive home.

On satellite radio I hear that a book about to be published on the pharmaceutical robbery has been optioned for a screen adaption—even though no one knows what *graphics have made warriors terrorists* means. Michael Bay is attached to direct. The studio is one of the Hollywood Hyena's.

CHAPTER SEVEN

HARDCORE

When I wake in the morning I check on Harlan's phone activity. He was up a little before me. Sheryl sent angry texts all night until he blocked her. He still hasn't called his mother back. But he has arranged to meet up with the woman he told his now ex-girlfriend was his mother.

I shower and dress in a Judas Priest shirt with a screaming mechanical eagle.

Self-help books make me sick. There's so little to them. The publishing companies just have to come up with the right title and the right personality for the author to wear while on tour. Truly, the contents of these books don't matter in any way. Most of the words are never even read. Buying them, ritually sacrificing a little money and sitting with them in Starbucks—that's enough to make most people feel better about whatever. Giving them as gifts is the same except two people feel better about whatever together. And when they are read, they just bestow a sense of having tried something. And that's more than enough for idiots to endlessly lend these book to other idiots and proclaim that all idiots should read them.

Marcia Cantrell's relationship books include: *He's Not Calling Right This Second Because He Hates You, Yes It Is Your Fault You're Single, Stop Crying and Start Trying: 60 Days to Marry the Man You Haven't Met Yet, Be A Bitch and Marry Rich, Get Them Hard and Then Play Hard to Get, Train Him to be A Good Lover in His Sleep, When You've Earned the Right to Cheat, Make Your Romantic*

Tragedy a Romantic Comedy and Be Jennifer Aniston, Why Cheating Makes You a Better Wife, Yes The Right Man Will Actually Solve All Of Your Problems, You Would Enjoy Sex if He Loved You More.

Her agent's secretary tells me she's on a photo-shoot for her upcoming book *He Can't Hear You with His Penis* this morning. The pictures are being shot in a fifties style diner. She's dressed as a pinup girl with her book on a platter.

I drive there and walk right onto the set.

She looks old and haggard under the hot lights. Photoshop is on standby.

"Marcia," I call. "I need to talk to you."

"You have the eyes of a divorce lawyer. I'm quite happy with my last divorce."

"I'm here to ask you some questions about Harlan."

She looks about the room for reactions to the wrestler's name. She steps out of the illumination and glow. She asks the photographer if she's done. He says almost. She moves outside of the diner and she sparks up a cigarette.

"His mother hired you?" she snaps as I join her.

"He told his girlfriend that you're his mother."

"You're looking at me pruriently." Big fucking writer. "You're shocked that a younger man would find me attractive?"

"No."

"You're disgusted that a younger man would want to be in a sexual relationship with me?"

"No. I find it a little weird that you are a friend of his mother."

"Was a friend."

"I bet."

She turns to yell at me but stops. "He had to tell the bimbo something. The girlfriend."

"That's how I always hear it. But why keep the girlfriend if the relationship the two of you have is so magically wonderful? They're not married. They don't have kids."

"They wrestle together. She is his—"

"Except she's not," I cut her off. "She didn't go with him to the WWE. And you know that. Try again Marcia."

"I give him what she can't."

"I hear that one a lot too. But it's just you now. She's done with him."

Marcia hasn't heard this news yet. The possibility burns like a chemical in her eyes.

"I knew Harlan had father issues. But mother issues too. That is what's going on with you. Right? I mean you're a menopausal self-help writer. You understand human psychology better than just about anyone."

"Why am I talking to you?"

"Harlan signed a contract last night with a Japanese businessman."

". . . he's going to Japan?"

"You tell me. Is that it? Is that all? He just signed up with Super Fire Pro Wrestling X Premium Japan? For legitimate and legal employment in his profession?"

"Yes and no," she says sadly.

"The Yakuza are involved."

"It's a double contract. He gets to go wrestle in the Super Fire whatever wrestling league in Tokyo. After. After he does a private hardcore match for the . . ."

"Yakuza?"

"A boss in the organized crime syndicate. Yes. It's going to be an ultimate extreme match. They offered it to him before Mr. Wrath took him to the WWE." She finishes her cigarette and folds her arms suddenly cold.

"He told you he was off the Raw tour. He didn't tell anyone else that."

"He called me from the road every night. We talked for hours. It wasn't just sex. And so what if the relationship included some mothering? He needs it. Why do you think he's trying to make a living hurting himself?"

"You're meeting him for lunch today."

"Who are you?"

"Chalk."

"That's not what I meant."

"Are you going to try and talk him out of this private hardcore fight?"

"I've been trying to do that for a long time. Now that the WWE dream is dead there's nothing anyone can say that will stop him. You said he signed the contract. Then it will happen soon."

"Don't tell him you spoke to me."

"Why the fuck shouldn't I? I have no idea who—"

"I'm a private investigator. My client asked me to find Harlan. He is going to want to meet him. I don't know when. But it's going to be good news when it happens. Don't scare him. Don't fuck it up for him."

"His biological father?"

I don't answer.

"When he tells me about the hardcore fight at lunch I will try and talk him out of it. When that fails I will support him. I will tell him that I love him. That I care about him. That I will be there at the end of the fight to help him heal."

"I'm going to go now," I say. "Before I do. I think you should know that I think your books are terrible. I believe that you're retarding our national intellectual development."

"That's nice of you to say."

"You're welcome."

I watch a text come through in the late afternoon that gives me an address for the fight.

After Hawaii, LA is the Yakuza's favorite American city.

Perfect white shirts and the tailored suits I've seen hide the full-body tattoos when they want them hidden. These intricate inks are done in the traditional manner with bamboo needles. Dragons, hangmen, geishas, shrines, masks, swords, devils, can each take years to complete. It is exceedingly rare for a Yakuza to survive a life of violence and become wealthy and fat enough to consider his tattoos done. Clogged with the inks of the tattoos their skin is unable to breathe and sweat. Toxins can't get out. These men drink all the time.

The Yakuza recently lost a bloody war with the Dub C Triad in LA.

There are no tickets for these irregularly scheduled hardcore wrestling matches. They are for the Oyabun and Kobuns only. I watch from the roof of an industrial building across the street with night vision binoculars. I witness vans unload barbed wire, chains, explosives, sheets of glass, gasoline containers, tool boxes that I know will include nails, staple guns, rat traps.

I see Harlan go in. He texts Marcia that he loves her before the bell.

Yakuza guards stand sentry outside among the black bikes and black Mercedes.

Harlan is helped out an hour later by the two assistants that were in the meeting, their tattoos now flowing free. Blood is matted on the wrestler's face and still dripping elsewhere. He has gashes and cuts in his arm and burns all over his legs. He is delirious.

I brought the good camera. And I have time to fit the lens and zoom. I snap.

Harlan's not going to Japan anytime too soon.

I know who he is and I have him under surveillance.

I'm ready to move onto the second of the three sons.

After I learn some more about my client.

On satellite radio they are talking about how technology has changed war. A veteran of the Iraq war is talking about a battlefield where the few remaining live soldiers see through eyes not their own and pull the triggers on weapons they don't control.

They're talking about this within the context of the message. Graphics have made warriors terrorists.

Chapter Eight

BOOKS

There is no paper in my life. That is by design.

Most of the paper that comes in the mail is just florid garbage. Bills should come electronically. Legal communications, municipal assessments, and all the rest can be scanned and destroyed. And that is what I do. I run them first through the scanner and then the shredder. I hate postcards. Personal letters are usually bad news: breakups, justifications, threats, laments. I read them once and that's enough to remember long enough to forget. People who hang onto paper are fooling themselves that they have some control over the blizzard of change and they don't.

It was harder to let my books go. I have always been a reader and so many of my books were presents from important people in my life. It was harder yes but necessary because of that. I donated them all and now rely solely on electronic devices to read. While the feel of a familiar book is nice, it is deceiving too. What matters is the words not what they are printed on. You can't really own books. If they're good, they own you.

I have eight tattoos on my body and they are all book covers.

On my right bicep is the original 1985 cover of *Ender's Game.* I was a teenager when my dad gave me this book to read. I was already an avid reader and books were well established as the main way that my father and I communicated. From the first words I knew it was a special book. I frequently turned from the last page back to the first, reading it in an endless cycle. It helped me survive high school as a weird kid. This book, like the other seven, owns me and is a part of who I am. The tattoo is dark and difficult to discern. I got it entering my first year of University, before my father died, before I crashed, before I was told that I have bipolar disorder.

On my left bicep is a recent cover of John Steinbeck's *Cannery Row*. The summer I was sixteen my father and I read everything by Steinbeck. We started with *The Grapes of Wrath* and ended with *East of Eden*. *Cannery Row* is a slim offering compared to those massive titles but it was our favorite. It is a collection of interlocking short stories and I read it whenever I have lost my faith in humanity. The denizens of *Cannery Row* are old friends. And Doc always reminds me of my father. I got this tattoo the week after he died.

On my left pectoral is my favorite cover of *The Sun Also Rises*. No truer words have been written about love and loss. I fell in love with a young woman called Diana in the University library. She was a writer while I was an academic. She was smart while I was just quick. She was a lover while I was still a boy. She took my love for her, cradled it, cared for it and then casually destroyed it. To this day she is the one person I always think I see at the grocery store or in the mall. Hemingway's book seemed to have been written about everything I'd experienced. When I read his words memories come of sheets and giggles and warmth and jealousy and pain.

On the left side of my back is the skull cover of *Trainspotting*. Welsh's prose taught me the power of experiencing a shared reality through rotating first person perspectives. It has helped me hear the voices of the desolate and the dead as I investigate. I got the tattoo after I met Special Agent Barrett.

On the right side of my back is the red cover for Brett Easton Ellis' infamous *American Psycho*. I got this tattoo when I was in the FBI. I honestly don't remember when which means it was after I started drinking and adjusting my meds myself. *American Psycho* is the only book I have ever read that made me vomit. It provides better insight into how a psychopath thinks than any academic treatise and is often found on the bookcases of serial killers and cult leaders.

On my lower back, together, are the covers for *A Clockwork Orange* and *Naked Lunch*. They represent my fear of madness, of waking up in that fucking psych ward with taped wrists bound to the bed, a melting brain, a breathless scream. I got these together before the end of my marriage, before my final banishment from any kind of normal life.

The last tattoo I have is on my right pectoral. It is the cover of the most powerful book I have encountered. I read it after my marriage was done and I couldn't see my son. This book destroyed me. I wept with every page and when I reached the end I was convinced I was going to die. Because the world was over and I would never see my son again. The cover I selected for Cormac McCarthy's *The Road* is the stark photography of the lines stretching into a dead forest.

Clients lie to me. They think my massive fee justifies it. Fair enough. But that cuts both ways. I feel justified in using some of that massive fee to investigate them. I learn a lot about motivation and stakes.

The Hollywood Hyena told me a moving story about a young man who was paid to jerk off into a cup and then took the money he earned to start a media empire. But then tragically his fertility was forever after cursed. He has been unable to conceive through marriage and affairs. And he's made himself sick trying.

But I wasn't the first person he came to. And that tale he told was not a first draft.

I remember hearing about a kidnapping case a couple of years back. My client's name was associated with it unofficially but not in the stories that ran. It's a more interesting place to start than the laudatory articles about what a business genius he is.

And it's been a while since I chewed the fat with Rose.

I met Rose when I was still with Behavioral and he was a pudgy prodigy LAPD Detective working with Homicide and Major Case. When I was forced out of the FBI he found me and we got drunk together in a strip club with good chicken wings. Since then he's quick to consult me. It's always a smart move. He gets access to FBI expertise without the FBI price tag. And in return he helps me disappear from LA crime scenes.

I call him.

"Chalk heh," he answers with a mouthful of food. "Let me ask you something. Try to be clever. What's the working distinction between a cult and a terrorist group?"

"The active FBI definition is pretty simple. Terrorists have guns and beards and Korans," I tell him.

"Cults have guns and beards and Bibles," he finishes it.

"That's about it."

"What's the real answer?"

"Quick and dirty?"

"You know that's how I like it Chalk."

"Cults define themselves in opposition to the outside world. The leader convinces everyone that those beyond the walls are out to get them. But the cult isn't at war with the outside world."

"Koresh wasn't looking to lead a crusade across Texas."

"Right. Terrorists want to bring the war to us. It doesn't get any quicker and dirtier than that. Why. What are you looking at?"

"Guess."

"You're working that pharmaceutical warehouse break-in with the strange message?"

"Everyone is working that my friend. It's a fucking gangbang: LAPD, FBI, DEA, ATF, Homeland. Dicks swinging everywhere."

"You think it was a cult?"

"There's talk. But what else are the experts going to do but talk? All I know is the robbers are going to have a hard time selling those pills."

"I'm sure."

"What can I help you with?" he asks me.

"I'm working for the Hollywood Hyena."

"Jesus Fucking Christ Chalk. When are you going to put a Porsche for me on one of these tabs?"

"When you get turfed out of the LAPD for suppressing evidence that implicates me, I'll put your name on my PI door. And give you your own Porsche."

"Promises." He coughs. "What do I know about the Hollywood Hyena? That's the question?"

"He was involved in a kidnapping situation a couple of years back."

"Yeah. Yeah. It was this. A woman comes to him and says she had his baby X years ago. She never told him. She didn't want his money."

"Right."

"Well he bought it. This supposedly brilliant businessman bought it."

"Desperation sells almost anything," I comment.

"Her hook? My girl—your daughter—has been kidnapped."

"How did that play out?"

"Bizarrely."

He tells me the rest and my afternoon takes shape.

CHAPTER NINE

KIDNAPPINGS

Glassell Park is not a stable place. When it is too wet there are hill slides. When it is too dry those same hills light up and burn. The demographics are volatile too. Laborers with work boots and shift workers with bags under their eyes nod hello to newly moved-in commuters taking mugged coffee for their morning drive to the land of 9 to 5.

For more than a decade there was a gang fortress on Drew Street. It was founded by a Latino woman who gave birth to a garrison of children. They sold drugs and used the money to arm themselves with guns. The matron was in and out of jail but her boys and girls kept the fortress running. The house cast a long shadow in the community. There were turf wars, drug deals that went bad, smashed syringes, pipes, and bullet casings. The police mostly contained it. But it took a politician seeking re-election to declare war. The LAPD had their own little Alamo with Mac-10s, Uzis and AK-47s. The family members who weren't dead after the concussed silence were put in jail and the city bulldozed the house.

The politician got re-elected.

Gangs are like mold: if the conditions that produced them in the first place are still there, it's only a matter of time before they return. The Lopez Covas gang returned to Glassell Park and they now hold an interesting position in the LA Gang Scene. They're associated with the Mexican Mafia in that they pay taxes and can rely on protection. They have understandings with the Aryans and secret agreements with both the Crips and Bloods.

Raul began rebuilding the family when he got out of juvenile by replenishing the genetic stock. They're all still in Glassell Park but distributed through a few different houses now. And they have found a business niche in the underworld of LA crime.

The Mexican Mafia asked Raul to nab the daughter of a dealer delinquent on his taxes. It worked and so he did it again. By the time he'd pulled it off half a dozen times, he'd started to understand the specialized work. Now the Lopez Covas gang does contract kidnappings for their friends and on spec for money.

Cherie Morris grew up in Glassell Park. Her looks got her a job as a hostess at Ceccioni's in West Hollywood. Her bright white smile and dazzling eyes caught the attention of the Hollywood Hyena. He started meeting her in hotel rooms. She was pregnant shortly after he ended the affair. The timing was such that she must have known her child wasn't his. But that's what she began jawing about to her boyfriend—how her son's real father was rich and successful. By the time the little girl was six the boyfriend had had enough. He hired the Lopez Covas gang to kidnap his kid. And Cherie contacted the Hollywood Hyena with the news just as Rose said.

I put on a Smashing Pumpkins shirt of a gas masked soldier in toxic green and take the elevator down to the parking garage where the 911 waits in my spot. I find Cherie at her new restaurant: Hugo's, still in West Hollywood.

It's early evening but near the end of her shift. I tell her she's going to talk to me about the Hollywood Hyena when she's done and I'm going to give her two hundred dollars for the information. She says she has to get home for her daughter. I ask her if she has a car. She doesn't. So I tell her I'll drive her. She's uneasy about the arrangement but I'm calm and consistent.

I sit with a Cuban sandwich while she finishes up.

The 911 impresses her. I put her home address into the GPS and drive slow.

"He paid the ransom," she explains. "He got the cash right away and paid."

"Your boyfriend split the score with the Lopez Covas gang?"

"I didn't know that he did."

"But you brought the Hyena a daughter you knew wasn't his. Could he tell right away?"

She shakes her head. "We stayed there for a month before he had the DNA test done."

"Stayed at his mansion?"

"At one of his mansions. It was always so clean. Tracy lived in the pool."

"Was Mr. Robertson married at the time?"

"I don't know. He never said."

"You didn't want to ask. You didn't want to do anything that would end the fantasy."

"We were a family. A kind of family anyway."

"You were sleeping with him again."

She's leaning against the passenger door, her face against the window.

"Your boyfriend is at home with his friends blowing through the ransom cash. And you're playing happy family in a Hollywood mansion. Until Mr. Robertson had the DNA test done."

"He had a doctor come to the house."

"How did he react when he was told the truth?"

"He called a car for us. He told my daughter to go to it and wait. He never yelled at me. He wanted to know what I knew about . . . about how the kidnapping happened. Who had done it."

"You grew up in Glassell. You knew everything about the Lopez Covas gang."

"He insisted on meeting them."

"So you went back to your boyfriend and explained the change. The new way to get money out of this rich guy."

"Mr. Robertson played with her for a week. Picked her up and threw her around and laughed. And then when the DNA test came back . . . he didn't see her. She wasn't there. He just wanted her gone."

"We did that part of the story. Your boyfriend arranged a meeting with who from the Lopez Covas gang?"

"He tried to arrange a talk with Alejo Lopez. But Alejo wasn't going to meet Mr. Robertson. He'd just taken his money for the kidnapping. He didn't trust it."

"Do you know what Mr. Robertson was going to ask the Lopez Covas gang to do?"

"He'd worked up a list of all the kids he said might be his. Women he'd slept with. There were like ten names on the list. He wanted the Lopezs to kidnap them, do DNA tests and if one was his . . . Keep it."

We drive through the silence. She sits up and I see that she was crying against the glass.

I summarize. "Instead of being angry that he'd been a victim of the kidnapping . . . he saw a way he could use it to his advantage. And right away tried it."

"He said he'd go to the police if the Lopezs didn't help him."

"But they didn't."

"No they reached a compromise. They told him about another kidnapper who would do it."

We've reached her home. And waiting on the step is the daughter who had a different dad for one confusing month in a Hollywood mansion. We just keep finding new ways to fuck up kids.

"Thanks for the ride."

I pay her the promised cash. She gets out. I pull away.

The Lopezs are the standard for professional kidnappers in LA. But it's generally a crime that appeals to slackers. I have a psychological theory on that. I think slacker kidnappers resent the happy childhoods of their rich target kids. Knowingly or unknowingly they want a little revenge before they get the gym bag of cash. They want to see that little prince piss his expensive clothes. They want to hear the princess cry in the dark and realize no one is coming.   Anjo Lopez foisted the Hyena off on a kidnapper who started as a slacker but then figured out an angle he could work over and over. Dejan Madar snatched children with diabetes. Three grabs a year earned him a decent annual salary. He got his leads from support groups, pharmacy records, book purchases. He followed the families for weeks waiting for a grab opportunity. Then he contacted the parents and told them he had their kid but he didn't have any insulin. There was no need for any threats or deadlines beyond that. The parents knew what would happen each hour after the first missed dose. Dejan just had to name a reasonable price—the careful consideration for any con or extortion. Any upper middle class professional can come up with a hundred thousand dollars.

And if he'd stuck to that smart game he'd likely still be alive.

But Alejo arranged for Dejan to meet with the Hollywood Hyena. Dejan got greedy.

He took the Hyena's money and the list of his potential children. The mother of the first kid on the list shot him dead when he tried to grab her son outside of daycare. The LAPD investigated but nothing traced back to the Hyena definitively—money gave everyone peripherally involved memory problems.

Rose thinks the Hyena gave up on the kidnapping plan after that.

None of this changes my approach to the work I've been hired to do. But it gives me a better sense of how ruthless my client is. He doesn't care about money and he doesn't care what people think about him. He didn't try and get his cash from the initial kidnapping con back. He twisted the idea and tried to make it work for him. He didn't flinch when this ill-advised plan led to a dead kidnapper. He just spent more money to make it go away.

And this was before he was sick.

He is desperate for blood and kin.

I owe him a call, a check-in.

"It's Chalk Mr. Robertson. Your first son is named Harlan. I have him under complete surveillance. I'm going to start on your second son tomorrow."

"Harlan." He says the name lightly.

"We haven't spoken about what's going to happen when I have all three of them."

"I want you to arrange a meet."

"Yes," I say. "And what are you going to tell them when you meet them?"

"That I'm their father. That I'm in their lives now. That I have money. That I can help them. That whatever they want to do or be I can make it happen."

"What if they don't want you in their lives?"

"That won't happen."

I pause. "Consider it."

"I didn't walk out on them."

"No. You were never in their lives to begin with."

"Does Harlan have a man he thinks is his father? A man he loves like a father?"

I decide to answer: "I don't know."

"No matter. I don't need to get rid of such a man if there is one. For any of them. Fake fathers or step-fathers are no threat to me. I am their real father. And when they know that . . . when my three sons know that . . . all the others will be nothing to them. It will be just me."

"I'm concerned that you—"

"What. You think I'm going to kill them if they don't love me?"

I hadn't thought that until just now. "You don't know how they will react Mr. Robertson. That's all I'm trying to say."

"I'm paying you to get my sons in a room. That's your job."

"Like it was Dejan's job to kidnap kids for you and have their blood tested."

He doesn't falter. "That kidnapping idea was wrong. This is right. These three young men are my sons, my blood. I will know them before I go. I'm not crazy Chalk."

"I don't mind crazy. I'm crazy myself. But I control it."

"I'm controlling it," he lies to me. "I'm fucking controlling it. Do you have pictures of Harlan?"

"Yes."

"Send them to me."

"I'll give you pictures for all three at once."

I'm frustrating him. "Fine."

This has not been a confidence inspiring conversation. I want to defuse it before I end it. "Tell me something as the Hollywood Hyena. How can you option the film rights to a book not yet written about a heist that just happened and no one understands?"

"It's a good way to make a strong claim on the story."

"Nobody knows anything about anything though."

"It's a great heist. With lots of action. People are interested. That's all I need to know. They'll read the book. And then go to see the movie. Or more accurately know about the book and go see the movie. What matters is we've staked our claim."

"We'll talk again." I click off.

CHAPTER TEN

COACH

Gloria Newsome went to California Cryo Futures after almost a decade of failing to conceive with her husband. They called their son Jason. Her husband died when Jason was a teenager. She's remarried now.

Jason has been locked up twice as a juvenile. And spent six months inside as an adult.

Gloria is a research accountant at UCLA. She has worked in both Science and Social Science. For the last five years she has been adding the numbers for the researchers in the Faculty of Medicine. Which is how she got in on the clinical trials for a special drug.

When I was a kid the best *Saturday Night Live* skit wasn't live—it was the parody advert that came after the opening. Some of the best lampoons were at the expense of the pharmaceutical industry. I remember Homicil: the drug to help parents cope with the anxiety of possibly gay children. I can still do the ad for Suppressex: the drug to stop surprise rogue erections. And I loved Annuale: the drug to conflate a year's worth of menstruation into a single murderous month. They were all just a little north by northwest of the actual reality.

Since Viagra made blue the new green, every drug company on earth has been working to engineer the second part of the sexual equation: a drug to enhance female libido. Pfizer has a new compound codenamed Flower. The clinical trials for Flower are being coordinated at Pfizer's research center on Wilshire. Public information retrieved from archived copies of their website and those of the agencies they use to recruit participants show that the overall study is moving quickly through the prescribed levels necessary for market approval.

I got this far dishonestly enough. Gloria's identifying information got me her work email which made it possible to target her work computer. UCLA network security always makes me smile—they just try so darn hard. Reading the email stored locally on her computer I connected to the dormant office computer of the UCLA prof who got her into the trials and has taken a sabbatical to work for the benevolent and loving Pfizer.

Cracking Pfizer's network security would require a little more effort. But it's not necessary. I know that Gloria is involved in the largest part of the study. She takes a determined dose of Flower daily and daily completes an online survey through which she rates both her sexual interest and her sexual activity. And of course she reports any perceived side effects. There is also space on the form for her to add qualitative impressions that don't fit into the standard structure. She cuts and pastes from the web tool used for the study into emails she sends her best friend in Spain.

Gloria's definitely interested in sex more. Sadly for monogamy fans, her second husband is not the only beneficiary of this change. First alluded to obliquely in her regular reports, and now openly discussed, Flower has helped Gloria resume an affair that had ended two years ago.

Every week she has a half hour appointment with one of the Pfizer researchers to discuss her submitted information. Before or after this she arranges to meet with her lover. Today it's going to be after.

I'm wearing a Pink Floyd shirt with the towering white bricks of *The Wall* behind a cartoon figure lost in a lunatic scream. Precisely parked, I watch Gloria go into the Wilshire building.

She's in there for forty five minutes: some waiting, a half hour interview with the researcher, and she's back out.

Now she's off to meet her lover.

I've observed two kinds of cheaters in my professional snooping. The first kind are the pros. They have different emails, secondary cellphones, secret credit cards, they know how to invent friends, events, problems at work, Facebook events, how to hide smells, how to pretend that everything is normal. These men and women have no trouble having a little on the side. They never get caught and they almost never leave their primary relationship. The second kind of cheaters have affairs for the drama. The emotional turmoil makes them feel alive. The anxiety and risk enables them to experience cleansing guilt. They may not know it but they always want to get caught. If they get away with it once, they'll be looser and looser until the desired disaster comes.

Having read her daily journal entries, I would say Gloria started out wanting the drama but is now becoming a pro. Is the drug part of that transformation? Is the increased desire for sex making her more mercenary about the pleasure?

The motel isn't far, still on Wilshire.

I park and watch her walk into the front office.

Flower started life as a new antidepressant. It's big side effect was increased interest in sex. So the company switched it up and began working on a pill to ameliorate "hypoactive sexual desire disorder" one of the side effects of which might be increased happiness.

I watch Gloria exit the motel office and walk down the line of doors, stopping at seven. She uses the key to open the door which means she's arrived first. Well her lover is arriving third because I'm showing up second. I beep the 911, stalk across the pavement and stand outside of the door. I give her a moment to light the candles and perfume the air or whatever bullshit helps her believe this is romance.

I knock. I hear her come to the door.

"Ken?"

"No but open the door Gloria."

"I'm not . . . I can't."

"I'm here to talk about Jason. Open up."

She unlatches the door and lets me in. She's wearing red and black lingerie. She either couldn't find a robe to cover up or mention of Jason's name made her not care. She sits down on the bed and doesn't look at me. I remain standing.

"I'm not the police," I answer as she starts to ask. "I'm a private investigator. Working for someone who wants to find and help Jason."

"Help him. Why?"

"You either want to believe that or you don't."

She rests her hands together in her lap.

"Jason has had some trouble with the law," I state.

"His father died when he was still just a kid. He reacted to that."

"He believes your late first husband was his biological father?"

She bites down on what she was going to ask and just answers, "Yes."

"Did he know about California Cryo Futures?"

"No."

"Has your new husband been able to be much of a step-father?"

"He's tried but no."

"Does Jason know you cheat on your husband?"

"How would knowing that help you find him?"

"There's finding him physically and finding who he is," I answer. "I need to do both."

"Count yourself lucky if you can find him at all."

"Who is he running with?"

"Bikers."

"They can be fun. Any particular club?"

"I wouldn't know."

"Is he into drugs?"

"Sometimes drugs. Dogs," she answers. "He fights dogs."

"Does he have a girlfriend that you know of?"

"He had one before he disappeared from . . . what do we call this? Jobs and lies and medication and affairs in motels? Oh yeah: normal life," she spits bitterly.

"What's her name?"

"Anita Lockhart. She's a Life Coach."

"Clearly a great one."

A knock comes on the door. Gloria is embarrassed.

I open the door for her lover Ken. He's brought flowers. Asshole.

I explain my presence by leaving.

Anita Lockhart is an actual Life Coach. She has a website that says so—so it must be true. Listed in her qualifications, right under her freshly inked degree in sociology, are the failures in life she has learned from: not making the cheerleading squad, a car accident her senior year, and overcoming bulimia. There is no bulleted point in which she brags about being born rich. But I don't understand how else she could pass this income fantasy off as a job.

Anita claims to have helped professional athletes and individuals released on probation with her inspiring message. That's likely how she met Jason. I call the contact number on her site. The assistant that answers is shocked that the phone has rung. She tells me that Anita is enjoying a small vacation between clients. I tell the assistant I'm from the Federal Department of Licensed Life Coaches and I am investigating Ms. Lockhart. The assistant rolls on her right away. She tells me the hotel Anita is at.

It's a hotel known for pampering dogs.

In-between the LA River and Glendale is Atwater Village. The San Fernando Road, Glendale Boulevard and the Golden State

Freeway all pass through and around. The Sunset Tower Hotel is a Gatsby great.

I leave the keys for the 911 with the valet and head for the Terrace with my MacBook. The decor achieves classic glamor with soft surfaces, rich appointments and an amazing view of the city. I order a California omelet with goat cheese, avocado and scallions. I eat by myself, thinking. I drink coffee. The bill comes. I place a hundred on top of it. The waiter returns, sees the hundred and pauses. I ask him about the amenities for dogs at the hotel. He explains that dogs staying at the hotel are treated to their own beds and bowls. He adds that they are run unleashed in the park left to the hotel by the silent film actor William Hart.

Eager to feel he's earned the hundred, the waiter says some dogs have gone missing recently. He confides that this has been an embarrassment for the hotel. He tells me knowingly that there may be a lawsuit.

He takes the hundred.

I put a second down.

I ask him if he knows Ms. Lockhart. He tells me her dog is being run now.

I leave the Terrace, find a perch just outside the dogwalk and open my MacBook. While I wait I run differentiated searches on Jason. I hear Anita's entitled voice before I see her. She's laughing with someone she's bumped into.

I shut my computer, stand up and stop her. "Where's Jason Anita?"

Her makeup cracks ugly. "Who are you?"

"Jason. Your boyfriend. Where is he?"

"He was never my boyfriend. He's a biker psycho."

"Which is more embarrassing? Admitting he was a boyfriend? Or a client?"

"I helped him as part of an outreach program." She tries to push past me.

"What's the dog connection? You like dogs. You like to come to the top hotel for dogs in the city. He fights dogs. What's going on with that?"

Anita can see that others are hearing this. She marches back to me. "I didn't know what he was doing."

"Sounds like you do now."

"That sick fuck . . . We used to come here. When we needed to get away and chill out. He stole dogs. And then used them . . ."

"To fight?"

"To train the fighting dogs," she hisses.

"There are dogs everywhere. Why not go to the pound?"

"That's where he got most of the bait dogs from. But he got a kick out of taking dogs from here."

"Rich pampered bitches like you?"

"He took Mickey Rourke's Dalmatian." She says this as if it were a war crime.

"So you're spending as much time as you can here to establish yourself as a good customer who didn't know the street urchin you'd let into LA's canine sanctum was—"

"I didn't know who he really was. He lied to me."

"I find that hard to believe. All your life coaching experience." I smile at her.

"If hotel management knew that Jason stole the dogs that disappeared. That he had them ripped apart," she enunciates. "I could not show my face around here ever again."

"Which surely would be the greatest cruelty in what you've described."

"Jason is a sick fuck."

"Yeah you said that. But. I mean. Is what he was doing with the pampered dogs that much different from you wanting to fuck a bad boy? Similar psychological needs, no?"

She wants to yell at me but doesn't want the scene. She wants to storm away but knows I will just call her back. She understands that I am in control. We will talk about what I want until I determine that we're done and then I will dismiss her. Maybe with a dog treat.

"You didn't know but you found out. About the dog fighting," I tell her.

"He hangs around the Mongols okay."

"Hangs around. He's not one of them?"

"He just organizes the dog fights. He trains the dogs and sets up the fights."

"Where?"

"They do them all the way up in Antelope Valley. He took my Mercedes there once and left the address in the GPS. And dog shit in the backseat."

"Get me the address and we're done."

We go to the lobby and tell the valet to get both of our cars. She gets the address from her GPS. I hold it in my memory for the time it takes me to enter it into the 911's GPS. And then I pull away.

CHAPTER ELEVEN

DOGS

I drive North for Antelope Valley, Kern County, in sight of the San Gabriel Mountains. The address is ranch styled. It's a new property but seemingly empty. There's no for sale sign but there are also no vehicles parked outside. Standing at the end of the drive I can see two other properties. But no one is here. And no one is watching.

Jason's half-brother is a hardcore wrestler.

Jason facilitates dog fighting.

It's a cruel carnival, dog fighting. Injected with steroids, fighting dogs are forced to tread water in pools and pull weights. They are hung by their jaws, taunted with lashes and starved. New fighters are brought to the pit strong and scared but usually unmodified. The animals that survive to fight again will have their ears cut off so other dogs can't wrestle them down. They will have their teeth sharpened with files. They will be fed meat coated with bug spray so their fur tastes wrong to their opponents. And just before a fight these animals may have an amphetamine rubbed into their anuses. A dog that wins one fight is a dead eyed killer. A dog that is alive after five opponents is an otherworldly monster.

Regular dogs are used as live training meat. Bait dogs. Like Mickey Rourke's Dalmatian.

I walk around the back of the house, pulling on gloves.

The bunchy lawn is wrong. Standing this close it's impossible not to see that it's a cover but it wouldn't be spotted from outside the property or from a helicopter. The grass is torn up and flattened except for a tidy and almost perfect circle. I check the edges and find the rope. I pull the cover away and there is the pit. It's twenty feet in diameter, ten feet deep. There is some structural bracing with wood but mostly the walls are dirt. The floor is a bloody mess of cheap rugs.

Are the dogs lowered in? Do they slide down crude ramps?

I see the footprints of a large tripod on the edge. Like for a heavy video camera.

I've never watched one of these fights live but I've seen the videos. They always record the carnage, sometimes even broadcast it. The ripping can end in seconds or go on for hours. This area isn't exactly the suburbs but how do they hide the activity? High fences, loud music. It is a known motorcycle club hangout—that could be all the answer that is needed. The neighbors can move, look away, or come on over for a cold brew and a little animal brutality.

No one lives here. It's a party house.

The MC keep the dogs somewhere else.

They bring them in to fight and then take away the carcasses when the fun is done.

I walk up to the back door and take my picks out to work the lock. But the door is not locked. I ease it open. The furniture and walls and floors are destroyed. Beer has been spilled everywhere and on everything. I move among scattered potato chips, cans, two used condoms close together on the floor, a pool of dried blood, hardened vomit in varied stages of decomposition. It would take me a day just to itemize all the DNA evidence.

Dogs were kept at least sometimes in the garage. The stench is unmistakable. There are food bottles and water. In the corner is a metal tub, jumper cables and a marine battery. This is where they kill the defeated. Or the dogs that refuse to fight.

I wander around the house with no idea what would be a good find. I find a book on Boerboels. It looks like it has actually been read. We better watch out—if bikers learn to read there's no way the forces of normal society can stop them.

It's getting dark out.

I know I should move on but I keep looking. The Mongol Nation is mostly Hispanic but they do count white boys in their numbers. They've been at war with the Hells Angels for years. Nothing would bar Jason from joining them if he made it through the initiation period.

The Mongols import and move guns in LA.

I've decided to go when I find a Sony Handycam in the kitchen. It's screen is cracked and it was left behind as broken. I walked by it at least once without noticing it. The battery is dead but I find a charger in another room. I play what's in the memory on the little fold-out screen. It's video of two Boerboels. A young white man is stroking them. They are panting and happy.

Whoever is holding the Handycam calls the young man on screen Jason.

Jason says these dogs are not going to fight. They're going to be guard dogs.

There's GPS data in the Handycam but I don't need it. I recognize the clubhouse from an ATF raid that made the news two years ago. I carry the Sony with me back to the 911 and start driving south as night comes.

Boerboels are bred for defense. They are massive, muscular, menacing dogs. They're superior guards because they understand who and what they are guarding. You wouldn't want to leave them around a child they don't know but if they understand that small human to be a part of their charge, they will defend little Tommy with all of their ferocious power.

I'm watching one through my binoculars from within the airtight 911.

Jason had two in that video. But I don't see a second.

Just as I have this thought the Boerboel stops patrolling and looks up. The second he detects my scent, my presence near the edge of his property, he will rush forward in the dark, teeth blared for blood. Even if I can keep my throat from being ripped out, the bikers will be alerted.

I need to prepare for this raid. I put the binoculars down and reach for first gear.

I query the navigation system to find me vets in the area. Several pins drop on the map and I take them in order. Vets have invested in security systems since the cat tranquilizer Special K became a popular club drug. The closest vet the GPS finds me is new and protected by a quality alarm system I don't have the patience to outwit right now. The second has closed since whenever the navigation data was last updated. The third seems to be open at this time of night which is strange. I'm thinking of doubling back and breaking into the first one with brute force but the fourth turns out to be perfect: a small old vet on a commercial street dark for the night. I back the 911 into the drive and leave it running. I pull plastic gloves on, a nylon mask, and I grab my picks and flashlight. I go to the side door. It's a simple residential lock battered and loose. I pop it and push the door in.

An old and cheap alarm sounds. Shit.

Barks and yowling come from the dark. There is a smell of urine and wet fur. I pan the flashlight around the cages, reflective eyes flashing back at me. There's a metal table and there is a counter and there is a sink and there is a fridge and there is a padlocked cabinet. I start to pick the padlock on the cabinet. It's a good one. I'm realizing this was a bad idea, that I should make a quick exit, go home and find what I'm trying to get online. I tell myself thirty more seconds, just thirty more seconds. A snake hisses. I trick the padlock with a click and the cabinet door swings open. Vials are aligned neatly with small font labels. Names I recognize: tylosin, phenobarbital, oxibendazole, panacur, lufenuron, no, no, no . . . .

there it is: acepromazine. I grab all the bottles there are, and a few needles, and I'm back outside and then back in the 911.

I pull away slow.

In the rearview mirror I see what might be a security car responding to the tripped alarm. I accelerate through one hundred, one hundred and twenty, blast through a red light, and then brake hard and pull into a vacant lot and cut all of my illumination.

I've made this much harder than it needed to be. It's a fucking dog drug. And this doesn't have to be done tonight. I scare myself when I get like this. I'm not going manic, I'm not, but it feels like I can't sense where the limits are.

I should go home, call it a night. I'm not making good decisions.

But now that I've gone this far . . .

Never a good sign when I'm arguing with myself.

My feet and hands make the decision for me: lights, clutch, gear, gas, back to the biker clubhouse. I park exactly where I was. I never took the plastic gloves off. I don't need the mask again. I unwrap a syringe, puncture the vial and pull the plunger back.

Acepromazine is a tranquilizer especially effective on large breed dogs. They used to use it on horses. It drops the animal's heart rate and blood pressure. But what's my plan here exactly? Get the dog to rush at me madly barking, jab it in the neck with the needle and hope for the best?

No. Fuck no.

This is a mistake about to become a disaster. I have to cut my losses.

I place the needle on the passenger seat and I start driving home. I drive the speed limit, the scanner and radio off. I park myself underground and go up to my condo. Somehow I'm completely ignorant of what time it is. Voraciously hungry, I go online and order a pizza. And then I search for sites that sell tranquilizer guns. Before the pizza arrives I've ordered a .62 caliber gun with a laser sight, a dozen compressed air canisters, and two dozen hypodermic darts. I pay for next day delivery just before midnight.

I could have got the Acepromazine online almost as easily. But no I had to fucking rob a vet. I had to trip a motion detector alarm like a shaking junkie kid. I had to hang around longer than I knew was safe and then tear up LA outrunning a security car that probably wasn't even real.

I buzz the pizza guy up, tip him cash, and eat the entire pie with a glass of water. The carbs and grease tire me but not enough to sleep. I feel like drinking. I feel like downing a bottle of vodka and counting down as oblivion comes for me, erasing the mistakes of tonight and propelling me to tomorrow. I can't. But. A little wine wouldn't hurt. That's not really drinking, it's just having a drink. One. Possibly two glasses. Because that never goes wrong right?

No. Fuck no.

I've got to end this day but not like that.

I take my meds with water. The Seroquel starts to bring me down. I move to the bedroom and think of reading. I make sure my MacBook and the phones on active duty are all plugged in and charging.

I sleep, I dream that I'm driving the 911 recklessly fast, trying to outrun something. The Porsche isn't its normal planted self. It's floating under throttle. As I dodge commuter cars, I begin to feel all four tires losing grip. I can't anticipate the chassis' reactions to steering input or braking. And just when I think I've caught it, I lose total control, the back comes around and I'm headed for a concrete underpass column.

I wake up, ravenously hungry again. There's cereal in the kitchen and I eat several bowls. I make coffee, shower, shave, move into my office. My tranquilizer gun order has shipped and I open a window to track the FedEx truck delivering it. It comes at lunch.

I sit on the couch and assemble the gun. It loads like a rifle and will take five syringe darts at a time. I load five empty ones, insert the air cartridge, aim with the laser and fire at the living room wall. It's quiet, quick. I fill five darts with the Acepromazine, get a fresh air cartridge and set the weapon by the door.

Hungry so hungry still. I order another pizza. The same delivery guy comes to my door. He makes a weak joke about my love of pizza, such a funny asshole. I tip him less. I eat most of this pizza. I think about drinking again, still, again, still. I decide to take a nap and stretch out on the couch. I wake up near dusk, not sure what just happened but feeling in control again and ready to work.

I drive back to the Mongols' clubhouse.

I wait where I was last night, in the dark, on the edge of the dog's concern, now with the tranquilizer gun. Every night's a party when you're a biker. There's activity in the club house but no one outside except the lone guard dog. I get out of the 911. I turn the laser sight on and walk it across the ground until it's on the dog's body. Unsure, the animal starts a low growl. I exhale and squeeze the trigger. The dart hits the beast's flesh and it whelps. I fire again. And then again. The last dart misses. No matter, the dog is asleep.

I calmly walk back to the 911 and drop the tranquilizer gun off. The plan is again to bluesnarf my target's phone. But I'm not going to bring my MacBook right now. I need to get a look first. See if Jason is even here. And if he is here what he's doing.

I approach the clubhouse. There are lights on in the main floor, Black Label Society blaring, angry laughter. I'm estimating no more than twelve bikers and associate women. Above the second floor is dark, as is the basement below. Yes this LA home has a basement. There are steps carved out of the ground, descending to a basement door that is wooden. I ooze down these steps and put my ear to the door to listen. I hear nothing, no one.

No wires here, no sensors, no alarm system.

The door creaks as it swings out. I wait and step in.

I'm surrounded by fighting dogs in the dark, panting, growling in their cages. They start barking and yelping at me but the party upstairs seems to take no notice. Then a door at the top of the inside stairs opens.

I move behind the water boiler.

Feet come down. The dogs calm.

Jason is standing among the animals. He's stumbling drunk. I hear him sit on the floor with a thud. I listen to him drink from the bottle he brought down with him. He's descended here alone. To be with the dogs. This feels like a ritual. He's one of them.

I risk a look. He's pushed himself against the wall. He's wearing a biker jacket.

"Barney is quiet outside tonight," Jason slurs. "You think I should bring him in here to sleep with us? To pass out with us?" He laughs. "Mongol or Marine. Do you think it matters? I don't think it matters. Both soldiers." He burps. "Both killers right? You guys are killers too aren't you you you you fuckers. You fucking vicious fuckers." He glugs from the bottle. "I'm making you killers. And life . . . life is making me a killer."

I hear an incoming text beep from his jacket. I hear him get his phone.

"I've got to pick up tomorrow." He's not talking on the phone. He's talking to the dogs. "While I'm out doing that I'll see if I can . . ." he burps. "I'll do my best to get you guys a rich poodle to rip apart."

Jason passes out. He tips over and starts snoring.

The dogs palpably relax. They don't bark when I come out.

I stand before Jason. I take his phone.

I float out of the basement and to the 911. Holding Jason's phone in one hand, I bluesnarf it like I did with his unknown half-brother's device. When I sneak back into the basement,

Jason has pissed himself and rolled over enough for me to see he has a Prospect rocker on the bottom of his Mongols jacket. I put his phone back on the floor where it was.

Just then he rolls over. I take a picture of his face with my phone.

Out in the night, the Boerboel is still sleeping. I pluck the darts from the breathing body and the one miss from the ground. I put them in my pocket. No one from the raging party sees me. I make it back to the 911.

I email a second clone order to Golden Earring.

I listen to satellite radio news on the drive home.

The drugs taken in the pharmaceutical warehouse robbery have been mailed to tens of thousands of veterans around the country. The same package to each individual: Lexapro, Prevacid and Vicodin. The packages all come with the same message: *Use or sell as you need. Courtesy of GR.*

The FBI have theories on how they identified the names and addresses of veterans and when and how the packages entered the postal grid. But these are just guesses. They don't know anything. It's an utterly amazing event in US history.

Forty million dollars' worth of pills dispersed at once.

Vets are being interviewed by every network and local TV station.

The treatment of our soldiers is now the only topic of political discussion.

Utterly amazing yes. But is it a distraction? The action doesn't seem to connect to the message. Graphics have made warriors terrorists. That's a statement about war not the care of veterans.

And who is GR?

Chapter Twelve

METH

Wearing T. Rex's *Electric Warrior* shirt with Marc Bolan in distorted perspective silhouette I drive to Playa del Rey and pay for the clone that enables me to watch Jason's communications. I then sit with Starbucks in the 911, windows rolled down, the cool air from the surf coming in.

Jason's morning texts are about the Boerboel called Barney that I drugged last night. Evidently the Mongols have fed the animal booze and drugs before. The dog is groggy but going to be okay.

I drive home and loiter in my office.

I assume most of Jason's morning is spent killing his hangover and washing his pants. After one in the afternoon he texts a number that is owned by a Vivian Spears. He informs her that he is going to be in Eagle Rock. He asks her if she wants to meet up at the mall food court. She writes back yes.

I drive to Eagle Rock Plaza and get orange chicken from BBQ Express. When I'm done eating I sit with the cloned phone. Jason arrives and hugs the blonde woman who was here waiting for him before I was. She kisses him on the lips. He is not flying the Mongol's colors at the moment. He's wearing just a windbreaker.

Vivian is better looking than the life coach.

They get Chinese. I don't move to sit closer. I don't need to hear.

Vivian is frustrated with Jason right from the start. She wants something from him that he won't or can't give her. He says he's sorry a lot. And that of course just makes her angrier. This could be a break-up except I don't know that they were dating. The situation has a high school vibe to it. Jason asks her if he can finish her food and she throws her hands up and leaves him. He doesn't run after her.

Jason finishes eating and then gets up and walks. I follow him at a distance.

He goes directly to the US Armed Forced Recruiting Center. He's standing well away from it but there's no question that this is what he is looking at. He starts moving again but circles right back. He doesn't go in any stores. He doesn't see me or anyone else.

It feels like the meeting with the woman was his excuse to come here. To be here.

He marches into the Recruiting Center. It's a Military Gap with posters and pamphlets. I watch his body language through the window. He's talking to a muscled sergeant with a bright white smile. The soldiers working in there are selected so carefully: happy and whole, crisp uniforms, medals. They'll talk to the kids that come in about education and training and a future. They don't talk a lot about combat. They say they do if asked but they just don't.

I think Army Recruitment offices should be exclusively staffed by injured soldiers. If a kid still wants to sign up after seeing what happens when you get pulled apart by an IED, then he's a fucking patriot and we should all salute him.

The muscled sergeant knows Jason. Their conversation is earnest and important.

Jason comes out with no materials. He must have got those the first time he came.

The Mongols prospect checks the time on his cellphone. He leaves the mall. He finds his bike. He kicks his leg over and puts on his helmet. He didn't park near my 911. But he takes his time firing the motorcycle up. And I'm able to find him by following the low rumbling.

Jason leads me to a bungalow in the nearby suburbs. He leans his bike on the kickstand at the curb and moves across the lawn. The grass is cut. The exterior paint is recent. There are no vehicles in the driveway.

I drive past the address once slow and then again faster. I see a single propane tank just outside the garage door, the fittings blue. It's a small mistake but enough to tell me what's going on here. There's a meth lab inside.

Jason likely has been charged with checking on the cookers or picking up product.

I park several blocks away. I can't use plastic gloves in the middle of suburbia in the middle of the day. I get a small backpack from the back seat and stuff it with my picks and the Glock. You have to be armed anywhere meth is being cooked or consumed.

I put earbuds in and move past the house like I'm a middle-aged man lost in music not quite jogging and not quite walking. I smell for that acrid cooking odor but it's not there which means they're venting it somehow. All the curtains are drawn on the main floor.

On my second pass coming the other way I move up the driveway and to the garage door. I take my earbuds out and listen at the cheap metal. No voices. I slip down the side of the house and to the back yard. There's a wooden gate with a latch. Beyond it in the back is an arrangement of plastic lawn furniture. Cigarette butts are everywhere on the stones. There is a garbage bag. Now there are voices coming from the back room. A woman is moaning and a man is screaming at her in German—the internationally known sounds of deviant porn.

There is the smell. I open the garbage bag. Inside are ripped boxes of cold tablets, bottles that contained acids, iodine and a metal can that was filled with paint thinner. An effort has been made to clean them. This information is valuable. Most home labs are set up by Martha Stewart chemists who are addicts themselves. They get the recipe online and buy the chemicals domestically. They cook and smoke and shoot. The more meth they do the more paranoid and crazy they get. It ends with the lab blowing up or a mad bloodbath. The fact that the cooks in the back room of this house are still making an effort to clean the empty containers and have figured out a way to vent the toxic fumes means they're hopefully not too far gone.

I put my ungloved hand on the back door knob and hold it for a second, feeling for a trap.

An ATF agent taught me how to do this. I talked about rock concerts with him the day I saw him blown up by the tripwire his feet found before his eyes. I wiggle the knob ever so slightly. I don't sense any sloppy extra weight or tension. But it is locked. I get my picks from the backpack. I take the tension wrench and enter it into the keyhole where the pins begin to show. I keep pressure on the wrench in the direction that the key would turn. Holding that, I slide in the rake pick and brush the pins with a downward motion. Next up is the half diamond pick to clean up the specific pins the rake didn't convince, again pushing downward as I work from the deepest pin to the one nearest the keyhole. The tension wrench gives and the lock clicks.

I trade the picks for the Glock and turn the knob. Waiting for the explosion that doesn't come I push the door inward. Extending my gun I look for wires near the floor. I move to my knees and look closer again. The porn screams coming from down the hall are loud. I step into the kitchen. Now the smell is unmistakable. There are more empty containers, dirt, powder residue.

Light is shining from the doorway at the end of the long hall, the back room. I look down into the psychotic abyss. I can hear glass being moved, bubbling, steam escaping. The old television flashing the porn is on a child's dresser just visible from my vantage. A hand reaches up and turns it off.

Jason and the man he came to see start talking.

"I told the Sergeant I've decided no."

"It's the right decision. The Mongol army is better bro."

"Safer. But what am I fighting for?"

"Pussy. Pussy and booze. Pussy and booze and drugs homey."

"All the major motorcycle gangs were founded by veterans returning from Vietnam. Did you know that?"

"So you skipped the sand in your ass part."

"Sand in Vietnam?"

"No I'm talking now. You're skipping the sand in Iraq and that other fucking place in the desert. . . . What do you think of my new pipe?"

"Damn son," Jason exclaims. "You are becoming like a glass-ware artisan."

I hear a lighter spark. The flame will be under the glass bowl. The meth will be melting. The friend will swivel the bowl about between his fingers. And he'll take the first hit while it's still heating.

His exhaled cloud drifts into the hall.

Jason's turn. Another cloud wafts back towards me.

"You know they piss test you when you're in the army," the cook says.

"That's what they have to say. To make people at home feel safe. You make it into an elite fighting unit they want you to be an optimal killer. Whatever that takes man. Hear me?"

"You've been on the internet again there homey."

I hear the lighter again. More smoke.

Jason was drinking last night. He doesn't have open sores.

"Invisible and invincible," he says.

"You and that fucking sword."

I haven't seen him scratching. His teeth are okay.

"That's how meth makes me feel man. Like I'm wielding the Honjo Masamune. Invisible and invincible. An unbeatable warrior."

"You want to watch *Ghost Dog* again?"

"We should get the job done first."

Jason's not a meth addict. At least not yet. But I'm still gripping my gun tight.

Done smoking their bowl, I hear the two moving around in the back room. Then I start to hear metal clicks and clacks and clunks. They're doing the work with rhythmic expertise and concentrated effort. They're assembling guns.

They will be AK-47s or AR-15s.

The ATF is a simple agency. They make all their trafficking cases as simply similar as they can. They get a tip on the movement of guns and then they setup surveillance. "Gunwalking" is a term they've preciously coined to let small sales go through in the hopes of catching the big bad guys like the Mongols. Sometimes the guns walking are even weapons put on the market by the ATF.

A chain of small sales allowed the ATF to get a confidential informant in the Mongols' Southern Cal gun business years back—long before Jason. The ATF raided the Mongols' warehouse with a tank. There were no guns to be found. But a wooden crate did contain the body of the confidential informant. He'd been dressed in the Russian uniform of Mikhail Kalashnikov, the inventor of the AK, and forced to swallow rounds for the weapon until the full metal jacket diet killed him.

I exit the house. I return to the 911.

I head home confident I have Jason under solid surveillance.

Horror movies are my choice for working out. But when I move to the couch for the evening I like my distractions layered. I have four televisions in the living room, all the same size, black windows into the cold expanse of space that is my loneliness.

The furthest on the left is my movie screen. I have about a thousand movies in rotation, all of which I've seen at least thirty times. I play them with no sound and they are like waking dreams which I remember I remember I remember. Turning the sound off is the best way to appreciate the artistry of the great directors. It makes you aware of the angles, the shots, the cuts, the choices.

To the right of the movie screen is my modern glass page, the screen on which I scroll novels. There are about five hundred books in this rotation, all read before and worthy of rereading over and over. I can set the words to scroll fast or slow and to jump to bookmarks or random pages. I'm never exclusively reading these novels but I'm never not reading them either. I don't know why this works for me but there's a telepathy at play, telling me when to glance, when to scan, when to block out everything else and read the words exactly and with purpose.

The next screen is my sports monitor which lately means classic Lakers games. I keep up with the current season and of course watch the playoffs but I adore watching the amazing performances from years gone by. I witness the historic happen. I watch men that are now dead or at least crippled fly through the air. Still no sound, no cheers, no whistles.

On the fourth and last screen are my mute news feeds: ABC, Al Jazeera, BBC, Reuters, CNN, Fox, selected RSS feeds. Thousands of bursts of information with only seconds to make an impression before the next jump.

These four screens flash and shimmer, a concerto of art and information. I'm engaged and distracted at once, both intensely interested and overwhelmingly confused. In this silent visual cacophony I hear my thoughts. No chirping police scanner, no blubbering radio, no intercepted conversations, no desperate cellular secrets, just the sounds of my movement in the condo. Good nights, I escape time for a little. Bad nights, I can't stop thinking about drinking. And disastrous nights I can't stop drinking.

Tonight is okay. I'm okay tonight.

I'm watching Ralph Sampson and the Rockets knock the Showtime Lakers out in the fifth game of the 86 Western Conference Finals. I've loaded up *The Great Gatsby* on the book screen and started it at the first Gatsby party Nick attends. It's rolling slowly. The prose is so light, the story so direct. And I'm watching Carne's *Les enfants* where the camera moves as the eyes of a child, eager to see everything but understanding almost nothing.

On the news there is mild chaos throughout the country. Veterans have made a principled stance of returning the stolen drugs they received to the company—in full uniform but without words that make any sense of the gesture.

Chapter Thirteen

INSURANCE

Insurance is metaphysical gambling. But the suited bookies of the industry invert the football paradigm: they pay the life losers with the money from the temporary life winners. The massive difference between the quick and the dying is enough to make billions. Yet the insurance companies aren't content with that. They want to make more. So they change the rules of the gamble.

Imagine placing a bet on the Patriots and winning but not being able to collect because of a pre-existing sporting enthusiasm you didn't disclose before making the wager. Imagine playing blackjack and the dealer busts except for this one hand the target number has been changed to twenty-four because well it just has. Imagine going to the casino cage to cash in your chips and being told that the house has decided to fight you in court even though they know they're going to lose because they'd like to hold on to your money for a little longer.

The "medical-loss ratio" is the insurance industry's calibration of costs. They call it something a little friendlier in their PR literature. But it means exactly what it sounds like: how much money the industry loses on paying out the medical expenses it entered into a contract to pay out. The pursuit to get that number down drives policy which forces life and death decisions on individuals every damn day. One example says it all: Caesarean sections are on the rise in the US because they're cheaper than vaginal deliveries.

The third California Cryo Futures mother is Ginger Petti. She called her son Alexander.

Ginger analyzes the medical-loss ratio for Blue Shield. She works seven days a week.

And this seems to have been her life forever.

I was once hired to manage a corporate defection. The executive was moving from Apple to Google. I approached her on a romantic weekend with her husband in Hawaii. I gave her a clean cellphone and a locked down notebook with an email address utilizing strong encryption. I told her and her husband to keep both devices hidden when they were inside and covered while they were moving outdoors. She liked the offer the enemy made her so I proceeded to arrange an in person meeting. I set it up at a downtown hotel and I advised her what to put in her calendar, the excuse to make when she disappeared. I ensured the three hour conversation was not monitored by bugs or laser microphones. The meeting ended in a printed contract and smiles. The final phase was the defection itself. I worked with her and her husband to plan when and how she quit. We consulted with a lawyer on what she could take from her office. And on D-Day I was there to walk her out of the building.

Ginger makes a fraction of what that tech executive did and I'm sure does. But Ginger is facing the end. She went to California Cryo Futures when her uterus was getting ready to retire. She's approaching retirement age for the rest of her body now. What will Blue Shield give her? A standard gift, a decent pension, and nothing to fill the emptiness that remains. If she has work friends they'll call less and less frequently to tell her how badly her replacement is doing. That will likely be all there is.

I think she thinks of nothing else but this end. I think I can trick her with an offer.

I call her. I tell her I'm a headhunter for another insurance company.

She invites me to her home in the evening. Just like that.

Stretches of Porter Ranch in the San Fernando Valley feel like a jail for homes. It's the fences and the walls of the gated communities. The gates open for the German and Japanese SUVs to commute to Simi Valley and Woodland Hills and Downtown LA. The vehicles leave to make their money and then drag it back within the walls like raiders. Some of the communities have little more than ornate gratings and cameras. Some referred to as "security zone" communities are nothing less than fortresses. They have high walls, lights, spikes—they stop short of moats, cauldrons of boiling oil and archers but it's a competitive and lucrative market so you never know what's coming next.

Ginger bought the cheapest house in the best neighborhood she can afford—always a smart real estate move for people who want to live in an investment. I give my name to the friendly guard at the gate and am waved through. There is a nine-hole golf course, an exercise complex and a spa on site. The lawns are absolute perfection, better than a baseball outfield.

I park in her driveway. The door opens before I can ring. She looks old.

I tell her that before we talk I need to scan her home for audio surveillance. I take my shoes off and she positions them perfectly by the door to wait. I walk around. The rooms seem as if they were just prepped for an open house. The choices of furniture and color and even personality are all about selling the investment. Almost no living takes place here.

When I'm done my fake scanning we sit in her kitchen.

"I can't tell you what company I'm with yet. I will give you that information as part of the package. The package will include a complete company portfolio, a statement of your responsibilities, a compensation package, and a transition plan. You will not be expected to bring any Blue Shield secrets with you."

"How can I express my interest if you can't tell me anything about the job?"

"You've expressed your initial interest by agreeing to meet with me. This interview is really for my employer. They want me to have this conversation with you before going any further."

"About what though?"

"About your morals."

She hates not understanding. "This doesn't sound like a job interview to me."

"It's not. It's a pre-screening defection conversation."

"You have no right to ask questions about my private life."

"That is true. And that is part of the reason I can't tell you what company I'm working for at this time. If you're not interested in having this discussion, I will leave."

"Why do my morals matter?"

"The company I represent is a new insurance business that is going to market itself as fair and moral."

"A religious insurance company?"

"No not religious. Moral. People's number one complaint about insurance companies is that they are not fair. And so my employers want to make sure that the top executive tier is beyond reproach."

Her eyes widen. "We're talking about the top executive tier?"

"I think I can reveal that yes." I wait for her to talk next.

"What do you want to ask me?"

"You've never been married."

"I'm a lesbian." The promise of money can be even more effective than money itself at getting people to talk. "Is that a problem?" she challenges me.

"Not at all. I take it you are not currently in a committed relationship?"

"Not now. Not for a long time."

"You have a son?"

"Yes. We went to a sperm bank. I went to a sperm bank. My partner left shortly after Alexander was born. I raised him myself."

"Do you do drugs?"

"No. Never."

"How is your relationship with your son?"

"He's an adult now."

"Do you talk to him?"

"Not very often. I tried to help him."

"What do you mean by that?"

"He got his girlfriend in high school pregnant when they were both fourteen. He moved out. Then the baby died. I tried to help him," she says again slower.

"What does he do?"

"Okay. Look. Alexander is the only thing in my life that might be a problem. If we're talking morality. He breaks the law. But I don't think it would be fair for him to jeopardize my chance at this job. I did my best. Now he's an adult."

"You have no idea what he does for a living?"

"He's a hacker. He makes money with computers illegally. I don't know more than that. He was always in trouble with computers when he was a kid. Hacking into the principal's desktop. Stealing games in development. Stealing credit card numbers."

"How did he get into that?" I ask.

"He got computers and books from this special charity. The digital something. And I sent him to a programmers camp one summer. I thought computers might keep him out of trouble with drugs and sex. He would type until he fell asleep on the keyboard."

"Help me find him," I tell her.

"Find Alexander? Why?"

"If he's breaking the law I will capture evidence and show my employers that it has nothing to do with you. If they are concerned about it but still want you then I can present the evidence to the police." It's a dubious extension. But she really wants the job.

"And then I'll get to see what your employer is offering?"

"Yes."

She tells me everything she knows about her son, his marriage, his boy who died, his cyber-crimes, his gang of teenagers, his gambling. She gives me a current picture of him and an address and a phone number.

Chapter Fourteen

PIN

I am wearing a Tool tour shirt of the mighty Penis Wrench.

Alexander's home is in Highland Park on Palm View Drive. He married the girl he got pregnant in high school and it appears that they are still joined in that blessed union. Neither of them are home when I stop on their street.

I let myself in and look around.

It's an old house with just two bedrooms. It looks like she works at McDonalds. I see a dirty uniform, a name tag, a printed out schedule with changes made in pencil. I find an old PC hooked up to a mag-stripe encoder. And a brand new Alienware rig with multiple monitors connected to a full NBS credit card printer.

The door to the second bedroom opens on a shrine filled with birthday presents that were purchased for the child that died. There are nine of them all swaddled in the same x-men paper, all with bows. It's easy to understand how the situation developed. The gifts were purchased in anticipation of a party, a few hours where the little man would have been a prince. But he died. Returning the gifts would have been wrong. They could have given them to another child. But they didn't. And then a year had passed and the presents hadn't been opened or touched or moved. So they became this ghostly collection. And eventually the pictures of the child were added.

It feels like my room for my son. And that makes me both angry and confused.

Then I see the cuts on the wrapping paper. The re-taping jobs.

I sense with sudden certainty Alexander is using these presents to hide money.

Even with a warrant no law enforcement officer would think of violating the sanctity of this sadness. I look at the presents for a long time and think through how Alexander might have done it. Would he have tracked down an extra roll of the same x-men paper in case he caused a rip? Would he have taken pictures of the original wrapping in case he had to do an entire rewrap? What did he do with the toys? How frequently does he make withdrawals and deposits from these shapes? How nervous had he been the first time his wife came home and entered the shrine? Does she kneel before them and pray? Or is it enough for her to know that they are here?

I pick one up. But I won't look inside.

Ginger told me that Alexander's wife knows about his hacking scams. Maybe she suspects the presents are full of cash. Or. It could be that he wants her to believe they are full of cash so she doesn't know how bad his gambling is. Because they couldn't ever talk about the gifts, could they? That's a twisted game of denial.

Ginger tried to resuscitate her relationship with her boy many times. She told me she would go and find Alexander in Garvanza Park. This is where her son had taken her grandson before his death and where he now organizes his gang of miscreant teenagers.

I exit the home and go back to the 911. I drive through Taco Bell.

I watch the house for part of the day. I see the wife come home tired and greasy.

I move to Garvanza Park and watch there with my MacBook. After dinner Alexander makes an appearance and sits on a picnic table. Two teenage boys, not older than fourteen, show up and talk with him for a bit.

Looking at him the entire time, I bluesnarf Alexander's phone from the street.

I put a third and final clone order into Golden Earring.

I pick up the cloned device two hours later. Eat. And get some sleep.

Alexander doesn't communicate much over breakfast. But after his wife has left for her shift at McDonalds he initiates four different text dialogues with two teams of two kids. They're using a shorthand code but it's apparent that both teams will be working at Santa Monica Place this morning.

It's out of my way but I take the time and drive along the Pacific Coast Highway. I arrive well in advance of Alexander's two teams. I get some coffee and a muffin. I sit with my MacBook outside of True Religion Brand Jeans: the identified target for Team A.

Team A appears to be the younger of the two units Alexander has working this fine morning for capitalism. But I sense they've still done this before. The two kids on the team enter True Religion Brand Jeans a few seconds apart. One is dressed in nice upper middle class clothes. He's clean. He belongs. He moves as close to the main point of sale terminal as he can. He's Clean Kid. The other kid is dressed in a dirty t-shirt with holes. His hair is unkempt and greasy. He's got a jagged addiction vibe. He moves for the back corner of the store very quickly. He's Dirty Kid.

There are three staff in the store and they all clock Dirty Kid as a shoplifter.

The Mighty Defenders of the Franchise react. Big Guy Geek, overweight and sweaty strong, moves to the store entrance to block an escape. I'd bet this guy lives at home. He spends everything he earns on DVDs and comics. A college-aged staff member, Efficiently Part-Time Asian, goes to Dirty Kid to see what he's doing. The third and last staff member is Menopausal Manager. She comes out from behind the counter and cash fully trained for this situation.

Dirty Kid steals. I don't see how exactly but he's made it as obvious as possible. Efficiently Part-Time Asian tries to stop him with her voice. Dirty Kid shouts back at her. Right away the situation is tense and potentially violent.

Menopausal Manager dials mall security from the counter phone. But before she's fully accomplished this words give way to tussling in the back of the store. Dirty Kid is wrestling Efficiently Part-Time Asian. She's screaming. Big Guy Geek leaves his sentry post at the front of the store and comes over to add his sweat to the fray.

Menopausal Manager abandons the counter and cash completely.

Clean Kid is standing watching all of this. He'll know where the cameras are, what the corner mirrors can see, and he'll have a notion of how long the rent-a-cops will take to arrive. But he only needs one minute.

The right minute.

Now.

Clean Kid moves behind the cash register and inserts a card into the point-of-sale terminal. He drops below the counter while the card loads the malware up. The two kids don't have a signal but having done this before their timing is close to perfect. Just as Clean Kid is pulling the customized card from the POS and returning to his role as a mildly shocked affluent young person, Dirty Kid gives up what he was trying to steal and starts threatening to murder the store staff. It's an over the top performance.

But it works. The Mighty Defenders of the Franchise back away.

Dirty Kid runs.

The mall cops have arrived wheezing. Clean Kid sees them and blocks for his teammate. He accidently gets tangled up with the mall cops and everyone hits the floor together. Dirty Kid makes it out of the store, turns the corner and hits escape speed.

Everyone wins. The rent-a-cops have an excuse. The Mighty Defenders of the Franchise defended the company's precious jeans. Team A did the job Alexander trusted them with. And everyone got a story.

The malware loaded on the point-of-sale device will now capture the information on every card inserted into it by dumping the memory after each sale. Alexander picked the store because they have wireless keypads for their customers. The malware will open a port that lets him retrieve the captured data with a notebook from outside the store whenever he wants. He'll likely sit right where I am now.

He can sell the numbers or use them.

Alexander watched it all from a vantage behind me. I just see him now as he leaves.

Team A can't be seen in the mall anymore now. They're done for the day.

Team B starts work before lunch. Their scam is going to take me a while to figure out.

There are great viral videos of idiots trying their collective grubby hands at bank robbery by yanking ATMs. They use trucks, fork lifts, motorcycles and chains to wrench the ATM away from the wall and get it to their country estate where they can, at a slow rural pace, perhaps over a few beers, crack through the shell of the metallic cash turtle with tools of flame and horsepower. And then happily divide the cash. Except that the metallic cash turtle notices that it's not where it's supposed to be and makes a cellular call to the police. And if the robbers do manage to crack through the shell without killing themselves, the money will be covered in red ink that makes it unusable.

It's much smarter to follow the bank's lead and rob the individual customers.

This is what Alexander's Team B are getting ready to do right now. Somehow.

On the third floor of Santa Monica Place there is a Bank of America ATM. I understand covert technology. But I don't see the extra lens until my third pass. It is the size of a coin and has no wires. Alexander placed it to the side where the deposit envelopes are kept. It's at an odd angle. It looks like a sensor of some kind.

The rubber sleeve that shields the keypad has been cut away cleanly.

I sit on a bench again. I take out my MacBook and look for the camera's signal in the congested invisible. It's there. It's not encrypted. It's not even hidden. Alexander named the device Bank of America Special Camera. I intercept the signal and display what it is seeing on my screen.

The camera is exactly pointed at the ATM PIN pad. Some people are too big for the camera to see past them. Some people's posture is too bad. But Alexander and Team B don't need to see everyone's PIN.

I close my MacBook and walk around. I consider the strength of the signal.

I go into the nearest men's bathroom. Alexander is in the handicap stall sitting on the toilet. I see his feet from under the stall door. I can hear him typing on his notebook. He's a smart fucker. But he doesn't know that I've cloned his phone.

I move back out and return to my seat in the mall.

When Alexander gets a usable PIN he text messages the two kids in Team B with a description of the freshly cashed target. One of the kids bumps into the target. Apologies are made. The target moves on.

I watch this happen four times before I realize what they're doing. The kids have RFID card readers under their clothes. These devices capture the bank card number of the person they've bumped into and any credit cards keeping it company in the wallet or purse. When they are done harvesting for the day, Team B will go home with Alexander and they will print new magnetized bank cards on the NBS printer I saw in his house.

It's fucking brilliant.

Except that no. Wait. A new fake bank card with the old PIN won't work in an ATM. PINs are matched to their cards. And then of course there's chip technology now as well. So how are they making money in the endgame?

Alexander texts the two kids when they're done at the mall. I watch them all load into his rusted GTI and drive away. They return to his home in Highland Park. Team A and Team B hang out in the house for the early afternoon. Pizza comes to the front door.

After their late lunch the boys jumble out of the house again and again fall into the GTI. Alexander emerges wearing a FedEx delivery uniform and carrying a box of newly printed bank cards.

I get it.

I follow the GTI to an address just off Ocean Avenue. The boys wait in the car while Alexander goes up to the front door. This will be the home of a bank customer who had his pocket digitally picked earlier at the mall. Alexander will tell the customer the ATM he visited was discovered to have a skimmer on it. To protect customers the bank has issued new bank cards to be delivered expeditiously. The new card has the right number. Alexander tells the customer it will use the same PIN. Should the other card be cut up? No the bank needs it back for the ongoing investigation. Maybe Alexander even makes the customer sign something.

He leaves with a working bank card that he knows the PIN for. And then he drives around LA having the boys hit the ATMs until the cash stops coming out. When the robbed customers discover their new cards don't work they'll assume it's part of the problem they were informed about and call their branch.

I've got to shake my head in admiration.

I get the good camera and take a picture of Alexander coming out in his FedEx uniform.

The third and final son is under surveillance and at least partially understood.

Home. I put on Kobe's 81 point athletic humiliation of the Toronto Raptors in 2006, Ingmar Bergman's *Persona*, and set the words of Nabakov's *Lolilta* floating. Kobe's sheer will drives again and again, changing physics, ordering reality. Bergman's close-ups dissect personality—they are unnerving, unwavering, each one a separate existential crisis. I speed *Lolita* up and then slow it to the part where Humbert receives the letter from the married and pregnant Lolita. It has always been a book that has made me uncomfortable, partly because of its brilliance. But mostly because the morality keeps shifting on the reader.

The chaos continues on the news. Veterans have overdosed on the stolen drugs.

Chapter Fifteen

GAMBLER

The year after I left the FBI was taken up with the divorce details, the custody battle, thoughts of suicide. I had no idea what I would do next. Working for another law enforcement agency might have been a possibility but I didn't have it in me to learn a new political game, especially considering I'd failed so badly at the FBI's. I considered going back to academics, finishing my doctorate, resuming the path that Dr. Fraser had shown me. And that probably would have worked. I was older but my FBI experience would have been interesting enough for a second or third rate college to let me do criminology lectures for freshman during the day and an edgy course about serial killers and madness for their menopausal mothers in the evenings.

I considered it but less than the bottle of sleeping pills.

I was depressed all those months, tired, afraid. I spent whole days in bed. I kept a scribbled journal of my dreams that was lucid nonsense. I was always looking for answers, reasons, and I felt like I was being watched.

I thought about the Bacchus killer all the time.

And then one day there came a knock on my door. My mind cycled through the paranoid possibilities first, then reluctantly the real ones: more court papers related to the divorce, a neighbor wanting to say hi, a friend worried that I was seemingly dead. I wanted it to be my son but knew it couldn't be.

After twenty minutes of knocking I got up and I turned the knob.

It was my new profession.

The persistent man was an attorney for a wealthy family. They were desperate to find a witness that they believed had disappeared into a cult. Asking questions of the right people the attorney had found my name. He came into the apartment, visibly concerned about the odor, the mess, the bottles, me. He gave me a file with pictures and notes.

It took me two weeks to find the witness, a week to get him out of the cult, and a final week to get him ready to testify—I never use the word "deprogram" because it is dangerously misleading. In a month's effort I had made my annual salary at the FBI. And it had pulled me out of my depression. And I knew what I was going to do.

I invested in some tools, moved out of that apartment and into the condo I have now. I bought my 911. In the back of my mind was the notion that I could work on the Bacchus killer myself, prove he existed, find him, show Barrett.

That's how I became a PI. I've got all my work since on the strength of my reputation.

As soon as his wife has gone to make sausage and Egg McMuffins at McDonalds, Alexander texts his teens. He tells them to come over for the game. There were four of them in the two teams yesterday but he invites eight kids in total.

I drive to the street in time to see a fanciful sight: boys arriving on bicycles and skateboards wearing tuxedos and carrying cases of cigars and bottles of scotch. He doesn't put a roof over their heads but Alexander is a true Fagin to these teens.

The text and call activity stops when everyone has arrived for the game.

I'm wearing a Placebo shirt with a neon blue and purple androgynous head blurred.

I drive away, park on the street and walk back. I get right on the property and near the windows with no difficulty. Stealing glances inside I can see Alexander and the teens playing poker on the kitchen table.

The boys are having the time of their lives, big cigars, important smoke, serious drinks.

Does Alexander just win all the money back from the kids he's made take the risks? It could be that's how it works out sometimes. But from what I can hear it's not like that by design. These are lost children. They either don't have dads or their dads aren't around. Alexander grew up without a father. And then he lost his own child so young. He gets as much from this as the boys do. It is real fun.

I return to the 911 not sure what to do next. It seems that the poker party will continue until twenty minutes before Alexander's wife returns from her shift. Do I need to wait around for that?

I should start thinking of how I am going to bring these three brothers together.

I drive home, make myself a bacon sandwich, and drop into my office.

I go for a nap. It's always smart to grab one when I can.

I wake up to the clone of Alexander's phone buzzing. I check it. He's texted his wife at work to tell her that he's going to be gone when she comes home from her shift and that he's going to stay overnight at his friend's. She replies just "ok."

Strange marriage. But who the fuck am I to judge?

Alexander then texts a number that a search exposes as a Verizon pay-as-you go burner. Alexander thumbs that he's given his kids their party and he wants to meet up for the OVB tonight. The respondent asks him how much cash he's bringing? Alexander texts back a smiley face.

OTB is an Off Track Betting establishment. I don't know what an OVB is.

I get back in the 911 and track the location of Alexander's phone. I catch his GTI up in Chinatown. I drive by his choice of parking spots and find one of my own. I tail him on foot at a distance. He was wearing a tuxedo with his kids but he has changed into jeans and a silk shirt now.

Chinatown is a smell for me more than a collection of streets or even ethnic faces. There's a base sickly sweet musk of garbage—it's different depending on the season but it never goes away. There's an aromatic sense of smoke and cheap oil. Above this foundation are the wafting odors of the vegetables and meats sold in the groceries and the dishes prepared in the restaurants. I can distinguish the smell of chilies, cinnamon, coriander, cumin, lemon grass, ginger and turmeric. Top of everything is the fish: dried, iced, burnt, pasted, rotting.

As night comes the lanterns are lit.

Zen Mei Bistro is on Alpine Street near Dodger Stadium. Alexander has just gone in. I wait until I see that he's taken a table through the window. And then I enter and ask for one myself. I've been around Alexander enough recently that his subconscious might register me. I have to be careful not to look directly at him.

Alexander and I have the same waitress. I order sizzling rice soup, eggplant, shrimp with spicy salt and Chinese broccoli. The waitress knows Alexander. She tells him that Xiong is almost done his shift.

There is a single thought that explains the wretched existence of every compulsive gambler I have encountered: She doesn't hate that you gamble—she hates that you lose. Early in the tragic fall that "she" will be a wife or girlfriend. Then the "she" will be a mother stolen from, a daughter abandoned, and down and deeper down. I've heard loan sharks say it almost word for word to their suckling addicts. I've seen it in the adverts for those phone services that will whisper the stone cold NFL locks on Sunday. The worst part is that there is truth in the statement. If a gambler never lost family and friends wouldn't know about the problem or wouldn't care. But the sickness would be the same. Gamblers aren't addicted to winning any more than they are addicted to losing. They are addicted to the rush of the anticipation, the moment in which the winning and the losing happens.

The turn of the card.

The horse's last stretch.

The numbers that come up on the dice.

The knockout count.

Smarter minds than mine have reached this conclusion. But I have a footnote. In my experience any attempt to understand an individual gambler is useless without understanding the stakes he plays for. A rich gambler gets no rush from playing dime slots. The stakes have to sting. And gamblers who win for a while always end up playing for their lives.

Alexander's wife has been disappointed by his gambling before. I don't need to do any digital snooping to know this. There will have been losses, debts, fights, threats to leave. They're not fighting now because he's generating enough cash flow that they can play the twisted game of denial with those unwrapped presents.

It won't last. He will disappoint his wife again.

Perhaps worse: he will disappoint the kids who look up to him.

Xiong is a cook. He comes out wearing his whites, carrying Alexander's food. He presents the dishes on the table as the waitress presents my food to me. Xiong then takes his whites off and joins Alexander to eat.

They're talking low, talking of gambling, cash.

I consider my waitress. She knows Xiong. She might know what they're talking about.

There are waitresses and bartenders in LA supporting themselves on tips while they run around for auditions. These kids and not-so-kids are chasing the American dream, working for a chance to be something more than they already are. They're Chasers.

Chasers are everything that's great about this country.

The Slash class is relatively new. They are mostly located in LA and New York.

A young woman from the Slash class will describe herself as a waitress-slash-actress and invoke the myth of the struggling Chaser but this is a lie. She doesn't need her tips to live. She's got breast implants that cost more than her tips for the entire year. She'll have an acting coach, a trainer, and always be going on vacations to get away from the stress. She'll be dating a C-list celebrity and exchanging flirty texts with a B-lister.

The young man who says he's a bartender-slash-screenwriter doesn't need the money either. He'll have a classic convertible and he'll have a family connection to a studio. For both archetypes the money will come from parents or trust funds—parents that have transformed into the highest form of existence for moms and dads: pure money representing love.

The salient point is that it is all a game for the Slash class. The waitress will take a job as a hostess to meet more celebrities and she will call in sick as often as she wants. The bartender will be writing a werewolf script about a bartender and each time he fucks up a drink he'll make a mental note to include that dialogue. Achievement is about sacrifice and these people sacrifice nothing. If they don't make it, they don't care. And honestly if they do make it, they probably don't care either. The BMWs and tans and sex are there no matter what.

My waitress is a member of the Slash class. She'll go through the motions of caring.

I get up to go to the bathroom and catch her in the hall.

"What's OVB?" I ask. "Xiong goes there."

"Why are you asking me?"

I clear my throat for the lie. "Fox is getting ready to shoot a new reality show called *Step Dad*. The show documents the challenges of a middle-aged man becoming the new step-father in a family of three children. Or so those children and their mother believe. In actuality the man is becoming a step-father in two separate families at the same time. The houses are identical but painted different. The children are symmetrically identical in their ages and genders. And the mothers have similar histories of divorce, heartache and trust issues. At the end of the season the true situation will be revealed to the two unwitting sets of children and their mothers. And the man will choose which family he wants. The production company has more lawyers on staff than psychologists and more psychologists than writers."

Her response is pretty vacancy.

I explain it. "They need actresses to play friends."

"Like what do you mean?"

"Like you would be a friend of the mothers. Or a friend of the oldest girls."

"How?"

"What do you mean how? The writers write something. The lawyers and psychologists say it's okay. You become a friend on the fucking show. You tell me what OVB is, what it means to Xiong, and I will take your portfolio when I leave here."

A Chaser would ask questions. But for a Slasher I've offered enough.

She looks to the cook and Alexander laughing together. "OVB is a joke," she tells me. "It stands for Otherworld Video Betting. It's a private room. Gamblers can bet on . . . anything. Like sick shit from around the world."

"How do you get in?"

"You've got to be vouched for. I've heard. I mean I don't know anything for sure or anything. I've just overheard Xiong talking to . . . well that guy over there. They go together. They're going tonight."

"Go get your portfolio."

I return to my table and finish up with my food. The waitress returns with her portfolio. Alexander and Xiong see me take it. I motion for her to come in close to my face and tell her not to talk to anyone about the questions I asked.

I peel off bills for the tab and leave. I go across the street, dump the portfolio in a trash can and wait on the Dodger Stadium side for Alexander and Xiong to emerge from Zen Mei Bistro. They do and I fall in behind them.

CHAPTER SIXTEEN

DEBTS

I always carry a lot of cash on me when I'm working. Right now I've got two thousand dollars in my roll. I should maybe get some more. I wouldn't be surprised if Alexander is holding ten large.

The gambling duo lead me into the dark heart of Chinatown and then they disappear down an alley in which lanterns are dim pastels warning and not guiding. They stop at a red lacquered door covered in golden symbols. A fat man in a black suit knocks on the wood for them. It is opened and they enter.

My face is not known. I don't have anyone to vouch for me.

I doubt the prospect of a part on a bullshit reality show will win this guard over.

I walk away and find a place to take a piss. I buy some coffee and return to the corner of the alley to watch. After two hours, Alexander and Xiong come out. Alexander is sweaty. Xiong is angry. They've busted out.

They're about to pass by me when I make the decision to blow my cover.

"Heh, guys wait a second."

Alexander slows and grabs his buddy's arm. "Yeah what?"

"I want to get into the OVB to gamble."

"Then you're even stupider than we are," Xiong answers.

"Would you get me in?" I ask them.

"We don't know you so uh no," Xiong snaps. "Let's go Alex."

"Wait wait," Alex says. "How much will you give us if we get you in?"

"Five hundred."

"Alex: you don't get someone in unless you know who the fuck they are."

"He's got money. I need money. Seems like a match to me."

"You get the wrong guy in there your life is worth nothing."

"Fuck off dude."

Xiong raises his hands in a gesture of giving up and walks off.

"You said five hundred. You're asking me to take a big risk for five hundred."

"Seven hundred."

"A thousand and we go in right now."

I count him out a thousand dollars. He takes it. We walk back to the red door and Alexander puts his arm around me. The guard knocks and we step into a darkness thick with smoke. I stumble down small steps.

The OVB is a single underground room with small old televisions on the walls and hanging from the ceilings. The space was carved out of the ground. There is a small cage in the corner for transactions. The dirt floor is plastered with dead betting slips.

Alexander forgets me right away.

There is bear baiting from Pakistan, zoomed cricket combat from China, cockfights from India. There is a full card of dog fighting. Alexander is betting on the dog fighting. The canine carnage is taking place in the pit I found in Antelope Valley. These are the Mongol dogs that Jason has trained.

There are also humans on the TV screens. There is a naked man in a padded cell with a gun and a knife within reach. He is lost to madness and sorrow and he could be anywhere in the world. I can't fathom what action is placed on this spectacle that is surely the end of his life. There is betting on the type of Yakuza hardcore wrestling Harlan participated in. The bets are made on when the wrestlers will pass out from blood loss and pain.

And there is Taiwanese death gambling.

Death gambling became an open but shocking secret in Taiwanese hospitals a decade back. Family, friends, and hospital staff were the usual gamblers. They could only bet that the patient would survive the week or month. If the patient didn't make it, the house took the money. If the patient lived on, the house paid out. Gamblers visited patients and paid to be notified of declining health metrics, changes in medications, calls to priests. Defenders said that by only allowing survival-positive bets the gamblers were rooting for the terminally ill patients to live on. But that's a moral blur, isn't it? You're terminally ill, you're in constant pain, you're trying to think your way through the end of this existence and possibly pray your way through to the next but could you just hang on long enough for us to pay off Susan's credit card, grandma?

It happens in hospitals here too but it's always kept quiet.

The standard kind of Taiwanese death gambling has been adapted for this OVB room and I would guess others like it. The location is still Taiwan. It's still an old person on the screen. But to keep the action quick the camera witnesses different injections. The bet is whether this next injection will kill the dying person in the next half hour. They run a timer on the screen.

I place a hundred dollar bet on a frog race, lose and leave.

Outside the red door I breathe fresh air.

"Wow," I say in an exaggerated Al Pacino way. "Some fucking place down there."

The guard looks on dumbly.

I take out my remaining cash. I count off five hundred. I tap the bills together on the red door. I hold the cash up. I shake it for emphasis. "The guy I went in with. Alexander. He dropped some money tonight."

"He likes to bet on the dogs."

"You're a valued employee in this organization. How does credit work?"

"I would advise you not to borrow to gamble."

"That makes sense to you and me. Because we're not gamblers. Alexander is a gambler. Who owns his debt?" And with this question I pass the cash.

The guard takes the money. "Alexander owes Dub-C."

"Not so much that they've stopped him from playing."

"He makes his payments."

"But he's not eating away at the principal."

"From what I hear."

"Does Dub-C keep or sell their debts?"

"They keep most. But they sell the ones that become trouble."

"I'd gauge the thousand I gave Alexander will last another twenty minutes tops. When he comes out, you're not going to talk to him about me."

"He won't talk to me when he comes out."

"Thanks."

I return to the 911 and drive home.

Companies operating in the debt buying sector purchase delinquent credit card debt, overdue cellphone contracts and car loans. Outstanding medical bills and secondary mortgages are the biggest buys. The sticker price is a percentage of the total potential recovery determined by calculated odds. Having secured their ownership of the debt, collectors then call the defaulters day and night to demand their motherfucking money.

These credit crusaders don't have any interest in maintaining good customer relations because they're not selling anything. They just want their motherfucking money. They harass the names on their list all times of the day and night and at work. They make threats. They lie about the consequences.

That's the legal debt buyers. The ones protected by legislation and the civil courts.

The basics of debt buying in the criminal underworld are the same: a bookie will sell a bad debt to a predatory collector for a percentage. It's the nature of the collection that differs. If broken limbs or raped family members aren't enough, a criminal holding a sizeable debt can simply convert the monetary figure to a non-negotiable action. Debtors are forced to walk into the police station and confess to a crime they didn't commit, plead guilty in court and do the time silently. There's a symmetry to it: money converted to years.

Dub C means Chinese Youth. Wah-ching. Chinese triad.

Bad people to owe.

I put on Game 6 of the 1980 finals when a rookie Magic replaced a hurt Kareem at center and began writing a legend. I set *Gravity's Rainbow* to jump around randomly. With over 400 characters and so many crazy plots it's a book ideally suited for my method of consumption. I know the stories and can remember some of the characters, but never the order and rarely the connections so the random scrolling makes it more prose poetry. And silently I watch Cary Grant and Irene Dunn in *The Awful Truth* trying to stop each other from finding new love before their divorce is final.

It's comforting to believe that your life is being written in the first person but it ain't. The narrative we're all toiling within is a sprawling Pynchon-esque novel. We're the comic relief more often than the protagonist. Trying to figure out the plot is maddening. The best most of us can hope for is guessing the current genre: bildungsroman, romance, comedy, tragedy.

I check the news before I take my meds.

Chaos out there still. Veterans have been arrested trying to sell their drugs.

CHAPTER SEVENTEEN

STANDUP

I call my client and tell him I'm ready to share what I've discovered. He doesn't want to meet at a restaurant and he doesn't want me to come to any of his mansions. He says he's going out to hear some standup comedy and that he will pick me up outside of my condo.

I offer to drive but he insists.

I stand outside my building wearing a Social Distortion shirt with a top hatted skeleton. A black limo pulls up and stops. The driver comes around and opens the door for me. I duck down and in.

The interior is a cave of confined sound and peaceful lighting.

The Hollywood Hyena is sitting at the back with a drink. He's dressed casually: open collar, light blue jacket. He has a drink with ice. As I get comfortable in my seat along the cushioned side he raises the light level and I see him better.

He looks sick.

I stretch and hand him a folder with pictures in it. I have written the names on the photos in pen: Harlan, Jason, Alexander. The Hyena puts his drink in its arm rest holder and he touches and loves the pictures each in turn.

He holds up Jason's picture first.

"Jason is a prospect in the Mongols biker gang. He trains dogs to fight. He's also involved in their gun running operation. Assembly. I don't think he cooks meth but he uses it sometimes."

"That's why he's passed out here? A crash?"

"No he was drunk there."

The limo is gliding through the night.

Next the Hyena holds up Alexander's picture.

"Alexander is a hacker. He got his girlfriend pregnant when they were really young. They got married. The kid died. There's a shrine to the boy in his house. Alexander uses local teens in a few different credit card and bank card scams. They're equal parts technology and con. He has a gambling problem. His high tech scams generate good cash flow. But there's no amount that's ever enough when you're hooked on the rush of the action. I've seen it. I'm sure you've seen it. He's likely in debt to a Chinese Triad."

"He works for FedEx as well?"

"No that's a disguise."

We're on West Sunset Boulevard. The Hyena holds up Harlan's picture last.

"Harlan is a professional wrestler. He was with the WWE for a short time without much impact. I saw him fight in Eugene. Right before he quit the company. He signed a contract to go wrestle in Japan. But part of the deal was that he would do a private hardcore match for a Yakuza boss. His injuries were quite severe. That has at least delayed his plans to fly to the land of the rising sun."

We've stopped outside The Comedy Store.

I sum my discoveries up: "They've all been drawn to fighting at the edges of society."

"Do you see the resemblance to me? I should have brought pictures of me when I was younger. I can see me in them so clearly. I could have picked them out of a crowd as my blood. They're all three risk takers."

"They're all three living very dangerous lives Mr. Robertson."

"They didn't have a father," he answers. "Don't tell me about step fathers. Boyfriends of their mothers. Those men mean nothing."

This again.

"These boys didn't have me to help them know the wild recklessness in our blood."

"I have to tell you, Mr. Robertson. I will help you arrange your meet but I think the worst thing you could do is give these three young men money."

"I hired you as a private investigator and not a psychologist."

"That is true."

"I owe them."

"You jerked off at a sperm bank."

"Blood is obliged to blood!" The force he says this with causes him to cough and gasp. "The only difference between a risky criminal and a daring businessman is money. If they'd had me as their father, had my money, my influence, my power … everything would be different for them now."

"None of their mothers were exactly poor."

"Mothers wipe noses and bums. Fathers make men."

He's convinced. I can't dissuade him. And I don't care to.

I take a deep breath. "This is what I suggest. I use three different lies to get them in a hotel room. When they are all there, I tell them the real reason and then you make your entrance."

"Will you stay to protect me?"

It's a strange question given what he's just said, his certainty. "If you want."

"Just until I convince them. Then your job is completed with my great thanks."

"How soon do you want the meet?" I ask him.

"As soon as possible."

"Fine."

The Hyena continues holding the pictures. "Do you know Kurt Davis?"

Through the tinted glass and the dark I can see this name in lights at The Comedy Store. "Not really," I answer.

"I started going to open mics with Kurt when we were both fifteen. I remember figuring out how to bus it to La Brea Ave, Hermosa Beach, Melrose, Pasadena, Hollywood, Sherman Oaks, Universal City. We would listen to Richard Pryor and Bill Hicks on our walkmans while getting to the clubs. The first few times I went up before him and I got some laughs. But nothing like Kurt did. It was obvious early that he had it and I didn't. It didn't bother me, honestly. I kept going along as Kurt's sortof manager. I got us to the club on time, made sure that my boy wasn't too high or too drunk to step up to the microphone and deliver."

The Hyena wants to tell me this story. So I listen.

"Kurt's act, even right back at the beginning, was not for everyone. He was as proud of pissing people off as he was of making them piss themselves laughing. And when he was bombing he wanted to fail so completely that no one ever forgot him. The worse the reaction, the more he baited the audience. He liked to single out the biggest dumbest guy and insult his clothes, hit on his girlfriend, parody his voice, mock his political views, jeer at his religious beliefs. Sometimes we had to run out of the club. Once he got the shit kicked out of him and we spent the night in emergency."

I reach for a water bottle, twist, drink.

"When Kurt had thirty solid minutes, he went out on the road to open for a few established comics who liked his fearlessness. He crafted a characteristic delivery and intonation. And he got good at being a standup. He auditioned for some TV shows—a lot of TV shows over the years. But he never got a part. . . . Eventually he gave up. He admitted to himself that he's just a good standup. That's what he is. That's all he will ever be. He goes out on the road and gets drunk. He stays in LA and gets drunk. And he's happy just being a good standup. That's the way he likes it. . . . That's what he says anyways."

He's left a pause for me to ask a question. "You never helped him make it on the screen? All the studios and companies you own?"

I've asked the question he wanted. He's grinning back at me. "Sure I could have. I didn't. He asked me lots of times. Not only have I not helped him Chalk . . . " he wets his lips. "I've actually thwarted him. Secretly. And he knows this finally. His entire career I've stopped him from ever being anything but a good standup. Do you know why?"

"He fucked your girlfriend and/or mother?"

"No."

"Why?"

"Because that's all I want him to be. I decided that. I cherish my memories of him doing

standup. And when I want to remember and laugh I drive where he is and watch his set. If he'd become anything else . . . well . . . well the experience would be ruined for me."

"You decided what he got to be."

"Yes." He's so very proud of himself. "Come on. He should be going on soon. I like to be there from the start."

There is a table waiting for the Hyena right near the stage. I sit with him. I ask for a diet coke. The Hyena asks for the best scotch they have. A female comedian that I don't know is finishing up her set. She recognizes my client immediately.

The quality of light in the club is harder than the limo. I can see just how sick the Hyena is now. He's drunker than I thought too. And everyone in the space is watching him: the King Midas in Hollywood's mediocracy.

"Enough of this cunt," the Hyena barks. "Bring on Kurt! We want Kurt!"

The female comic looks offstage. She looks to the bar. She looks throughout the club. Somewhere she finds the eyes that tell her what to do. She gets off the stage. The MC comes on and tries his best to not look at the Hyena as he introduces the headliner.

Kurt is pushed out. His skin is bloated and discolored. He's hunched and overweight. His nose is florid. He's an alcoholic. But his hands are steady as he takes the microphone. He stands right in front of the Hyena and welcomes him by name.

Kurt goes through his set. He riffs on the last night of sex before a breakup, how guys get excited when one of their friends is getting divorced, about what old people think of twitter and blogs, why women join emotional celebrity cults where they care what kind of day Angelina Jolie is having, how and when to share a sexual fantasy correctly.

The Hyena heckles him throughout. He interrupts jokes, he hurls insults, he hates.

Then Kurt starts joking about AIDs. My client throws his scotch glass at the comedian.

And the headliner is done for the night at The Comedy Store.

I tell my client I will get a cab home and contact him tomorrow.

I've booked a Becker Suite at the Millennium Biltmore. It's a luxury one bedroom just under a thousand square feet. It is opulently appointed. It is regal. It has a dining table that seats six.

The lies have to be good enough to hook but not so good that the truth is a letdown.

I phone Harlan and tell him that the TNA wants to talk to him about a contract. He doesn't give anything away about his situation but says he will come at the time I repeat three times.

Jason calls me back. I tell him that I'm a corporate gun engineer looking to move prototype ammunition. I got his name from a Mongols associate at a dog fight. I want to deal with him and no one else in the Mongols. It's the kind of deal that would earn him his full patch if it were real. He agrees to come alone.

I have to leave three intriguing voicemails before I get Alexander on the phone. I tell him I'm selling hundreds of clean credit card numbers and matched PINs at a crazy price. I'll let him have them on consignment—he pays me when they work. It doesn't sound like he trusts the offer but he says he'll show up.

I check into the room two hours in advance of the time I gave the three half-brothers, and an hour before when I expect my client. I scan the room for electronic snooping devices. I don't expect to find any and I don't. It's a routine.

The Hyena arrives. He has foolishly brought a gym bag of cash with him. He's shaking uncontrollably and pallid. He asks me about the room. I explain that I've only booked it for the one night. He starts to fuss over this. He calls down to the front desk and gives them his credit card to hold the room indefinitely. I manage to get him hidden behind a door to wait.

Alexander knocks fifteen minutes early. He recognizes me from Chinatown. This makes him hesitate. He likely checked his exit routes before he knocked. But he doesn't run. He listens to me and he stays for now.

Jason and Harlan arrive almost together. Jason doesn't appear to be at all suspicious. He takes in the rich room, makes smart cracks. Harlan is still badly beaten. He's bandaged and bruised. He's skittish.

I get them all to sit down at the table.

I'm wearing a Rage Against the Machine shirt with the kid in the evil empire super suit.

"I lied to get you here," I tell them. "The three of you are brothers."

"Fuck this," Alexander says as he stands.

"Have you ever heard of the Hollywood Hyena?"

Alexander stops leaving but he stays standing.

"I have," Jason says.

Harlan shakes his head.

"The Hollywood Hyena is your father. He was a sperm donor at California Cryo Futures. He hired me to find you."

"I don't need a dad now. I know how to ride a bike."

"He's here in this suite. He wants to meet you."

The three young men appraise each other. They do look similar. It could be true.

I'm about to get my client but he's already standing behind me. He's holding his bag.

"I know your names. I know a little about you. I'm a dying man with a lot of money."

Alexander sits down. My client takes his seat at the head of the table. The four of them talk for an hour. At the end of those sixty minutes the three brothers have formed a bond that the Hyena has mistaken for duty to a father. He has promised them money over and over. To secure this money Harlan promises to give up hardcore wrestling, Jason vows to leave the Mongols and Alexander assures daddy dearest that he's done breaking the law.

What has really happened is quite sinister. Through glances and tone, reactions and eyebrows, these newly found brothers have entered into a conspiracy to take this dying fool for as much money as they can.

I can see it. My client cannot. Maybe if he was a nicer guy I'd care.

But my job is done.

Yet after the handshake, after I've left the Biltmore, I know this isn't done with me.

I order in Thai food and sit on the couch. On the game screen I watch Kobe sink the game tying shot and then the game winner against the Suns in the first round of the 2006 playoffs. The book TV is scrolling *Under the Volcano*. It's such a messy book, such a heap of words and thoughts and ideas. But every now and then there is a perfect moment of consciousness in the narrative. If I was drinking I would raise a glass to Geoffrey Firmin, one of the grandest literary boozers of all time. And the silent movie tonight is Howard Hawk's *His Girl Friday*. It's a different kind of funny without the dialogue, seeing how animated people can be when they talk to each other. They could be discussing almost anything. They could be discussing me and this strange case. At least they're smiling about it.

Chaos is still top on the TV news. Punks have tried to rob veterans of their mailed drugs.

Chapter Eighteen

JOBS

There's nothing in my fridge and yet there's no room. It's been at least two years since I cleaned it, maybe even as much as three. My relationship history can be explained and possibly understood through Great Condiment Purges and it seems time for another.

I start with a jar of fancy French Garlic Mayonnaise. The label is done with an impressionist pastel background. I wasn't seeing anyone when I bought this but I wanted to be. I was anxious about my weight and I made the decision to eat less meat and more tuna. The mayonnaise was to be used to make tuna sandwiches on healthy bread bursting with seeds. I don't open it, just drop it into the garbage bag.

The A1 Steak Sauce, Budweiser BBQ Sauce and Sweet Bay Ray's BBQ Sauce all stand together. I purchased them with Larissa, the woman from Texas. I bought a grill and set it up on the balcony. I burnt steaks and ribs and she boiled corn. We met in a bar. She had been relocated by her company to LA and didn't know anyone. I'd lived here almost all my life and didn't know anyone. We had happy months. I wasn't working much then. We started out laughing when we were drunk and ended up fighting when we were drunk. Her company moved her again and we promised to keep in touch which translates as goodbye for now and forever babe. I don't have propane for the grill and can't be bothered to get any more. All these bottles go in the garbage.

The tartar sauce was for Ruth. She was a valley girl who'd lived in England for two years with a fiancée who never married her. She'd been on the rebound for five years and as much as she liked me I fumbled her and she kept rebounding. She knew a Fish and Chips place that delivered. It was always a cold greasy mess when it arrived but she kept ordering it and I kept covering it with tartar sauce. It made sense when she left but it still made me sad. I twist the top and give it a smell but what would tartar sauce smell like if it went bad? What else did Ruth leave here? Yes, Gentlemen's Relish and Marmite. The Relish is ground up anchovies and Marmite is a yeast spread. They're both usually for toast and I don't think she liked them but they were English so she pretended to. All in the garbage now.

Salad dressings: There's Artichoke Parmesan, Roasted Red Pepper, Herb Balsamic, Greek, Cowgirl Ranch, Raspberry Hazelnut, Lemon and Chive, Harvest French. I was seeing Vera longer than most but she never lived here. She had a marriage habit. She was on her third marriage when she started seeing me. We had afternoons, a few evenings, and several special weekends. I stopped even asking what she told her husband. Vera took care of herself. She exercised every day and she ate nothing but salads. She made salads for me. They were flavorful surprises. She drank only water. It started to fall apart when I asked her if she would leave her husband. She did leave him but not until after she'd left me. She was married again shortly after. When she asked if I wanted to start seeing her again when her newest husband wasn't around, I said no. I said goodbye. And now I say goodbye to these dressings.

Sriracha, the red bottle with the rooster and the green top, Viet Huong fish sauce and Roothman gourmet dipping sauce came with Madison. She was much younger than me. The sex was amazing, we both kept each other laughing, but we didn't have much in common and little to talk about. We were always out seeing theatre, movies, concerts, so we'd have something to talk about but she was too eager to agree with me on everything. We both liked Thai food so that became one of our things, trying every Thai restaurant in LA. For her birthday I bought her a Kindle loaded with Asian Cooking books. We attempted to recreate the magic in my condo. We went from the bed to the kitchen and back. We both wanted it to work but it just didn't it just couldn't. She was too young to see that so I had to tell her. She threw food at me but she left.

The garbage bag is getting heavy.

Strange salsa, wing sauce, onion chip dip, bean chip dip, jalapeno nacho cheese, are all from different attempts to be one of the guys. There was a guy in the building who watched football with another guy and I watched a game with them and then invited them back here to watch another. There was one time I had three LAPD guys and one LAPD girl trying to be an LAPD guy over and we watched the fight. I'm sure they all thought of me as one of the guys but I wasn't and won't ever be and I've learned to live with that.

Soy sauce and ketchup alone survive the purge. I walk the garbage down the hall.

I'm wearing a Grateful Dead shirt with a space skull, a bone globe of galaxies.

There is a backlog of small jobs waiting for me.

I'm hired to find a hard drive, generate a report of the data on that drive, and then document the complete and utter destruction of it. I've done jobs like this before. I set a condition. I tell my employer that if I find kiddie porn, the drive will be delivered to the LAPD. He agrees to this.

After the owner's death, the contents of his apartment were donated to charity. The computer ended up on the operating table of a refurbishing company. They didn't reformat the drive fully because they usually don't. They just wiped the top layer and rein-stalled Windows. The machine was donated to a Boys and Girls club where it is used for general surfing and flash games.

It takes me half a day to track the computer down. I walk into the Boys and Girls club and replace it with a new PC that I've loaded with games. There are no complaints from kids or staff when I carry the target machine out.

The report I generate itemizes the kinds of files that are still there like a garrison of the undead: the text files, the doc files, the system files. There are a lot of pictures but they aren't of forbidden sexual acts. They are images of schematics, designs, and PDFs with confidential watermarks—engineering data. In addition to the itemized list, I provide a paragraph of my qualitative impressions on the likelihood of the data have being accessed or copied.

I take pictures of the identifying numbers on the hard drive. I then use a tripod to film myself drilling holes through the case and into the platter. I punch six holes through. And then I put the drive into an immersion of hydrochloric acid. I do this in a rented garage. I sit in a folding chair, in the shot, while the data bubbles away.

Secrets gone. Job done. Fee paid.

The three cloned phones are still working. I keep watching the brothers' texts. I keep tracking their calls. Then at first once, and after as a compulsive routine, I take the added risk of tracking their locations in the city.

Dad has certainly brought the brothers together. They have all three surrendered their normal lives—to an even greater extent than they promised. Harlan has stopped communicating with the women in his life: the clinging girlfriend, the desperate mother, the needy surrogate mother. He's abandoned his plans to fly to Japan. Jason is missing in action from all Mongols activity: dogs, meth, guns, bikes. Alexander is not responding to texts or calls from his hard knock teens or his wife.

The Hyena is spending. He has given Alexander money to pay his gambling debts with Dub C. He's purchased the hacker new computers and hardware delivered to the suite at the Millennium Biltmore. He's bought a massive new house that Jason and Harlan are sharing. Dad has also given the three white BMW M3s—divine driving machines if specced properly.

What is the Hyena getting for this outlay of cash? Is it enough for him that his boys hug and thank him? Does he want them to play basketball in the driveway? Will there be family movie night? Wrestling with Harlan? Picking out a puppy with Jason? Betting on the game with Alexander? How much Brady Bunch time is enough before he dies?

Because he's not going to run out of money. And they're not going to stop taking it.

They did a new study . . .

Studies have shown . . .

Did you hear about the latest study?

These phrases will prepare listeners to believe anything. Speakers once had to reference that they had heard about the study on *60 Minutes* or *Oprah*. But if that was ever true, it isn't now. Listeners just assume when they hear the word "study" that the wisdom coming next is sourced from those twin towers of veracity: TV and/or the internet. Not only do people not care about the size or method of the study, they spontaneously just make these fucking details up. It's like we have all become improv research scientists. Yes, oh yeah, they uh interviewed mothers who exhibited symptoms of postpartum depression—sounds good but it's pure bullshit. Yes they gave the drug to people trying to quit smoking, you know, people who had failed with other methods—believable but you just invented it. I know of no other piece of discourse in which people do this. They hit the word study hard, make claims of what was discovered, and then invent the methodology to back it. It's a security flaw in the cultural OS our brains are currently running.

I'm hired by a corporation to trace the internet origin of a non-study being referenced in memes. It is killing the sales of their new energy drink. Twitter to Facebook to blogs to tumblr to podcasts to reddit to product reviews and back through the online digestive system again and again I go.

I find it. The fake study was a plant, corporate espionage. I write it up in my report. The company wants me to advise them on a strategic reprisal. I sigh physically and then virtually and give them a quick opinion.

Traced. Job done. Fee paid.

I see myself in the mirror, the Zeppelin shirt with the mysterious Zoso symbols.

I look and feel old. And tired. This is not the work that lights me up.

Chapter Nineteen

ATTACK

The house the Hyena bought for Jason is 10,000 square feet in the Pacific Palisades. Anyone who inherited or earned the money to buy such a home would know it needs a maid to come in every day. Jason doesn't know that. And when I track all three cell phones as being elsewhere I know there will be no one home.

I park out front in the driveway and take a gym bag of electronics up to the front door.

There is an alarm system. It's using midrange Honeywell hardware.

I put my bag down and take out my picks and a wire cutter.

I pick the lock, push the front door in. After a beat the alarm goes off.

These home systems are engineered with a delay that allows the owner to get through the door and to the central keypad inside the house. That gives me as an intruder the same amount of time to trick it. On a midrange system like this one the all-in-one controller on the wall is also the brain. So when I tear it off its mount and cut the right wire in the mess behind there is no brain to send the signal to the company's response center. It's kind of a big flaw.

The alarm stops sounding.

I wait a minute, dig for more tools. I re-splice the wire I just cut, tape it, and remount the panel to the wall. Back online the system thinks all is well. I won't be able to arm it on my way out but it's unlikely that will seem wrong to anyone.

I check on my cloned phones. The brothers are still far away.

The spaces in the house are vast. I focus my attention on rooms that appear lived in, that have some furniture, empty pizza boxes, dead beer bottles. I wire five rooms with ghost transmitters: the great room, the kitchen, and the three bedrooms with beds.

I pack my stuff up, exit out the front, sit in the 911 and check the signals.

Ghost transmitters are my preferred audio surveillance devices. They listen like normal bugs but they don't immediately broadcast the salacious gossip they're hearing. They store the recorded audio in internal memory and wait for a requesting signal to transfer what has been captured. These two distinct steps allow the ghost transmitters to maintain a low enough profile to avoid detection from basic bug scanners. But this comes with a unique risk. If they are found, the recordings can be retrieved by the people who were being spied upon. The targets may gain an idea of how long they have been unwittingly performing in a radio play.

I won't be able to listen live. But a quick park on the street and I'll be caught up.

I pull away hard for home.

I wake to the country going crazy. Four more pharmaceutical warehouses were hit last night. These weren't stealth missions. These were military operations. Four separate parts of the country all hit at once with the same attack plan. The assaults began with shoulder launched missiles. Gas came next. Then the shock troopers went in. They were supported by overwatch from snipers. The soldiers killed efficiently. The perimeters were secured. The trucks rolled in and were loaded with the drugs.

Forty minutes from start to finish.

The black armored forces killed twenty one guards and wounded three dozen more. Some of the action was caught on shaky video. I watch interviewed survivors try to connect the events with words. The soldiers had full gas masks and protective eyewear. They displayed no symbols, they flew no flags.

The first warehouse was a distribution point for Pfizer. The force took Lyrica which is for neuropathic pain, Celebrex for arthritis, Viagra for erectile dysfunction, Lipitor for cholesterol, Zyvox for bacterial infections and Stelara for inflammation.

The second warehouse was owned by Astra Zeneca. They made off with Nexium for Gastrointestinal problems, Crestor for cholesterol, Symbicort for Asthma, and Seroquel for psychos like me.

The third warehouse was Purdue Pharma's. They make Oxycodone.

The fourth warehouse was owned by a company that produces generic drugs to be sold under different labels and used at hospitals. The most dangerous of the many drugs taken from this warehouse were Methylphenidate for ADD and Fentanyl for severe pain.

Four hundred and seventy million dollars in meds is the estimate.

Dead electronic screens were left behind again: six in each location. Just as before the different sized shapes were written on with red soap. Just as before each screen has a mysteriously identifying letter or number circled before the message.

At the first warehouse the screens read:

F: War is the original and only true game.

D: War is the original and only true game.

G: War is the original and only true game.

3: War is the original and only true game.

1: War is the original and only true game.

5: War is the original and only true game.

This is not a quote from Cormac McCarthy's *Blood Meridian* but the sentiment makes me bring the book up and find the master's careful words on the subject: "War was always here. Before man was, war waited for him. The ultimate trade awaiting its ulti-mate practitioner." That's the august and terrible Judge speaking.

At the second warehouse the messages are:

F: Peace was never our profession.

D: Peace was never our profession.

G: Peace was never our profession.

3: Peace was never our profession.

1: Peace was never our profession.

5: Peace was never our profession.

Peace is our profession is the motto of the 843rd Bombardment Wing flying out of Burpelson Air Force Base in Kubrick's *Dr. Strangelove*.

At the third warehouse the words are:

1: RTS w BBEG . . . L8tr

5: RTS w BBEG . . . L8tr

D: RTS w BBEG . . . L8tr

F: RTS w BBEG . . . L8tr

3: RTS w BBEG . . . L8tr

G: RTS w BBEG . . . L8tr

This is an incoherent stream of gamer slang: Real Time Strategy with Big Boss Evil Guy . . . Later.

At the fourth warehouse:

3: Death is a flash of light.

5: Death is a flash of light.

F: Death is a flash of light.

G: Death is a flash of light.

D: Death is a flash of light.

1: Death is a flash of light.

I have no idea what this is referencing.

There are talking heads on all of my screens. A medical doc-tor on CNN is lecturing the country about the dangers of using these drugs without proper medical guidance should the cap-tured pills be mailed to veterans again. An economist on MSNBC is prophesizing doom about what this is going to do the stock of pharmaceutical companies. A four star general on Fox is saying that this is an important skirmish in our two big ongoing wars— you remember those: the ever-so-winnable crusades against the words "drugs" and "terror. " On PBS the widow of one of the guards who died last night is jawing about legalizing marijuana because we wouldn't need any of these pills in the first place if everyone had easy access to ganja.

The President is going to speak soon. Let's see if I can guess how that will go. Deplorable actions. Our thoughts and prayers are with the families of the killed. I'm taking this extremely fucking seriously America so just chill out. Or words to that effect.

CHAPTER TWENTY

ENLISTING

I'm hired to find and retrieve a set of pearl earrings. They were stolen from a wealthy couple's home while they were away on a vacation to celebrate the wife becoming cancer free. The earrings were heirlooms.

I determine that the attendants at one of LAX's long term parking services are involved in a criminal conspiracy. Owners don't turn in keys when they park to fly but Mercedes, BMW, Audi, Cadillac, Lincoln, Lexus and Acura all offer variations of the same remote start technology. An engineering student built the attendants a radio box that works on a varied list of models. When this device tricks a car into opening and starting, the attendants check the ticket to see how long the owners will be gone. The car's GPS tells them how far away home is. And when the attendants decide to take the road trip the same GPS guides them directly to the home garage where another trusted button rolls up the garage door.

The attendants know they have days to manage their break in and theft.

I figure this out from observation and interviews.

I am able to surmise more. The attendants will have started off with frequency rules: no more than one rip a month say. But not getting caught is an even greater rush than the money and that rule would have fallen first. That customer was a total asshole—we should rip him off. That car is worth at least two hundred thousand—we should check out her place. There may have been a rule about who was involved and what they took and how they fenced the spoils. A few scares—teenagers who didn't go on the vacation and were home, a tough alarm system, LAPD questions—would have been enough to justify taking what they can whenever they can.

I finger the ring leader and accost him for an interrogation in an LAX bathroom. I tell him I won't sell him to LAPD Robbery Homicide if he helps me track down the pearl earrings. We find them in a shoe box of jewelry at his fence—aspiring fence really: the son of a pawn broker and failed drug dealer.

Found. Job done. Fee paid.

Sometimes I wish these jobs didn't pay so well.

I wake up from the depths of Seroquel slumber to my iPhone ringing. I sit up and grab for it. I've missed twenty calls, one after another, all from my former client the Hyena. It's him calling now.

I hit the green button.

"Chalk. Chalk. You have to help me. These boys are wild. . . aggressive . . . I've given them everything . . . but it's not enough. They're planning something criminal."

"What?"

"I don't know. It's like they're at war with society."

"Do you fear for your safety?"

"I . . . I am scared," he confesses.

"I don't know what to tell you Mr. Robertson. You have made millions as a risk taker and a raider. These are your sons. You were prepared to have children kidnapped and subjected to blood tests. These are your sons. You are wild and aggressive. These are your sons."

"What if they're not?"

"But we know that they are."

He seethes into the phone. "What if they are not?"

"How can I help you Mr. Robertson?"

"You get their DNA. My DNA. You have the tests done. And then I'll know."

"You want me to ask them for DNA samples?"

"No! They can't know that I have doubts."

"Alright. I can get DNA in a number of different ways."

"However. I'll start paying your fee again."

"But what will change Mr. Robertson? The paternity tests will come back positive for all three. Because they will. What will have changed? They'll still be out of control. They'll still be spending your money. This is what you asked for. You brought a fucking bag of cash to your first meeting with them."

"I know," he whines. "I was stupid. Now I'm scared Chalk. Tell me you will do it."

"If you want to hire me to secretly obtain their DNA I will do that."

"Thank you! Can you start tomorrow?"

"I have other cases."

"I will pay you double."

I sigh. "You pay me the rate I quoted you originally. I'll start tomorrow. Which is today."

I drive to the Hyena's home first thing. I figure taking a proper DNA swab will calm him down a little. It doesn't. He's a disaster. He's lost a lot of weight since I saw him last. His skin is bleached white and his shaking has gotten bad.

I have him rub the swab in his mouth for thirty seconds. I pop it in a sample container.   I don't try to reassure him with words. I just get on with it by leaving.

Once again I watch the cloned phones to know when the brothers are away from the Pacific Palisades home—which it appears they are all three living in now. When I can see that they are each a twenty minute drive away I return to the house with my tools. I work the same trick on the alarm system and start roaming. I take a shirt of Harlan's with a blood stain. I bag clipped fingernails and a disposable razor from Jason's room. I capture hairs plucked from a comb and a snotty tissue in the room Alexander has moved his computers and specialist hardware into.

Sitting in the 911 ready to go, I retrieve my ghost transmitter audio.

My electronic specters send me what they've heard.

I drive to ARCpoint labs in the Beverlywood Health & Medi Center because I trust their work. I tell the girl the tests don't need to be court admissible but I want to pay extra for their 24 hour service. The total is more cash than I have so I have to put it on a credit card.

She says they will call me.

I start listening to my surveillance audio on the drive home. I listen to the brothers complain about the mothers and girlfriends and wife that have let them down. Then they get to it—what the Hyena possibly heard a little about and now suspects.

"Being together has felt right from the start. Before that detective guy even told us that we were brothers I felt a strong connection in the room." It's Alexander talking. "Since then I've been thinking about what is the same about us. I think I know what it is."

They're drinking. There's a game on the TV, sound low.

"We're waiting Alex."

"We all want to be a part of something more. Something bigger than just us."

"Uh okay."

"Harlan," Alexander says. "You are a warrior."

"I hate to ruin it for you Alex but professional wrestling is fake."

"Don't diminish yourself like that. You are a warrior dancer."

Harlan and Jason laugh at this but Alexander does not.

"You Jason."

"I'm not a warrior Alex."

"Not in the same way as Harlan. But how desperate are you to wear a uniform?"

"The Mongols aren't warriors. They're fat guys who like bikes, beer and sluts."

The laughter is uneasy now because they all sense Alexander is building to a good point.

"It's a uniform," he says. "You wanted to wear it. To be in that brotherhood."

"So why am I here with you assholes then? I was on the verge of getting patched."

Alexander leaves a pause. "I bet the both of you have come close to joining the army."

"Okay I have," Jason agrees. "So what?" Someone turns the game off.

"That's wanting to be a part of something more."

"I was going to enlist too," Harlan admits.

"Well I did enlist," Alexander tops them. "After my son died." If this is true I missed it.

"Where did they ship you?"

"Texas. I got out before my unit went overseas." It sounds like a lie.

"Yeah Alexander we're great warriors," Harlan sneers. "Two brothers that have almost enlisted. And one that did and then got out right away. Sounds more like we're cowards to me."

"You support the troops?" Alexander asks them.

"Yes," Harlan answers.

"Of course," Jason follows.

"A severely mentally challenged child in a motorized wheelchair chanting USA USA USA while waving a stupid little paper flag. That's what I think of when I hear people say they support the troops. What they usually mean is that they don't want to talk about the wars our country is currently engaged in and the wars we're contemplating starting. These good citizens have been told that any challenge to why the troops have been deployed undermines them, weakens our resolve. The best way to truly support the troops is to be sure they're fighting the right goddamn wars. Because righteous wars do exist. I'm no pacifist. America needs to project power throughout the world. And the best way to support the brave soldiers who deliver that force is to question the conflicts lined up and how we fucking fight them."

"Ah fuck politics man," Jason says.

"Sure fuck politics. Let's talk about flags instead then. Precious work has been done by nations to convince us all that warriors fight for flags. They didn't used to. And they don't have to."

"Is this how you get your army of teens to do shit?"

"They're boys. I'm talking to you as men."

There's a little residual nervous laughter—the last of it I think.

"What if . . ." Alexander starts and then waits. "What if the something more had been waiting for us? Waiting until we became men. . . . You watched the coverage of those pharmaceutical warehouse robberies. Yes?"

"Some cool Robin Hood shit. Straight up," Harlan says.

"The soldiers that did that are the first of two armies. Following the leadership of one man."

"The fucking FBI and CNN don't know this. But you know this."

"I've received encrypted emails."

"From?"

"General Ripper."

"Jack the Ripper?" Harlan questions.

"General Jack Ripper. It's an allusion to a character in a movie. *Dr. Strangelove.*"

"Never heard of it," Jason says.

"Two armies," Alexander repeats. "The first is doing the work on the news now. They are veterans from America's recent and dumbest conflicts. General Ripper wants young men for the second army. He is recruiting now."

"He wants us?"

"He wants me. He wants my technical skills. But he will take all three of us. If we can prove we're up to it. I know because I've asked."

"How long have you been chatting with this super villain?"

"I was contacted just before we were brought together. I've told you everything that I know. Which isn't much I admit. But it's enough for me to know I want to be in the second army. If you want to come with me, then we'll get in together. If you don't then that's cool too. Just keep your mouths shut."

"What is the second army going to do?" Harlan asks.

"He hasn't told me. But it is something important. Something that will be remembered. Something that will change how we think about war in this country. Something he needs hackers for."

"What does *Graphics have made warriors terrorists mean?*" Jason cites the news.

"Something to do with how technology has distanced warriors from war. I don't know."

"That's a lot of somethings Alex," Jason comes back. "You want to go fight for him. But you don't even know the big fucking point he's trying to make to the country."

"What do we have to do to prove ourselves?" Harlan asks.

There's air. I check to see if the audio file has ended but it hasn't.

"General Ripper has been watching me for a while," Alexander says. "He seems to know a lot about me. And not just biographic information. What kind of films do we all love?"

"Kungfu films," Harlan answers.

"Kungfu and Samurai films. Right. There is a Samurai Sword. A special Samurai Sword. If we get it, the General will take us all into the second army."

"What Samurai Sword?" Jason asks.

"The Honjo Masamuni."

This is the sword Jason talked about when he was smoking meth. . . . Maybe General Ripper has been watching Jason and Harlan too. . . . Jason doesn't say anything about his interest in the Honjo.

"The sword has been in LA for three years now. The Yakuza boss Yoshinori Narita owned it until last year. Dub C killed him and most of his leadership. Jian Chin, the triad boss, now owns it. He carries it with him everywhere."

"You know this because you owed them money?"

"No. This has all come from my encrypted emails with General Ripper."

"Do we get to see these emails?" This is Harlan.

"If you want."

They're just breathing and thinking. But they're still there.

"I'm in," Harlan says. "Fuck it yeah I'm in."

There's edgy, daring laughter now. "Me too," says Jason.

I stop it and listen to it all again.

CHAPTER TWENTY-ONE

SUICIDE

Rose's name comes up on my iPhone. I answer with the car's Bluetooth.

"You were working for the Hollywood Hyena?"

"I am working for him."

"He's dead Chalk."

"Murdered?"

"Well. We're going to investigate it. We like to do that at the LAPD. But it doesn't look like a homicide."

"He did himself?"

"That's what it seems like."

"You're there?" I ask him.

"Heh fuck you. I call you with a hot tip like this and you want me to go spend half my day at the crime scene writing a summary haiku for you?"

"Would I be welcome if I showed up at the scene?"

"What kind of dumbass question is that?"

"Are the detectives and possible brass on the scene Chalk fans?"

He exhales. "Let me check who was dispatched." I hear him talking to someone. He's covering the phone with his hand. And then he's back. "You would not be beloved."

"Screw it. I'm going anyway."

"Thank you Rose."

"Thank you Rose."

The call ends, I take my bearings. I can make it to the house in twenty.

Rose was right. I'm not welcome at the crime scene. The two detectives who caught the case are Wooldridge and Camper. Wooldridge knows who I am. Camper just made detective and is following Wooldridge's lead on everything—including being a dick to me.

But they let me see the Hyena's end.

He blew his brains out with a revolver that was a gift from David Mamet. Self-inflicted gunshot suicides are hard to stage right. It looks like a legitimate self-exit to me. He wanted to die before he found the results of the DNA tests.

My phone rings. It's the lab.

The Hyena was father to none of the three young men. There could have been a records error at the sperm bank. It's possible that all three mothers were impregnated by other men around the same time. I don't know and at this point it doesn't seem to matter.

I turn down all my outstanding small jobs.

I've got enough money in buffer to work on this for interest. I read about the sword.

Centuries ago a Shogun demanded that Muramasa and Masamune have a competition to see who could craft the greatest sword. A year later on the same day they both completed their blades. Both weapons were to be hung downward in the water of a creek. The first sword cut everything that touched it: leaves, branches, floating flowers, fish. The second sword seemed to cut nothing. The first was the sword of the student, the second that of his master. The student believed he had won the contest. But a monk who had stood witness explained. The first sword was an amazing blade but evil as it cut everything without discernment. The second blade was superior because it did not kill the inno-cents of nature. So the master won the contest.

The Honjo Masamune is the most perfect katana ever forged. The legend is that it can cut light and make the warrior wielding it both invisible and invincible. This is what Jason was talking about when he was smoking meth. It has a magical presence in samurai fiction and films but it is a real sword.

Ancient records show the steel passed from Shogun to Shogun over the centuries. The Tokugawa family owned it at the time of World War II. A US Cavalry Sergeant possessed it for time then. And then it was gone. It might have been melted down along with other worthless blades. But that was not its fate. Since the nuclear end of Japan, the katana has been the prize possession of warlords. It has spent time in Africa, South America and Eastern Europe. Millions have been paid for it but it is more often taken with violence.

Rose calls me. The investigation is done. Wooldridge and Camper interviewed the three brothers. They all had alibis and there was no motive that made any sense. The death has been ruled a suicide.

I don't tell Rose about the job the brothers are planning.

I'm wearing a shirt with Marilyn Manson's name in white, his eagle symbol in red, an icon ready to lead deluded masses to massacre. I select the first *Saw* movie for my needed sweat tonight. If they hadn't made any other *Saw* movies the original would have to rank up there as one of the most authentic scares ever made. The rising madness does not come from the chains, the modernized devices of the inquisition or the spooky little doll. The horror derives from the nature of the games, the knowledge that there is a way to escape a gruesome end but that there is not enough concentration, enough strength, enough time, enough moral resolve to work out an escape. Is this a glib perspective on life? Or is this what we make of our existence?

The game master, Jigsaw, is an ego projection of every serial killer and cult leader I have hunted. He believes he is in control, that his power over life and death is righteous. He even goes so far in the movies as to state that he has murdered no one. No, he's just crafted the games in which they die.

The twist at the end of *Saw* has the dead man in the center of the room rising to reveal himself as the cancer patient, the real Jigsaw. And his last act is to leave the shackled photographer in the room to die. This is the simplest murder in the movie and yet it is the cruelest because there is no game here, just one man leaving another to die alone in a dark and cold room.

General Ripper is playing a game with America.

Chapter Twenty-Two

BOILER

The Chinese don't do organized crime like the Italians. The Triads aren't about family or even race. They're more like criminal clubs. There are benefits and obligations to being affiliated and different levels of membership.

Wah Ching or Dub C opened up business in San Francisco in the sixties and now divide their power between there, LA and loosely across Southern California. All Triads use Chinese numerology to indicate rank within the secret society. The gang leader, the Mountain Lord, the Dragon Head, is number 489. The initiation he, all of his soldiers, and every other member of the Triad took included drinking a cocktail of wine and the blood of a sacrificed animal while reciting 36 oaths before passing through a gate of swords.

Jian Chin is the Dragon Head.

Jian Chin has the Honjo Masamune.

Jian Chin has a reputation as a very paranoid man.

I've gone beyond the risk of routinely tracking the location of the brothers' phones and am now listening in to their live calls. In addition to this real time surveillance, I am still retrieving the captured audio from my ghost transmitters.

Alexander is learning the names and ranks in Dub-C's organization. He's getting a sense for when and how Jian Chin moves. He's thinking through the technology tricks he's going to have to pull off for the heist to work: a 911 service blackout, killing street security cameras.

Harlan is planning the choreography of the grab. It's going to have to happen in daylight.

Jason is getting guns and armor from his Mongol contacts.

The brothers' plan is coming together. I haven't a damn clue what mine is.

I decide that I need some of my own intelligence on Jian Chin.

As I saw the other night at the OVB, the only thing older than the Chinese inclination toward secrecy is the Chinese love of gambling. The biggest gambling house in the world is the stock market. And in recent years Dub C has been making serious money through telemarketing stock fraud. The Dragon Head has put his youngest son, Chi, in charge of the newest and biggest boiler room. This information is not that hard to get because the brokerage is a real business entity. It has to be—people look that shit up. It's called—seriously—Merrill Sachs.

I retrieve a logo and a font from the internet and print myself a laminated ID card.

I resolve a phone number to office space in Century City. It's too late for the telecrooks to be phoning suckers now. I pull on a Slipknot shirt of a nonogram with a red border, grab my jacket and drive there.

It's yet another standard corporate tower in LA. The evening security guard couldn't give a shit who I am or why I'm here. There will be four new corporations signed up for leases each month in a tower like this. Cubicle walls, generic business furniture and phones are the real tenants.

I follow the signs to Merrill Sachs' entrance. I pick the door lock and set the alarm off.

The guard from the front desk comes to see what's up. He's not suspicious just annoyed. I show him my fake ID. The picture is me. It doesn't say that I'm Captain Picard from the United Federation of Planets. So yeah that's good enough. I tell him I forgot the code. He grunts. He kills the alarm and leaves me alone.

Beyond the door is a tight space crammed with phones and the residue of ruthless young men: coffee rings, phone chargers and cables. The vinegar smell of panic distilled drop by drop into anger clings to the air. There are no name plates on these desks, no pictures of family, no individual personality at all. These telecrooks are what they rip from the suckers and only that. Every screaming moment in this space is a competition and each one of the telecrooks will know who is top dog at all times. If I gave the surfaces a close inspection I'd find lines where cocaine has been chopped up, areas of the floor cleared and flattened for craps dice to fall amongst cash, drops of blood that have dripped from unbalanced swings delivered as payment in full on brash boasts.

All the dropped snack wrappers and discarded cans are for Asian products.

Each phone in this boiler room has a black tablet next to it. This allows the individual salesman to change the number that displays when he calls and likely pump in some ambient sound. And what do the telecrooks promise the suckers they call? What everyone wants: guaranteed, no risk, high percentage returns. But you have to buy right now. This secret inside information about the gold, the pharmaceutical promise, the technology, the change in regulations—it just isn't going to be secret for many more hours. The company, the banks, the government are going to clamp down. They don't want you to be rich. I do. You have to buy right now Mr. Chalk.

Telecrooks often refer to the stock they're selling as their girlfriend because they are pumping and dumping her. The brokerage buys large quantities of microcap or penny stocks cheap. They sell these to their sucker list at a higher price. The ongoing activity keeps pumping the price up until the dump comes.

Salesmen are only as good as their leads. The sucker list is everything. These lists often target a specific profession for a run. Everyone being a chiropractor has its advantages. The telecrooks learn about their customers on every call. And chiropractors and dentists and professors and pension fund managers talk to each other.

So what has Merrill Sachs been selling? And to whom?

I pick a spot, sit, and turn a computer on. The machines are cheap Windows all-in-ones without logins. There are no user profiles, no security. I bring the browser up first and look through the surfing history. Whatever telecrook was sitting here today accessed ESPN, streaming porn, the Audi site, William Hill's online Sportsbook. He emailed a revealing article called "10 Signs that It's Time for You to Come Out and Admit You Are Gay" to seven different email addresses.

The program that matters on the machine is accessed through a shortcut called "Call List." It is a custom written program, simple in its interface, quite advanced in its function. The main screen displays itemized names and phone numbers in Excel-like columns. The default view shows leads not yet called. Clicking on a name pushes the number to the tablet by the phone where I can then select what office I want to be calling from: New York, Hong Kong, LA, Tokyo, London, Toronto, Madrid. When the number dials the number containing cell on the screen turns green and is locked so no one else can call that number.

When I hang up the tablet prompts me to select a result: Sale, No Answer, Fail. Just three options. These boys won't be leaving voicemail messages so I guess that No Answer puts the lead back in rotation, maybe on a delay. Fail results turn red. The Sale selection turns the number a money green and transitions the telecrook to a new screen where he provides the monetary details of his financial homicide. Once these details have been verified by the manager the win goes right onto the leaderboard. Here the telecrooks are ranked on sales percentage, sales volume, average time to sale, minutes to dollars, by hour and by day and by week.

It seems the young Asian American men of Merrill Sachs have been selling to their own people: Chinese doctors, naturopaths, acupuncturists. They have been selling stock in a drug company developing a rival to Pfizer's magic female libido cure.

The drug company will be real. Their drug will not be.

There is only one office in the entire space. It is Chi's. His computer is the same as the ones out there just with more monitors. I look through the sales made today and start clicking on numbers to dial. It's three in the morning and most of these numbers are in this time zone. But everyone answers the three in the morning call if they're not blackout drunk or switched off under the right drugs. I make the first ten calls as a Merrill Sachs broker calling to correct details. I explain that if we correct a clerical mistake before the markets open tomorrow then all is good but that if we don't then the price has gone up. Two of my answers want to back out of their purchases entirely. I make the next ten calls as an investigator from the Securities and Exchange Commission. I share the bad and the good news. We're investigating Merrill Sachs. Your money is gone but you can help others.

I give everyone Chi's personal work phone number. I leave my number on a post-it note on one of his monitors. I walk out of the building at dawn, drive home and take my meds. I make sure my phone is plugged in and near my ear.

Chi calls me over my late breakfast. "You know who I'm connected with, asshole?"

"I do Chi. That's why I paid your office a visit. Your dad has five sons. You're the youngest. He's entrusted this business to you. I know you don't want to let him down."

"Some unhappy customers called me this morning."

"Not strange in your business though surely."

"It would be very easy for me to have you hurt."

"Sure. You just have to call your dad. Say you fucked up. Again. And you need him to bail you out. Again." I let that sting. "I have your sucker list," I lie. "I have all of your sales," I continue the lie. "I can call them all. I'm Larry from the Securities and Exchange Commission. Larry? Larry. Larry? No. Maybe I'll go with Jim. Jim. I like Jim. Hi. I'm Jim from the Securities and Exchange Commission. You were recently defrauded by—"

"We close the boiler room earlier than planned and move on. You can't kill this business. We are America's fat bloated body wheezing and gasping."

"I'm not threatening to kill your business Chi. I'm threatening to get you in trouble with your dad. And I don't even want money. I just want a little information. About your dad."

"He is a great and terrible man you should fear. There is your information."

"He's an old man to have the top job."

"He has a young heart," Chi says dryly.

"He carries the Honjo Masamune with him at all times?"

"Everyone knows he carries that which he took from the dead hand of his enemy. Nothing greater is earned in this life."

"Japanese steel for a Chinese Gangster. Seems strange to me."

"I'm not going to tell you anything you can use to hurt him."

"I don't want to hurt him Chi. I want to understand him. I have heard that your father is a very paranoid man."

"Words his enemies use. They breathe because my father allows them to breathe."

I'm not getting anything here. "You grew up with him. Was he always this paranoid? Or did it come with the crown?"

"Great men are paranoid because others want to take their greatness."

"Can we give the fucking aphorisms a rest? I'm the one with the leverage here."

"Except after talking to you, I don't think you have any real leverage."

"He has a young heart. What did that mean?"
"Goodbye." He hangs up.
That was a failure. No other way to score it.
But. Jian Chin has a young heart. That means something.

Chapter Twenty-Three

HEART

I call Rose and ask about the Dub C Head Dragon. He doesn't know as much as I do already. But he gives me the names of some confidential informants Organized Crime were working with recently. I make three calls. They all go to voicemail. I say I want to hear the heart story and I'm willing to pay cash.

I get a hit. I meet up in Hollywood with a thin grey haired Asian boy who says he worked in one of Dub C's boiler rooms. He tells me the heart story. He tells me that it happened just before Jian became the boss.

Getting someone else's heart legally is a demeaning and personally invasive process. In assessing the physical health of a candidate the doctors ask probing questions about smoking, drinking and drug abuse. They delve into a patient's psychological history and current mental stability. They sit supreme in judgment, jealously guarding access to More Life. How many dying people give up their cigarettes to show these judges they can live clean only to spend their last weeks grouchy and irritable? How many drinkers die craving a last sip of whiskey because they thought a 60 day chip might help them make the list? How many of my people, the crazies, are forced to pretend they are normal right until the end when they die not being themselves?

When an individual is determined to be a good candidate for a transplant, he or she makes it on the national waiting list that is coordinated out of Richmond, VA. They then wait in good life purgatory.

The black market for organ transplants is far less judgmental. The basic assumption made is that if you have the money to buy an organ then you're probably an okay person. Simple and smart and it works well.

Brokers source the warm and wet from the third world and arrange for the transplants to be performed in major US hospitals. Donors can be flown to the US to assuage the recipient's guilt. They can receive cash after a removal performed in their home country. They can be drugged and wake up with stitches. Or they can be ripped open with rusty tools and left to die. A kidney harvested from a living donor will keep a recipient alive twice as long as one taken from a corpse.

Livers, eyes and lungs sell well.

Hearts are the big ticket item.

Jian Chin could have purchased his heart from a black market broker here in LA. And that broker could have arranged for the transplant to take place in Cedars-Sinai, Keck, Kaiser or the UCLA Medical Center. The total cost might have been half a million—including a plausible paper trail and the proper hospital bribes.

But Jian didn't do that. Because he knew the exact heart he wanted. It was beating inside the chest of the young man his wife had been having an affair with. He had the handsome but untalented actor kidnapped. His doctors ran all the tests and they determined that miraculously the heart was a viable candidate to be transferred to the crime lord. The actor only woke up once more, long enough for Jian to explain why he was dying.

The surgical team set-up the necessary machines in a veterinary operating theatre. Jian was shaved and anaesthetized. The surgeon opened his chest, sawing the breastbone and spreading the ribs. A heart-lung machine took over for his breathing and pumping. Circulation was rerouted. His blood was cooled. His bad heart was removed. And the young clean heart of the young actor was enthroned in his chest cavity.

His blood was rewarmed. A shock got his new heart beating.

The actor's empty chest cavity was stuffed with valentine chocolates and left waiting for Jian's wife at the fuckpad she thought was a secret. A weakened Jian found her there and made his wife eat his dead heart before he killed her.

Much of this story has to be embellished. But even so. As a myth it fucking works.

I push the scared kid to tell me more about Jian. He gets shifty. And more cash doesn't help. He doesn't look like a junkie but he has some place he wants to get. He runs away with my money balled into his fist.

I drive home listening to satellite radio. Veterans are clamoring for the new stolen drugs.

I make it home but can't get out of the 911. I just sit in my parking spot.

I check on the cloned phones. The boys are all home in the Pacific Palisades.

I jam the Porsche into reverse and roar backwards and around and then select first and squeal up from the underground parking and back out into the night. I'm telling myself that I'm headed to the Pacific Palisades to retrieve audio from the ghost transmitters but I'm not.

I get there, I pull up to the front. I arm myself with the Glock and go ring the doorbell.

Harlan answers the door and lets me in.

"It's the detective," Harlan says.

He leads me into the great room. Jason is putting an AK-47 together. There is body armor near him. He is smoking. Alexander is surrounded by notebook screens. The one I can see is displaying Google street view.

"How can we help you?" Alexander asks me.

"The Hyena wasn't your father after all."

Jason and Harlan both look to Alexander. His features remain neutral to this news.

"I came in here and took DNA samples from the three of you. I had a lab do three tests. He killed himself because he knew."

"That's sad," Alexander says. "But it doesn't change anything now. The Hyena brought us together as brothers. That's what matters."

"You're likely not brothers."

Harlan shoots back: "Did you do *that* test?"

"No. But it can easily be done."

"We don't need it done," Alexander answers for all three of them. "We're brothers."

"Fine. You're brothers. Whatever. But you don't need to do what you're planning. . . .

General Ripper is just another attempt to find a father. You are going to get killed."

Alexander eyes me with respect. "You've been watching us. Listening."

"You are not warriors. Jian Chin is a paranoid crime lord. You will die trying to get that sword."

Jason finishes putting the AK together. He slams in a clip.

"We are going to take that sword," Alexander assures me.

"And then what? General Ripper appears in a beam of light and takes you away to play army? Whoever that man is he is a wanted terrorist. It is only a matter of days before he is found and brought to justice."

Jason points the AK at me.

Alexander stops giving me attention and talks just to his brothers. "We'll get new cellphones tomorrow. I'll get the equipment for a proper bug scan of all our rooms and cars. I should have done it before. I'm sorry. I'll fix my mistake."

"You should upgrade the home alarm system too. It was trivial to bypass. Twice."

Still just talking to his brothers and ignoring me, Alexander responds to this as if the idea just came to him. "We should upgrade the home alarm system too. You never know when a pesky PI is going to come around and bother us."

"No," I spit at him. "You didn't know. You wouldn't know if I hadn't rung the doorbell. I came here to warn you. To save you. Have you heard Jian's heart story?"

"Heart story?" Harlan asks confused.

"Yes," Alexander commands, talking to me again. "We have."

Jason shoulders the assault rifle and clicks it hot.

"I hunted serial killers. Cult leaders. I would not fuck with Jian."

"Why do you care?" Alexander yells at me. "We're looking for a father—that's your pathetic two cent psych diagnosis? Well you are *not* that father. So fuck off."

"I warned you," I say.

Jason fires a bullet past me and into the wall. The crack of the AK stuns us all.

"You don't think we're at the level to pull off a heist like this," Jason says evenly. "If we were world class thieves, combat veterans, shock and awe specialists. If we were at that level. We'd never let a man who had us under surveillance walk away with his life."

I feel the shape and weight of the Glock under my arm. Did I walk into a firefight?

"He has a point," Alexander agrees.

"We're going to kill him?" Harlan asks nervously.

Jason aims again and waits for the command from Alexander.

But Alexander raises his hand. "No Harlan. We're not. However: we are done with him."

"We see you again and you die," Jason promises me. "Got that Chalk?"

"Don't try going after the General's encrypted emails," Alexander adds. "They're gone forever."

I back away and leave, tense until I'm past the front door and outside.

My cloned phones are dead before I get back the condo.

I put on my sweat gear and pick a scare for my sixty minutes. I adore Romero but the 2004 remake of *Dawn of the Dead* is an amazing horror flick in its own right. Classic zombies are slow, contemporary zombies are fast—they're still coming for all of us. So many scare set-ups are about location: a house, a camp, a forest, a prison, and if the protagonists escape and make it back to the real world then they're safe at least until the sequel. But Zombie movies are about there being no place that is safe, no escape, just temporary respite.

The best sequence in the film is when Luda is both in labor and turning into a zombie. She dies to then be reanimated and give birth to a Zombie baby. They have to kill her and then they have to kill the baby too. It's a brutal scene. With the zombie infection closing in from the outside, the survivors have to be ruthless about it growing from within as well.

I felt that terror tonight. But now I've sweated it out.

I should let these three fools go.

I'm going to call the FBI and pass what I know on.

CHAPTER TWENTY-FOUR

DIAMONDS

"Thanks for coming in Chalk."

The Federal Building on Wilshire is home to the LA Division of the FBI. There are satellite offices throughout the area code but Wilshire is where the Assistant Director has his throne room.

I still know a lot of agents who work in LA. I chose to call Special Agent Paula Danson. We trained together at Quantico and we both spent time in Cyber. We lost touch when I joined the Behavioral unit. She's been all over the country and now she's here in LA. I didn't have to ask if she was detailed to the pharmaceutical warehouse robberies because I know that everyone is.

The FBI works like that. Everyone over here on this right fucking now.

Wait wait wait over here—this is suddenly more important.

I gave Paula an outline of what I have and she asked me to come in. I parked in the visitor's lot. At the front desk I was given a temporary photo ID slightly better than the fake ones I make for myself. Paula came down and escorted me up and into the labyrinth.

We're in a conference room. I'm wearing a Depeche Mode shirt with the violator flower in red, small bloom, many petals. There is one other agent in the room, an athlete type. He has positioned a video camera on a small tripod that is connected to a notebook. This is a live video feed streaming to the desktops of men who want to see me but don't want me to see them.

I tell Paula the story about the three brothers.

Done, I drink an entire glass of water and pour myself more.

"Why does this domestic terrorist want these three young men to enlist with him?"

"He wants Alexander's hacking skills. Alexander wants to bring the other two with him."

"Do you have the encrypted emails Alexander referred to?"

"No. The way it went down . . ." I'm feeling defensive. "No. I didn't try and get the emails. And now he says they've been erased."

"You believe him?"

"Yes. But you can use the Patriot Act to find out for sure. Right?"

At once I feel it. I came here thinking I was bringing them vital information, that I would be welcomed as a lost son returned. But the organization sees me as a fool or even worse: that guy who was fired but still wants to hang with his former colleagues on the bowling team.

That's why no one is here.

Paula is doing this out of mercy.

"The bottom line is this: I think you should watch Jian Chin." I swallow. "But what do I know right?" I stand up and knock my water over. The liquid runs across the table and dribbles to the carpet. Paula motions for the athlete agent to cut the video. "I'm going to go now," I say pulling at my visitor credentials.

"Can I take you to lunch Chalk?" Paula asks.

We get out of the building. We take the 911 West of the San Diego Freeway to a new indie wrap place on South Barrington, across from the Social Security Disability Benefits office. We get baskets and drinks and sit outside.

"I just thought I should share what I'd discovered," I say.

"Stop apologizing. You were right to come in. If it's something it will be something big."

"But."

Paula puts her wrap down and wipes her mouth. "Let me tell you what we've got so far. I want to hear what you think."

"Go," I say.

"The pharmaceutical jobs are not their first heists. They've been hijacking diamonds for years. Diamonds on their way to Surat, diamonds being processed in Surat and diamonds trying to leave Surat. We've connected their work through the attack profiles and ballistics. We're estimating they've scored about 400 million dollars."

Five billion dollars in diamonds make it to India each year. They are escorted by private security companies and mercenaries. The gems come in from Africa, Russia, Australia and elsewhere, fully ninety five percent of the world's supply. During their stay they will be owned and sold and owned and sold by warlords, street dealers, governments, corporations, organized crime, cartels. Half a million of Surat's five million residents are employed in the processing of these diamonds. They are paid almost nothing and protected by few workplace regulations. Crunched together in hot factories these workers sort the diamonds by the characteristics that will be referenced to sell to men ready to pop the question: size, shape, color, clarity. After sorting comes the cutting and polishing. The thousands of polishing companies have tight security. Armed gunmen watch over boys who squint through magnifiers hour upon hour. Their eyesight fails just as they develop respiratory problems from the diamond grains in the air. The polishers make no real distinctions between stones obtained through slavery and crime and those that come with specialized documents that lie about fair trade in that special way the Western world cares for. Possibly final sales and distributions take place on the trading floors of the diamond exchanges. It is the only place in the world that multimillion fortunes can be amassed without any trail being left behind.

"They've been building capital," I say.

"A war chest Chalk."

"To buy the guns and armor."

"The weaponry we've seen would still just cost a fraction of what they've amassed."

"How much of that money have they laundered?"

"We don't know because we're not sure how they're doing their cleaning. But. And this is strange. We think they're cycling out new cash from Surat for old cash in the US."

"How old are we talking?"

"Old enough to ring alarm bells if spent."

"Why would they want to do that?"

Paula raises her eyebrows. "We don't know."

The Treasury Department ships freshly cooked paper money to Federal Reserve Banks where the bills are then divided and shared as allowance with the kids: credit unions and lesser banks. Just as the Fed distributes the new bills eager to make a positive difference in the economy, it collects the sweaty, rumpled ones that have given up on our grotesque national lifestyle. Cash is taken out of circulation far more often than people believe. Collected cash is shredded and replaced with paper money that has ever more advanced anti-counterfeiting technology.

Trying to counterfeit modern US currency on any kind of scale is a stupid crime. The investment it takes to be bad at it requires so much money and intelligence that you might as well launch a tech start-up and earn the money legitimately. When Marky Mark & The Funky Bunch were putting words to a new generation's feelings about good vibrations, the counterfeit prevention technology in US Bills relied on threads, watermarks and advanced ink. The same bill coming from the Treasury today has ultraviolet secrets, hidden graphics and mystery textures. And those are just the technologies that have been disclosed.

There are people who maintain that any US bill printed after the Civil War is legal tender and must be accepted. But it doesn't work exactly like that. Older bills can be returned to a Federal Bank to be exchanged for a straight trade to the modern equivalent. But any stack of significance will require a case number to be created. The government will want to know where the money came from, if tax was paid on it, why was it not in circulation, and who are you again? And big transactions with old bills get noticed at businesses as well.

"What if they're counterfeiting old bills?" I think aloud.

"They have four hundred million real dollars. Why would they want to counterfeit more?"

"They could mix the counterfeit old bills in with the real old money."

"What would that accomplish?"

"It could double or triple their cash."

"How are they going to spend it?"

"Maybe they're not," I answer.

We're both quiet.

"These guys have got to be ex-soldiers."

"Yes they absolutely have to be. But we don't know who or how."

"I can't believe nothing has turned up from the mailings."

"Nothing Chalk. Thousands of different mail drops around the country. No fingerprints on the packages. Nothing revealed in the inks or the postage or the routing. Nothing."

"What about the initials on the drug care packages. GR. That is for General Ripper?"

"Yes. You're right about that. And that lends some credibility to your story about the brothers."

"Peace is not our profession. That was on one of the screens in the recent hits. That's an allusion to *Dr. Strangelove* as well."

"There's more than that. We haven't released this to the media yet but it's only a matter of time before someone else figures it out. Those letters and numbers circled on the screens? FGD 135 when put in the right order. That's the code in *Dr. Strangelove* that General Ripper sends to the bomb wing. It decodes as Wing Attack Plan R."

"Which is the code that orders them to drop their bombs in Russia and start World War III," I say.

"The go code," Paula confirms.

"The go code," I repeat. "Which has what to do with stealing pills?"

Paula shrugs.

"Alexander's encrypted emails are the first two way communication with this General Ripper. The offer to join the second army is real. You have to put the three bothers under surveillance. You have to watch Jian."

Paula checks her watch and then her phone. "I should have asked more questions before I had you come in. . . . If I 'd known what you had. . . ." She looks straight at me and articulates: "I believe you Chalk."

"But."

"But I don't think anyone else in the FBI does or is going to."

"I'm Fox Mulder all of a sudden."

"Come on. Not all of a sudden Chalk. You know that. And you're much worse. Fox Mulder kept his office in the basement."

"I'm a pariah. So you're not going to use good solid intelligence."

"My superiors don't want to use it and that means I can't. I have to get back Chalk."

I drop Paula off, still stunned. She says bye and goes. It's awkward.

I should return home and start again with the small jobs. But instead I drive by the brothers' Pacific Palisades home. All my ghost transmitters are discovered and dead. And all three brothers have new cellphones so I can't listen that way either.

They are unknown to me right now.

How close are they to hitting Jian?

CHAPTER TWENTY-FIVE

STINGRAY

Driving home I think about the Unabomber.

John Douglas, one of the founding fathers in Behavioral Science, did a 1995 profile of the mail madman. The tone in the document is that of a carnival gypsy uttering the obvious in a spooky voice hoping for a reaction that can be used to sell an impression of otherworldly prescience. It risked almost no insights and for that simplicity was deemed perfect. Because the secret about profiles is this: they are valuable hunting tools only because they tell us what the monsters we have caught have in common with the monsters we're catching—it's circular success. I've studied them, I've used them, I've authored them.

There will be a profile of General Ripper in the works down in Virginia now.

I park for Starbucks and drink my coffee at a table outside. There's a busker on the street with dirty hair and a military jacket. He has a worn Epiphone acoustic in tobacco sunburst, the case open for donations. While I sit with my coffee he plays *Wish You Were Here* by Pink Floyd, *Runaway Train* by Soul Asylum, *Wishlist* by Pearl Jam and *Summertime* by My Chemical Romance. I immediately recognize the songs but don't dismiss them as background noise because he's added a Beach Boys harmonic quality.

I often wonder if the Bacchus killer is a musician himself, failed or otherwise. When I do I consider that he might be a busker just like this guy. Maybe playing outside concert venues. Setting up, tuning up, singing to the fans as they enter the venue—any of which might be his next victim.

A profile will never catch the Bacchus killer. Even if the FBI believed in him long enough to draft one. No. He's a more portentous and mysterious monster . . . beyond mere psychology.

A profile will never catch General Ripper either. He's like the Bacchus killer in that respect. But unlike the Bacchus killer General Ripper is real right now. The FBI believe in him, believe in the threat his activity poses to the country. How could they not? But they're still going about it all wrong. He's not another Unabomber or Timothy McVeigh. He is a member of the Dark Pantheon that I've always known exists in this country . . . another monster beyond mere psychology.

I'm not the only one who can catch this domestic terrorist.

But I can catch him faster than anyone else. And given the stakes that's important.

I finish my coffee and make the decision. I'm going after General Ripper.

I give the busker twenty bucks.

I need to put the three brothers under surveillance again and find out how close they are to grabbing the sword that will somehow get them into the second army. Bluesnarfing IDs and cloning phones ain't going to cut it this time.

I'm going to need a Stingray.

A Stingray presents itself as a legit cellphone tower. Attracted to its strong signal, cellphones in the area connect. The fake tower is then able to monitor all traffic: calls, SMS, location and data traffic. The Stingray routes the communication streams through the regular telecom networks ensuring there is no suspicious service disruption.

The FBI has been using this surveillance technology for years.

The main reason it still works is that the phone companies are reluctant to make technology changes. They've labored to make roaming reliable and they don't want to add security that would jeopardize the constitutionally protected right to stream funny cat videos anywhere and everywhere they are needed.

I don't need the resources of the FBI's Tracking Technology Unit to run a Stingray.

I have Harry. Six months ago Harry said he could build me a Stingray if I brought him the right parts. He backed the promise by giving me a shopping list I now retrieve from the glove box.

I drive to Fry's, the Ham Radio Outlet and Deal Extreme.

Harry owns a small cinema in West Beverly that caters to cult showings of horror movies. He is the owner and only employee although he lets a few film school rejects pour fountain drinks and dispense popcorn covered in good old chemical butter. The tight and dirty lobby is plastered with great posters: *Werewolf in a Girl's Dormitory*, *Voodoo Woman*, *The Hooker Cult Movies*, *The Black Sleep*, *Carnival of Souls*, *Murder Mansion*, *Oasis of the Zombies*, *I Eat Your Skin*, *Tower of Screaming Virgins*, *Shriek of the Mutilated* and one of my favorites: *In The Mouth of Madness*. The theatre itself seats a hundred. I believe Harry cleans the floor with a hose.

There is an office upstairs awash in bad screenplays. Harry will read anything and tell the kid who he ripped off and why it's not as good as the original. He has a hookah in there. He draws on it now as I appear before him with a small suitcase of just purchased electronics.

Harry is an aged master of special effects. He's made horrific death believable for a few dollars and spent millions of studio bucks on science fiction dystopias. He doesn't work that much anymore. But every FX man in LA knows Harry. I met him while hunting a serial killer who collected and made amateur torture flicks.

Horror movies are the visual representation of our cultural nightmares. Films don't turn normal people into killers but a psychopath gets more out of *Cannibal Holocaust*, *Texas Chainsaw Massacre* and *Human Centipede* than you or I.

I watch Harry work with the circuit boards. He creates a black box with two attached directional antennas managed by a subnotebook running Asterisk on OpenBTS. The specialized open source software saves information to a micro SD card that can easily be lost should I need to appear innocent.

Harry and I discuss important movie questions. How much does the contemporary Batman owe to Bond?

"There. Done. I think. Mostly. Probably. If you have any trouble just jiggle this. . . . Take a flyer on the way out. New festival coming up."

I set the Stingray up on the passenger seat, power plugged into the 911's grid.

I drive straight back to the brothers' Pacific Palisades home. Alexander is there talking to Jason and Harlan who are out running different errands. When the two get home I use the Stingray to remotely control the radio processor on Harlan's device. And I just turn his microphone on.

Instant bug. I'm soon caught up with the brothers' plans.

They've determined the street on which they're going to hit Jian Chin's convoy. Alexander has figured out how to engineer several moments of invisibility from the security cameras on the street and how to jam 911 calls in the area. Jason has finalized the armor and armaments. Harlan seems to be mostly just taking orders.

The final piece has just fallen into place: the inside man.

Park Tang has been Jian's lieutenant for many years. His hands were bloody in the murderous heart transplant. He aided Jian in becoming the Triad leader, in massacring their Yakuza rivals, and in taking the Honjo Masamune.

Park and Jian were like brothers until Jian jailed Park's actual brother.

The Dragon Head did not send Park's sibling to a corrections facility run by the county.

No. Jian sent Park's brother to the Keister Penthouse: a prison built by criminals. It's under the earth somewhere in LA, deep enough for the dirt to hide the noise of caged existence. The stories heard on the street never reference less than six cells but sometimes more than two dozen. The cages are singles. They have metal bars, cots, chemical toilets.

It gets better. Every cell has a TV enclosed in a hard plastic box. The inmates are given their own remotes and can request movies. The food is procured from the surface and inmate choice is taken into account. Phone calls are not allowed but inmates are permitted to make video recordings that are delivered to loved ones. Prostitutes are brought in for conjugal dates according to a schedule. Alcohol, cigarettes and weed are abundant.

And then it gets worse.

There is no outside time allowed ever.

There are no days to count down because there are no sentences.

Inmates can be executed at any time.

It started out as an idea of the Irish Mob. They needed a place to hold brothers they didn't entirely trust but weren't ready to kill. The basic idea was improved upon by others but it never really worked until the Aryans took it over. The white supremacists know cages better than anyone—spiritual, mental and physical.

They made the Keister Penthouse a functioning business.

They will take warm bodies from any OC if they come with the required fees.

No good reason was given when Jian jailed Park's brother and none has been offered since. Park is still smiles and bows. But he has had enough of his leader's unpredictable paranoia. He knows that if the Dragon Head is killed during the armed theft of the Honjo Masamune then he can get his brother released.

So he has turned. He has taken the role of the inside man. He is going to give the three brothers all of the up-to-the minute information they need to hit the convoy and take the sword. Soon.

Maybe I am wrong. Maybe they can pull it off.

Back in the know I drive home.

Shorts. Running shoes. Elliptical. Earphones. Movie: *Jacob's Ladder*.

A soldier returns from the Vietnam war. He has memories of his former family life while living with his new girlfriend and working as a mailman in New York. Hallucinations go from the disturbing to the grotesque. He learns that another man from his army unit is having the same visions. He discovers a conspiracy concerning a secret drug that the army administered to his unit to increase aggression in battle. As the horror becomes intense, he finds himself back with his wife and their son who had died but is now alive. The movie ends in Vietnam where it is suggested that everything that has transpired was a fevered deathbed dream.

What scares me about this film is the point in the story where it becomes impossible to discern reality from nightmare, conspiracy from paranoid madness, drug hallucinations from biblical end times, the present from the past or even the hoped for future.

This is how extreme terror ends.

I turn the news on before I go to sleep.

Veterans are clamoring for the newest drugs stolen to be sent to them. They are pleading and preparing. The chaos from the first pharmaceutical packages is bleeding into the chaos of the anticipation, the desperation for more. There are already hateful confrontations, crimes. This is the nightmare of a veteran's personal existence being visited on normal society: the blur between what is real and safe and what can become a violent nightmare at any moment.

General Ripper is playing with the line.

Nothing terrible has happened yet . . . but the rising national tension is palpable.

This is how extreme terror starts.

I'm crazy for deciding to go after this man. There's just no question.

But I'm doing it.

Chapter Twenty-Six

SHELLS

The Los Angeles Gun Club is an indoor range on East 6th Street. It's open to 11 PM seven days a week. There's good parking. Inside it's a warehouse. The lane rentals are fair. They sell standard human outline targets and life-size photographic sheets of bad guys frozen in positions of aggression sufficient to justify a hail of bullets. Visitors and tourists rent guns. Regulars bring their own firearms but usually buy their ammunition on site.

I followed the brothers here.

I watched them set up and start shooting. And then I came out to the parking lot to wait.

Just when I think they are aspiring pros they do something stupid like this—firing off hundreds of AK rounds days or scant hours before a daylight raid with AKs goes down in the city. It's dumb. But maybe they are that sure General Ripper is going to take them away to the Valhalla where his forces are successfully hiding from all the law enforcement agencies of the most powerful country on earth.

I watch them come out, guns in bags. They drive away in Alexander's M3.

I go back into the range. The club's shop has Glocks, Springfields, Berettas. They have shotguns, rifles, HKs, AKs and an Uzi. Most of the lanes are occupied. There is a small group of people waiting, cleaning, lubing, preparing their weapons.

There is one man standing alone in this loud and violent menagerie. He's my age, much fitter, he has the calm of combat.

His gun is a Smith & Wesson 500: an artillery piece disguised as a hand-gun. It has a five round capacity. The finish is satin stainless.

The two lanes the brothers were using are about to be cleaned and released to the next paying customer. I only need a few seconds to pick up a pocketful of AK shell casings—evidence that I can maybe use later.

No one saw me drop down to my haunches.

But as I leave I catch the man with the Smith & Wesson 500 watch me go.

I see that he has a long scar down his left cheek.

I tuck the shell casings away in the 911. And drive back to the Pacific Palisades.

Everything is ready for the heist. The brothers are just waiting on the call from Park.

Listening through their phones I hear them stripping and loading their guns, checking the tautness of their armor, going over the street plans, the timing. It's grimly tense and there is no joking around.

It's early afternoon when a courier delivers a package to the front door.

I listen to Alexander rip it open.

"A USB key?" Harlan asks.

Alexander plugs it into a computer. There are clicks.

"A picture?" Harlan asks.

"Yes and no," Alexander answers.

I hear typing. I hear the two brothers not at the keyboard breathing.

"Digital Steganography," Alexander determines. "There's a text file and a picture in this image. They're hidden but not encrypted. There are lots of programs that will do a decent reveal. Give me five minutes."

I'm thinking through how I might get into Alexander's computers in the house and see the image delivered by the courier when the call from Park comes in. He tells the brothers when Jian Chin's convoy will be passing through the designated target zone, the order of the vehicles, the number of bodyguards, the weapons they have at the ready.

Park confirms that Jian has the sword with him.

Just as Jason hangs up on the inside man, Alexander announces success.

They are looking at the screen.

"We saw him," Harlan says in a whisper.

"Yeah," Alexander answers.

"We're going to see him again real soon," Jason orders. "Let's go."

There are no words after this. Just preparations.

Five minutes later the brothers pull out of their driveway in Jason's M3.

I know where the target zone is, where they're going. But I want that digital picture.

I roll into the driveway, leave the 911 running, and rush up to the front door with my Glock. No time for a pick. I shoot the lock and charge the hard wood with my shoulder. The door caves inward and I trip and fall to the floor.

They didn't arm the alarm.

I'm up. Alexander was working in the kitchen. There are three of his notebook computers on the main table. Just the one is open. It has a USB key in the side. The bubble package it came in has fallen to the floor.

Whatever they saw is not on the screen anymore. I don't have time to retrieve it.

I yank the USB key and hurry back to the 911.

I drive with insane aggression to reach the target zone in Chinatown, twice actually popping onto the sidewalk to get around slower drivers. I've made it before the show has started. There are other people here but I'm the only who came with a ticket.

I have a good seat in the Porsche. But I'm deliberately not in the front row.

Jason's M3 is illegally parked and empty. The brothers are not visible.

The 911 emergency service works like this. Cell and landline calls are routed to a dedicated 9-1-1 switch that sends the call through to a Public Safety Answering Point. The operator who receives the call triages the problem and determines whether police, fire, medical or all three are needed. Operators see call information on their screens but there is no special detail. 911 calls are just regular calls routed differently—as such there is no 911 network to hack.

So. Alexander has planned to overwhelm the service with automated calls from the area.

He set this up in a rented apartment last week with an open source PBX system connected to multiple VoIP lines. He wrote custom code to cycle through a call file pushed to a spooling directory that blasts the emergency number.

I call 911 and get through.

I call 911 and get through.

I call 911 and don't get through.

Because Jian Chin's convoy has turned onto the street.

There are five vehicles. Leading and at the back are white Nissan Armadas. Between them is a white Infiniti QX. All the vehicle windows are tinted black but only the QX is armored. Two Suzuki bikes are buzzing around. They are either side of the QX when the first explosion comes.

A pipe bomb knocks the lead Armada over and on its side. The blast came from a gym bag on the curb. Two pedestrians were destroyed in a hurricane of blood and skin and white bone. There are five full seconds of shocked silence before the second pipe bomb knocks the trailing Armada over. This one covers my Porsche in debris, cracking my windshield and partially covering my view.

The convoy is now trapped.

Jason emerges from a building archway firing his AK. He cuts down both wounded bikers as they flop and fumble to get their submachine guns out. Jason turns his barrel on the untouched QX. He doesn't fire on it because he knows his bullets will just bounce off the hardened exterior.

Jason nods.

Harlan appears and approaches the SUV tank. He has a knife and a large plastic container filled with gas. Harlan uses his strength to puncture the tires of the trapped vehicle. And then he pours the liquid under the refined truck and lights it.

Jason has covered the big wrestler the entire time.

The doors of the SUV finally open. Park comes out raging. He has a submachine gun, an HK. He fires wildly and uselessly and falls as if he's been shot even though Jason has not pulled the trigger and Harlan has not even brought his AK up yet.

The SUV door that opened shuts again.

I've heard most of the parts of this plan put together. But I don't know what's next.

The three bodyguards in the Dragon Head's vehicle have not been quivering in fear while inside. They've been arming and discussing how best to enter the battle. The passenger side window opens now just enough for two smoke grenades to drop out and bounce and skitter across the pavement.

The billowing grey adds to the burning black of the gas fire.

Three immense men come out of the SUV at once. I hear a shotgun. I see a staccato muzzle flash. It's a ballistic slug fest in the smoke. Which Alexander ends. His position was hidden until this moment. He comes up the other side of the SUV and murders the bodyguards before they even see him.

Just as I was the only with a ticket I am the only one in the audience left—everyone has either run away or been killed in the crossfire. Right now I wish my seat was worse. The brothers have not hesitated to kill. Shells are everywhere.

Alexander puts out the fire under the SUV with an extinguisher. They had to have been only seconds away from the gas tank blowing up. Park stands up, resurrected in his master's eyes as the traitor he is.

Jian Chin comes out of the SUV holding the Honjo Masamune. Park pulls a Ruger and shoots his boss in the side of the head without movement from his lips. Alexander catches the katana as its former owner falls.

The three brothers stand together. Park says a single word to them and then twitches standing. His worried face goes a white blank and he collapses as if his entire skeleton had been removed. He's been brought down by a sniper.

The boys bring up their guns and spin around looking for the shooter.

A man starts walking toward them through the smoke and carnage. He's wearing the same black armor of the men seen in the coordinated pharmaceutical robberies. He's got a Smith & Wesson 500 holstered.

It's the man I saw from the shooting range. I can just see his scar.

The brothers were told that they could enlist with General Ripper if they got the Honjo Masamune. They did and now this solider has come for them. Few words are spoken. Alexander hands the solider the Honjo Masamune and they follow him at a run, they follow him away.

They've left the M3 like they will be leaving the house and everything else.

They've enlisted with General Ripper.

The scarred soldier knew my face. The brothers knew my face.

If it wasn't for the debris covering the 911 I would have been killed by that sniper too.

CHAPTER TWENTY-SEVEN

EXCOMMUNICATED

I drive the battered 911 to my Porsche dealership. They give me a Cayenne Diesel as a loaner. I take the keys with disgust but drive it home. The Chinatown firefight is on the news. The media have no security camera footage but witnesses had their cellphones out and they couldn't reach 911. So there are clips of confused sound and shaky video.

No one has any idea what happened or why.

I drop into my office and plug the couriered USB key from the brothers' house into a Windows desktop I keep isolated from my network. There's one image. It's a high quality jpeg of the cover for the upcoming *Call of Duty: Black Ops* game. The title is centered in block white letters. Behind the title is a masked soldier armed for urban combat, partially covered in darkness.

I check online. This is indeed the official cover for the upcoming video game.

The character could almost be one of General Ripper's soldiers.

There are several freeware programs for steganography. Most will both encode and decode. Running an inspector on the file I determine that this steganography was done with the popular S-Tools. Within the video game image is another picture and a tiny text file just as I heard Alexander say. The picture is a headshot of the solider that approached the brothers in the aftermath of their heist: the recruiting sergeant with the massive Smith and Wesson and the scar.

General Ripper sent this so they knew who would be coming for them if they succeeded.

The text file has one sentence: *Come to me and we will bring the game to them. GR.*

I eat, take my meds and crash.

I wake to what I want to be a safe day inside climate controlled air.

I get cereal and turn the news back on.

A few hours is all the coverage the hit on Jian Chin got. Because veterans have started receiving the new stolen drugs in the mail. And this time there is cash in the packages as well: tens of thousands of dollars for each recipient.

The FBI has already confirmed that the currency bundles are a mix of real older bills and counterfeit older bills. My guess at lunch with Paula was right. This allowed them to multiply the hundreds of millions in cash.

But that's not why General Ripper did it. Again, always, his motive is chaos.

Veterans are having their money scrutinized and in some cases rejected. From restaurants. From grocery stores. From Walmarts. From liquor stores. From gun stores. Soldiers who fought for their country, many of whom have been self-medicating, are being publicly insulted.

They are becoming angry. They are arming. They are ready to fight back.

Gunfights will happen soon.

I take inventory. I have surveillance evidence that the brothers planned the robbery of the Honjo Masamune. I have shell casings. I have a digital picture of General Ripper's recruiting sergeant.

But just the one picture. Which doesn't connect.

I bring up Google street view of where the attack took place. I mentally position where the three brothers stood when they handed over the katana to the recruiting sergeant. The hand off was made. And then they ran away.

There. In that direction.

Security cameras on the street where the firefight took place were brought down. But what about a business a little further along? Just beyond the target area of the heist? Might a camera there have caught the brothers running away with the recruiting sergeant? Might I be able to get a second connecting picture?

There's a chance, an outside shot.

So much for my day inside. I pull on a shirt of a fetish pilot's mask done in stone with the band's red initials stamped on it: STP. I head down and get into the Diesel Cayenne which I hate. I drive to Chinatown and park.

The LAPD have taped off the exact area that Alexander blinded. Uniforms are collecting evidence. Crime scene techs are taking pictures. I walk around the block and come out the other side of the tape.

There is a variety store here with an outward facing security camera. It's on now. I stand and watch it watch me. It's a model a few years old, not expensive but decent. It wasn't just slapped up there as a visual deterrent. Thought was put into its placement and the programmed sweep it performs. Its cable tail is thick and blue.

When all the evidence has been tagged in the primary crime scene the detectives in charge will expand their scrutiny. They will see this camera. They will want to determine if it was brought down as well and if not they will found out what it saw.

I'm just a little ahead of them.

I move into the store and look for the interior camera. It is at the back, same model, same thick blue cable. The owner is staring at me. I grab a basket and start filling it with items. I spend no time considering my selections. I am a spending locomotive chugging directly for his cash register. I reach the glass topped counter and dump the items out. I point behind him at the cigarettes and booze. I make rapid requests. As his back is turned to me, I take out my roll of cash. I peel off three hundreds and tell him to work it out while I use the bathroom.

He nods okay and tells me it's in the back.

I move around the counter and to the back.

There are two doors in the tight back hallway. I open the one without the bathroom sign. The office is little more than a closet. The desk surface is clear but everywhere else there are stacks of paper, invoices, receipts. Two blue cables descend from the ceiling and run down the wall to a tower PC. I pull on gloves, open my little screwdriver and take the computer's metal case off. There are two hard drives nestled in the ribs of the machine. I can't tell which one the video card is feeding with the security footage so I take out both and slide them inside my jacket. I hurriedly peel off five hundreds and set them on the desk as compensation.

I emerge from the office and return to the counter just as the owner is finishing my total.

I forgot to take my gloves off. He looks at them strangely.

I tell him to keep the change, take my bag of stuff and walk out.

There is a homeless man on the street. He's working on a new topical sign that states he's a veteran without a mailing address. I hand him the bag of goods. He gives me a gummy smile and starts seeing what he's got. I walk back around the block, back around the tape perimeter and to the Cayenne that I hate.

And I drive home.

I take coffee into my study. The first drive was running the shop owner's OS. It has personal files, including spreadsheets for his business. I find his store online and print out an address label that will go on a bubble package to return this.

The second drive has the video footage I want. There are thirty days of 24/7 capture inside and out. It's low resolution but it is color. I zoom through it, watching the long string of numbers that indicate the time sequence rolling on.

The exterior camera caught the periphery of the heist. There is the explosion at the start, people running, flashes. There's no sound yet I can see screaming faces. I try to sync up what I'm watching with the timing of what I witnessed from my vantage in the debris covered 911.

There they are: the three brothers and the recruiting sergeant that came for them. I can't see where they're headed to. But with this I'm on their trail. I have the connection. I have two images of the recruiting sergeant's face. And it's his face that I will chase.

I'm thinking through how best to start when Paula calls. They're sending a car for me.

It's not a request and I don't see any reason to argue.

They don't dick around with a visitor's badge at the front desk this time. I'm brought directly to the executive conference room. Paula is there with the Assistant Director and attending special agents. There are three video feeds: identical conference rooms in Quantico and Washington and from the sky on one of the FBI's planes. Dark suits, tired eyes, impatient ears.

This time the powerful men are not hiding from me.

I'd just decided to do this alone. And now they want to listen to me.

Sure. Fuck it. Let's see where this goes.

It takes me twenty minutes to connect everything I have. But I make the dumb mistake every mid-level manager advancing through power point slides does. I focus on what I'm presenting and not who I'm presenting to.

When I'm done all three video feeds cut out immediately.

The Assistant Director clears his throat and pronounces judgment. "Thanks for bringing this information to us Chaucer. We'll see if we can use it."

All the attendant special agents start packing up. Everyone but Paula.

"No. Naw. Uh-huh. Sit the fuck down," I command. Everyone freezes. "I am not ending like this again. General Ripper is directing a complicated terrorist attack against this country. I have brought you a connection that—"

"What you've brought us is a massive legal problem." The AD waves his hand for everyone but him and Paula to go. "Breaking into databases. Illegal surveillance. Stealing hard drives."

"I'm not an FBI agent anymore."

"And there is a reason for that, I can assure you."

Paula looks at me finally. She can't help me. She's sorry.

I keep my anger focused on the AD. "Tell me that your ten thousand agents have got you anything as good as what I just gifted you out of the goodness of my goddamn heart."

"I can't discuss our case with you."

"Because I'm not an FBI agent."

"Yes."

I slam the table with my fists. "You had nothing before I walked in here the first time and you treated me like shit. You asked me to come back. And I did. I brought you the connection. Just to be treated like shit again. Fuck the legal situation! Catch him! And then write it up however you have to!"

"I read your personnel file. Twice," the AD says with ice surety. "I'd heard about you of course. Paula came to me. She said you might have information of value. So I read your personnel file. Quickly. I glanced at it. Because we've been a little busy. And I watched you come in the first time with the story about the brothers and the sword."

"And I was right about that!"

"About the heist you were right. But the connection to General Ripper was tenuous at best."

"Then—maybe. Not this time. This time even a bureaucrat like you has to see it."

The AD continues telling his story. "Paula came to me again. She told me you'd made a clever guess about the counterfeit money and we should have you return. I said yes." He stares at me. "Then I went back and read your file again. And this time I read it carefully. Mental illness. Domestic violence. Strange conspiracy theories."

"Fuck you asshole!"

"Now we're done. Alright? Let's just leave it at that. Now we are done. You can go."

"No thank you at all. I didn't expect a cake. But this level of disrespect is stunning."

"You're not under arrest!" he finally yells back. "You should consider that your thank you, Chaucer."

"It's Chalk asshole."

"Keep talking to me like that and I will have you arrested!" he screams at me.

"This meeting is done," Paula tries.

"You want to arrest me, you prick?! Try it! Just fucking try it! I will release what I just shared with you to the media." I'm laughing at him.

"If any of this makes it to the media I will have you picked up on everything we can write. That is not a threat psycho."

My body charges with violent energy. I want to rush at him, beat him, break him.

But I don't. I grin maniacally. "I'd decided after my last visit here. But now I am resolved. I am going to beat you to him. Even with what I just gave you, I am going to get to him first."

"You are not authorized to investigate any of—"

"I'm going to beat you to him."

"I would advise you to consider—"

"Now the meeting is done. Now. Because I say it is." As I gather myself, I know I have to help Paula out before I exit. "Just FYI Assistant Director Asshole. Paula had nothing to do with my investigation at all. I called her because I knew her. That's how it started. That's all there was to it. She told me almost nothing. I don't even like her," I lie. "She's a fucking cunt."

I'm escorted out of the building. I call a cab for the ride home.

I want to drink but I don't. It would be dangerous. I let the adrenaline surf through me.

I watch one of the best Laker's buzzer beaters ever in the 2004 semifinals as Fisher puts it up in the last half second and the backboard goes red. *Slaughterhouse Five* is rolling on the book screen relaying Billy Pilgrim's abstract time travel through his own life. The classic movie playing silently is *Some Like it Hot*: Billy Wilder's funny attempt to not draw attention to the craft of directing in such a funny, perfect, director's movie.

Billy Pilgrim knew his entire life.

Most people wouldn't want to know how they will die. There are only two ways for me: a bullet in the dark or a swallow of the last sleeping pill and a final wait alone. That's it, that's all. And the which will be answered by the when.

I take my meds and wait for sleep.

I almost forgot. How could I forget? I see my son tomorrow.

Good I didn't drink.

Because I will tomorrow.

CHAPTER TWENTY-EIGHT

SON

My supervised visits happen at a Family Services Agency. It looks like a daycare from the outside but it's not. They do counseling, parent child interactive therapy, foster mentoring, the whole sad opera. There's parking outside. I don't mean to come early but I do, I always do, and I'm sitting in the stupid Diesel Cayenne watching, waiting, like every other day of my life except that this time it is my life.

I parked away from the front door but at such an angle that I can observe. I didn't think about the positioning, I just did it on auto-pilot—like noticing where the exterior video cameras are and how quickly they pivot.

My ex-wife's silver Honda CR-V pulls in. She's driving. Her guy, my replacement, is sitting in the passenger seat. She parks right in front. I see my son get out of the back seat. He's happy. His mother comes around and takes his hand. The three of them go into the building, a family.

I'm wearing an Iron Maiden Trooper shirt.

Still twenty minutes to go before my scheduled appearance. I feel sick.

A few months back I read an investment prospective for a pharmaceutical company that is designing a drug to erase painful memories. The sales pitch referenced the billions of dollars spent every year on therapy that never ends and anti-depressants that just mask the problem. The company claims that traumatic memories can be erased by isolating the right neurotransmitters and addressing the specific processes by which individuals remember the same bad events over and over. Analysts were quoted as saying the company is three to five years away from reaching the market.

But how could the drug be exact enough to erase memories of my ex-wife and keep the memories of my infant son? He is her mother. And as much as I hate her, he loves her, and she is a bigger part of his life than I am.

My ex-wife comes out again with the boyfriend. I know they've both seen me. Regular citizens would have and they're both FBI agents. They don't acknowledge my presence. The CR-V pulls away.

Today's assigned social worker is Tammy. She will sit in the corner and watch all of my interaction with him. When I've left, she will write up a report and file it with the court. This is because I am mentally ill and violently dangerous.

I have of course learned Tammy's entire life story. I know that she failed at pre-med, failed at psychology and eventually convinced herself and everyone else that she'd always wanted to be a social worker. It's been three years since her long term boyfriend left her and I suspect she hasn't had a single date since. I hate her because she holds my fate in her hands. She gets to decide whether I see my son more or less—this childless failure of a bitter hag. Too harsh? Fuck her. I doubt she even knows the lies that were told in court, just that a judge has decided I'm not fit to spend alone time with my son.

With five minutes to go before my access starts, I get out of the Cayenne and start walking toward the building. I'm jittery. I show my ID at the desk and am walked down a hall to the room. Tammy is there at the door and she tells me all the rules that I already know. I smile and nod and hate her. My son is behind the next door. He is waiting for me.

The last door opens and there he is, playing with some Lego on the floor. I stop.

I hear Tammy shut the door behind us.

"Hey son."

"Dad!" He jumps up and comes to me with a big warm hug.

I sit down on the floor with him. We play with the Lego as we talk.

Every moment is bliss and heartbreak and the seconds slip away in my head.

I feel so sad when I leave. I don't watch him get back in her CR-V. I just start driving home, absently, slow, so slow. My gentle weeping doesn't become sobbing but it also doesn't cease.

I stop at a liquor store. I wipe my eyes and hold myself together long enough to come out again with beer and whiskey. I'm thinking: this was inevitable, it happens every time, he doesn't know you, he never will.

When I get home I go into his room and sit on his made bed.

I start drinking Jamesons from the bottle and chasing the inexact shots with cold beer.

I drink until I'm on the edge of blackness and it is there that I think about the Bacchus killer. Like the drinking this is a ritual after a supervised visit with my son. I remember the two times I saw the monster, when I began to realize what he was. And I think when, how, if, I will ever be able to hunt him down.

In the first encounter he was just a weird slightly older guy lost with the crowd in the music. I hadn't studied Greek mythology. I hadn't read about cults or cannibalism. I hadn't learned about deviant psychology. I hadn't practiced the black art of serial killer profiling.

I was a kid at a rock concert. I was years away from being diagnosed as bipolar but I understand now what my emotional state was then. I'd had my heart broken the week before and was bouncing back manic. I was drunk and high on sweet west coast pot.

It was 1987.

The band was Guns n Roses. The venue was close and hot and dangerous. There was the hypnotic drums, the terrified heartbeat of the bass, the wailing paranoia of the guitars, and the urgent voice of the god Axl bringing breath to ecstasy. The band achieved a mystical state, the kind only a few acts are ever able to accomplish. We the concert goers were outside of ourselves and floating in a trance of mayhem. Within the drowning waves of moving arms and frenzied visages, he was there: a still and predatory presence. His dark burnt eyes fixed on me and I felt him make the decision that I would live. Those evil eyes judged me as a sacrifice and found me not worthy of the rite to be enacted.

I remembered the man in passing from before the band hit the stage. He'd been giving out brownies. The drunk and debauched assumed the treats were baked with drugs and they probably had been laced with some illegal substance as well. But the real secret ingredient, I believe, was the human flesh of his last victim from another concert—a ritual chain of rock n roll cannibalism.

There were no facts to connect, no evidence to work with after the concert but my diseased brain put different details together and I read and read. I remember the moment I understood it, the very second I grasped it, and in the same instance knew that no one would believe me. I had been in the presence of a serial killer who frequents rock concerts searching for transcendent performances of ecstasy necessary for his murderous ritual. I had seen the modern incarnation of the god Bacchus.

How long has he been operating? Decades.

Why has no one else discovered this pattern? I have guesses but they are no more.

How does the ritual work? I've made assumptions, leaps of imagination. But just that.

It was the work of years to figure out who the victim was at that Guns concert. I engaged with the bootleg community. I sent emails, letters, and exchanged tapes and CDs. I communicated with fans who had been there. Many remembered the weird guy handing out strange tasting psychedelic brownies. Two knew of a girl that had been seen with him near the end. She was not from LA. She was a UCLA student who had dropped out and thought she was a singer. She wasn't listed as missing at the time of the concert but she was two weeks later. Her body was never found. He would have killed her during the performance but I don't know the method and I have never figured out how he gets the bodies out of the venues.

My second encounter with the Bacchus killer was at an Alice in Chains concert. The same intuition that had led me to presume his godhead had got me thinking that the psychedelic baking might be a cannibalistic element of his ritual. So when I heard a rumor at the event about an older man handing out brownies, I tried to find him. It was insane except that I felt it, felt the change he was waiting to feel too: that moment in which the band reached the right level of ecstatic trance for the ritual.

I saw him in the crowd and remembered those eyes. And I swear he recognized me. One face out of a heaving mass remembered as the same face from another heaving mass years before. Impossible. Improbable. And yet he knew me and he knew that I was looking for him, that I was the first person who understood who he was and what he was doing at these concerts. He raised a single eyebrow. And then he disappeared. I jostled my way forward trying to reach him, desperate to get out and free and find him.

But he was gone.

I may have saved the selected sacrificial victim. I can't know.

I had doubted myself. But that second sighting took away all question. There was still nothing that I could share with anyone else then. Yet when I joined the FBI, when I became a hunter, I came to understand that we almost never catch even a glimpse of the most heinous killers. The amateurs get caught because for them it's just about sex and twisted gratification. For the mighty and malevolent, the truly evil, it is about myths and sacred rituals. There is a Dark Pantheon of evil figures in this country. The Bacchus killer is in that Dark Pantheon. I believe General Ripper is in the Dark Pantheon also. And as I always observe: these demons know each other, they find each other, they communicate with each other.

Barrett was the first and only person I told about the Bacchus killer. That didn't go well.

I haven't given up the hunt. But I also haven't made any real progress.

My two long term goals: to have my son, to find the Bacchus killer.

General Ripper is a short term goal.

And I when I sober up tomorrow I'm coming for him.

Chapter Twenty-Nine

SERVER

IT for The Department of Veterans Affairs is managed by The Office of Information and Technology. They have several data centers. The big one is in Austin. The smaller ones are in Boston, Seattle and LA.

OI&T has an exclusive hardware contract with Dell. They've purchased millions of dollars of desktops and servers from the hardware provider. Because these procurements are funded with tax dollars the details are a matter of public record. The government views these PDFs as mere fiscal disclosure. But with careful consideration the information can be extended and made more.

I mentally map recent hardware purchases for the LA Data Centre against the network architecture that was presented twice at staff conferences with almost unchanged presentation slides. This allows me to make educated guesses without scanning or probing. I don't know anything. But I'm reasonably certain about a lot.

Medical files for hundreds of thousands of veterans that include x-rays and scanned reports, imaged documents for treatment, insurance statements—this all requires huge amounts of storage. I can logically identify the servers purchased to do this work by their arrays of huge drives. Inversely it follows that the machines handling the gatekeeping and security have conspicuously smaller amounts of storage and lighter price tags.

Knowing the possible Dell models I'm looking for in the LA Data Centre, I come in from a proxied connection off the East

Coast. I patiently craft nmap scans over and over. After three hours I've fingered the specific machine I want.

I back out and cut off. It is the model I'd guessed but with slightly different specs. They must have had a failure and turned a replacement into an upgrade. I find the right Dell manuals online and read through them. They're boringly byzantine but it's necessary work.

Dell has to send out firmware updates for their servers occasionally. The model I'm going after was patched within the last month. I want to create a new fake patch that shuts down the server's fan.

This is far beyond my programming ability.

Known to few, and constantly disappearing, there is a hacker's bounty board called Bobba's Wake. It works like this. A trusted member or vouched for noob authenticates into the board and posts a job title. Regular titles request help in finding credit card numbers, network maps, circuit diagrams, hardware manuals for switches, source code, advanced kernel information, specialized Trojans, worms, viruses. The job title is accompanied by a price. To look at the job's details an interested hacker makes a commitment to the price. If he reads the details and chooses to decline the opportunity then five percent of that job's posted price is taken from his credit account and added to the advertised bounty. This smart system accomplishes two related goals. Low level hackers are scared off from jobs they're not ready for without learning anything they can blab about. Difficult jobs start at a premium price and as that price increases they draw the attention of the elite. The bounty hunter hacker who elects to take a job gets half the money up front and the rest when the satisfied job poster says the job is done. Hackers understand e-commerce better than anyone and all of this is done through honest PayPal transactions and not bitcoin. A user found to be using a stolen account or credit card is forever banished from the group.

The job title I post is: "Dell Server Firmware Fan Fuck Needed." I set the price at seventy five percent of the top job on the board which is a request for internal Oracle security documents. My job should be a welcome payday for a hacker with the right connections and skills.

It turns out this fan trick is not an original idea. Other hackers have used the gambit. And someone called JumpMan64 has made it his programming specialty. It doesn't take him long to deliver after he commits to the job.

He emails me the patch. I pay him his money.

I try to find a Dell Technician uniform of some kind on eBay. There isn't one. So I go online and create a corporate branded golf shirt, a nametag and a security lanyard. I also buy the exact model of drive that is in that server. It takes a day for these purchases to come to me.

In that time I spear-phish a low level clerical employee at the LA Data Centre. She clicks on a link embedded in an email that looks like it's from her bank. This gives me control of her desktop. Her computer is weak and restricted. But it's on the network and with the created tunnel I am able to work at convincing the ARP tables on their network that my computer proxied in from the East Coast is actually the Dell update server.

And then I upload the trap patch and announce it.

The server I want and two other identical models pull down the patch right away. They won't update automatically though. I know that before it doesn't happen. An administrator will have to make the decision.

If he or she checks Dell's site they will be able to determine all is not right.

If he or she inspects the patch they'll see that all is not right.

But whoever it is does not. They just apply the patch. Because that's what admins do.

I get dressed and grab some tools.

With the fan turned off the server I am going after and the two that are collateral damage will start to heat up. When their internal temperature reaches the cutoff point the servers will shut down. Lights on monitoring software, panels within the server room and on the exterior of the blade servers themselves will flash red.

I suffer through LA afternoon traffic to get to the Data Centre. I park, check my disguise and walk in through the front doors to cheerfully rob them. I present myself at the desk. "Hi, I'm from Dell. I'm here to look at some of your servers that are having problems."

The security guard calls to the server room. All this technical sorcery and it's still a fifty fifty proposition. There's back and forth confusion about my presence. The security guy gets tired of being middle man and he hands me the phone. I talk to the NOC Admin who reluctantly answered the phone and tell him I'm here to do a spot check on server models that have been failing. I tell him the model number.

He says they have three of them and they all just went down.

I am escorted to the server room where I pull the blade server I'm after. The NOC Admin stays to watch me but he misses the trick. I switch out the hot drive loaded with the data I've come for and replace it with the new empty drive I brought with me.

I then just unscrew and rescrew parts until the guy starts to get impatient.

"You almost done?"

"Yeah but there's nothing I can do. These models are just going to be down."

"What's the problem?"

"Fans."

"You guys suck," he tells me.

"We'll ship you three new servers."

"Which I will have to rebuild."

"You've got RAIDs."

"Thanks for telling me what I already know."

I stand up. "Listen dude. We're sending you three new servers. Identical except that the fans aren't fucked."

"You said that. Can we go?"

"When the new ones arrive you ship the duds back."

"Uh-huh and what? Throw me a bone here."

"And because the drives have had sensitive corporate slash government data on them, Dell doesn't expect them to be in the blades. So you can take the drives out, wipe them to your satisfaction and use them for whatever. These are fast pricey drives dude. Put them in your gaming rig at home. Torrent every movie and TV show ever made."

This has stripped his surliness away. "Thanks for the tip."

This last deception doesn't have to work. If he notices the blank drive then he'll know he fucked up and maybe want to hide it. If he cleans the drives on auto-pilot with no thought that he's been tricked then he has his own reasons to explain away what just happened. Either way I'm driving home with the drive in this bloated Cayenne that I hate.

And when I return to my lair I plug it in and bring the data up.

Chapter Thirty

PATRIOTS

The server this drive came from runs the access control gateway for the VA records system. The drive contains account profiles and password hashes used for authentication. Time for more encryption silly math. I set my crack program to attack the hashes. The weakest passwords are defeated in minutes. All of them will be known in time.

I reset my proxy and come in from Arizona.

Entering the VA records system again and again as different staff members, I start to become familiar with the software: what it knows, what it can do. There is facial recognition search functionality.

I use Photoshop to clean up first the picture of the recruiting sergeant that was hidden inside the video game cover and secondly the best photographic still I can lift from the variety store security video. Together these two images will obtain the optimal results from the facial recognition algorithm.

I set the scan running, change out of my disguise and into a shirt with The Who's minimalist name in mod font. I drive to the Porsche dealership and return the deeply offensive Cayenne for my restored 911. They fiscally rape me because that's what these German motherfuckers do. But it's worth it.

The 911 feels amazing and alive. My feet are connected directly to the drivetrain through the pedals. My hands feel the road through the roll of the wheels and the twitches that come back through the steering.

I return home happy to find Evan Cave staring at me from a monitor. Evan Cave: General Ripper's recruiting sergeant. He fought with the Rangers. His injuries are documented. His scar is explained.

He's listed as dead. But there's no question it's him that I saw.

I click and type. Evan supposedly died five years ago. He had a wife. He had a son. I run their names through the big public databases. His wife has not remarried. She still lives in the LA area. His son is in Michigan.

I drive out to Westmont and park in front of a single family home with bars on the windows. The widow who isn't a widow is named Maribel. She answers the door after my knock but keeps the latch on. She has large glasses and a pronounced stoop. I tell her I want to talk to her about her late husband Evan.

She lets me in.

The house feels like a cave, like the living space was carved out of clutter and weakening wood. She smokes in here. She drinks in here. And she works in here. The furniture and surfaces are covered in colored cotton and silk and cones of thread. A metal chair with a cracked brown leather blister of a seat is close to a table with an industrial sewing machine atop it.

I interrupted her sewing an American flag with a coiled snake rampant.

"My husband died in a fire."

"That's what the world believes. But you don't."

"Shouldn't you show me a badge or something?" she asks.

"Do you have any of Evan's stuff?"

"No."

"You kept nothing?"

"He had so little. The military life," she explains. "I gave what there was to charity."

"I saw him recently," I tell her. "He's in LA."

"His death was our divorce. Is that a better answer? I don't know anything about what he's doing now."

I push again. "But you knew he'd faked his death."

She sits like a bag of bones on her couch. "They'd talked about it before. Some of the men and women in our militia. How it could be done with the right corpses and a little luck. It was just campfire talk when I heard it."

The seeds of hate—unemployment, ethnic ignorance, poverty—are abundant everywhere in this fecund nation. But California just seems to have the best combination of soil, sun and smog to grow these seeds.

I put my hands in my pockets. "This militia?"

"Patriots in Christ and the Constitution. Evan and Floyd founded it. They had been in the Rangers together. They convinced others to come out into the woods with us. It was like most other militias I guess."

"I've never been in one. Angry camping?"

"That's a good enough description. Evan ranted about globalization, unjust wars, the poor treatment of veterans. . . . I made flags for us. I made badges. I made uniforms right before the end. . . . Now I sew for other groups. They change all the time. One militia joins up with another. Or a new leader comes in and wants to change the symbols. It pays my bills. I don't belong to any of them."

"Does PCC still exist?"

"It still exists in name. It's all new people now though. They believe in different things. Or they believe in the same things in different ways. I've done lots of sewing for them. They seem nice."

"Evan left the militia he helped found. And you. In that fire."

"Evan and Floyd left together," she answers. "They did it to join up with . . . " She holds me with her eyes. "General Ripper."

I give her a cool nod. "Who do you think General Ripper is?"

"He's the one behind everything that's happening now." She lights a cigarette.

"General Ripper had another militia?"

She shakes her head. "Not a militia."

"What then?"

"I think we're all finding out."

"Do people in the other militias know about General Ripper?"

"Just his reputation. They don't know anything that would help the FBI find him. And that's God's honest truth. The FBI has interviewed everyone affiliated with a California militia five and six times in the last weeks."

"How did Evan and Floyd get in contact with General Ripper?"

"I was just his wife. He didn't tell me anything." She coughs. "But I noticed when his thinking started to change. I heard him working out stuff in his head. He stopped blaming the government for everything that was wrong. He talked more about the warrior's way and authentic violence."

"Authentic violence?"

"There were other phrases like that. That's one I remembered."

"Was there a text? Like a manifesto?" I ask.

"No."

I stop and breathe. "Why are you talking to me, Maribel?"

"You found me."

"The FBI came and talked to you as well."

"They came and asked questions just because I know people in the militias. They didn't ask anything about my husband or Floyd or the fire."

"Would you have told them if they did?"

"I likely would have," she admits. "But I ain't going to make it easy for them now am I?"

"No," I say.

It seems like she's making it easy for me. But I think that's deceiving. She knows more. I move her work chair and sit on it. "Tell me about the people who were in PCC when you and Evan and Floyd founded it."

She appreciates that I've included her.

No one has listened to Maribel for a long time. I listen to her now—patiently and with interest. She tells me how Evan returned from active duty, their failures to get pregnant again, the problems with their distant son, the violence within the home that damaged the dishes and the walls and the furniture. Remembering it all makes her a little sad. But then she smiles as she remembers the start of the PCC—how amazing it felt to be at the beginning of something important and vital.

I order Chinese food. Maribel gets beer from the fridge. As we eat and drink she reveals how just this one time in human history noble ideals were undone by petty disagreements and jealousy. They'd almost all left PCC's Eden of green tents and hushed talk of insurrection when Floyd introduced a woman to the group called Angie Navarro.

Angie was beautiful and smart. Angie worked at the LAPD morgue.

This is the lead she didn't make easy. This is my reward for spending time with her.

That seems to be how Maribel is.

"Angie helped Evan and Floyd out with the dead bodies for the fire?" I ask.

"I don't have any proof of that."

"But she must have."

"She left after. I haven't seen her since."

"Have you ever told anyone else this?"

Maribel says no. And I believe her.

We finish eating and clean up together. I tell her a little about me.

Then we're sitting close and talking slow. And I know I have to go.

I thank her. She's a little embarrassed at what we've shared. Tenderness from me now would only make it harder. I remain gentle but distant. I thank her for her time and the information she's given me. I go to the 911 without checking to see if she's watching me from the window because I know that she is.

I drive away thinking.

The LAPD Morgue lists unclaimed bodies on their website. Sad economics are what prevent most of these bodies from being claimed. If they are left long enough they will be cremated. It costs a few hundred dollars for a family to pick up the ashes—much, much less than to claim a preserved body and pay for transportation and a funeral and burial.

Angie Navarro could have watched the roster of dead bodies not being claimed. She could have listed two bodies suitable for Evan and Floyd's needs as cremated and then given the poor family someone else's ashes.

I park in an open lot and pull my MacBook toward me. I search LA news sites until I find the fire from five years ago. Evan and Floyd are described as veteran Rangers. There was an arson investigation. The suspicion was limited and extinguished right away.

It's been a long damn day. But I want to try and talk to Angie Navarro before I rest.

I call Rose. It's the LAPD's morgue—Angie will be in the LAPD's HR system.

Rose calls me back. She's still employed there. He has a phone number and an address.

I call Angie. I haven't thought of a great lie before she answers. I tell her I'm an old friend of Floyd's and I just heard he died. The FBI told me. They asked me questions about his time in PCC and how he died. That works. She tells me to meet her at the Outpost Hollywood Bar on Cahuenga Ave.

I describe the Who shirt I'm wearing.

Chapter Thirty-One

CARTRIDGES

The place is styled as a western themed sports bar, a saloon with big TVs. A waitress shows me to a table. I order a basket of fries, corn fritters, sweet whiskey wings and a cowboy boot of beer. I accomplish this transaction with the minimal amount of western roleplaying. The boot is 45 ounces of cold goodness.

Angie Navarro arrives, looks around, sees me.

She walks up to my table and says: "You don't look army."

I swallow the last of a wing. I take a drink of beer.

She's still standing. Each silent second is making her feel dumber.

"You provided Evan and Floyd with corpses that made it possible for them to stage their own deaths."

"You can't prove that."

"I can't. But I could. If I wanted to. The good news for you is that I don't want to. Sit."

She sits. She closes her eyes. She fights tears. She knows she's in trouble.

"Help yourself."

"They just told me they wanted to start again."

"Why did they want to do that?"

"I don't know."

"I've done my gentle interview for the day Angie," I warn. "They were enlisting again. But not with Uncle Sam." I sit back and look at her.

"They didn't tell me anything," she pleads.

"So they paid you then."

"Yes," she grabs at the motivation. "I needed money."

"How much did they pay you?"

"Ten thousand," she lies.

"Ten thousand. For such a risk. Wow. Well. Everyone's price is different. What did you do with this ten thousand dollars?"

"I spent some. And put the rest away."

"In the bank."

"Yeah."

"How was the cash constituted? All twenties? Hundreds?"

"Twenties."

"You're lying. You didn't do it for money."

"I—"

"You work at the morgue Angie," I cut her off. "This is my job. This is what I do. I interrogate. Computers and people. I will figure out that you're lying to me every time that you lie to me. So. All that lying does is make this take longer. And piss me off more. I have no interest in shopping you to the LAPD or the FBI. I can come up with more inventive threats if it comes to that. But we don't have to go there if you tell me the truth."

I push the fries toward her. "Just tell me what happened."

She grabs my beer boot and takes a swig. "I was Floyd's girl. He brought me into the Patriots. The militia. I'd never been a part of anything like that before."

"Floyd knew you worked at the morgue right from the beginning?"

"Well sure. You know someone's job when you start dating them. Why? What. You think he was just interested in me to . . . No."

"He needs two bodies. He starts dating a woman who works at the morgue. Lucky coincidence?"

"No. That's not why."

"Come on Angie. This isn't the first time the thought has occurred to you."

But it still embarrasses her.

"He didn't just ask you, did he? He introduced the idea."

"He talked about the bodies that come back from Iraq and Afghanistan. He told me the army makes mistakes all the time. Family and friends don't know they are burying the wrong jumbled pieces. He said that's how it's always been for soldiers. They die in the mud. They're blown apart. They're scattered over the desert. Soldiers are anonymous in death. All they are is what they fight for. . . . When I believed that he talked about how the right to bear arms is a distraction. Because the contemporary construct of identity shackles individuals from any real rebellion."

"Did these sound like his words? Or did it sound like this was rhetoric he'd heard and was repeating?"

"They didn't sound like his words," she admits. "Then at last he asked me straight. He told me he and Evan needed to die to prove themselves and . . . "

"Yes?"

"Join the first army."

If she knew about General Ripper she would tell me now. She doesn't.

"Authentic violence," I say. "Did Floyd talk about that?"

"All the time."

"What is it?"

"War is becoming a video game. Our young men are becoming soldiers who will see their enemy only through screens and kill them only with buttons. There was more but."

"Has the FBI contacted you Angie?"

"No. Will they?"

"Eventually yes."

She starts to cry. "Then I'm fucked. I am fucked."

"Stop blubbering and listen. When they find you and start asking questions . . . You tell them Floyd threatened your life. He put a gun to your head. He swore he would kill everyone in your family."

"That will save me?"

"It's your best shot," I say.

She eats a little now. I finish my beer.

"I have a key. For a storage place in Laurel Canyon. It was Floyd's."

"What's in there?"

"I haven't opened it."

"You've been there?"

"But I haven't gone in. I brought it. Because I thought you were an army buddy."

She produces the key. I take it. She eats more and then she goes.

One last stop.

Laurel Canyon is famous for the musicians who lived, partied and died here—each of these three acts requiring different drugs and different chords. Vito from Vito and the Freakers was the prophet of the Hippies here. He loved sex and convinced women to join his family and love sex with him. It was a promising cult. But instead of building a compound and stockpiling weapons, Vito shared his orgies with the musicians and artists in LA. And he started an accidental revolution called "Free Love"—the greatest oxymoron in any language ever.

The Storage Company has 24 hour controlled access that allows customers to come and go without going to the office. Every door is alarmed with a separate system and there is centrally monitored closed circuit video.

The key is for one of the smallest storage units.

Inside it are boxes of video games: cartridges, floppy discs, CDs, DVDs.

The titles I recognize are: *Call of Duty 4: Modern Warfare, Splinter Cell: Chaos Theory, Red Faction: Guerrilla, Metal Gear Solid, Silent Hunter 3, Tom Clancy's Ghost Recon Advanced Warfighter 2, Enemy Front, Commando, Counter-Strike: Source, Battlefield, Medal of Honor: Allied Assault, Company of Heroes Online, America's Army.*

America's Army was the game developed by the U.S. Army. The avowed intention of this initiative was to provide better information to prospective soldiers. It was supposed to usher in a new era of propaganda. But it ended up just being another first person shooter—no more or less authentic than the others to be found in this strange museum.

Angie said that Evan and Floyd had to prove themselves to join the first army. That makes sense from what I know. But could the faked deaths really have been the challenge General Ripper gave the two Rangers? Floyd lied to a woman and they staged a fire. That doesn't seem like much. Especially when I consider the three brothers were charged with stealing a mythical sword from a paranoid underworld leader.

I continue looking through the collection but I don't find much more. There is a box stuffed with game manuals. There is a box full of old controllers and joysticks. There is a box with shirts and posters.

I'm not making any connections here.

I drive home and hit the couch, too tired to sleep right away.

Tomorrow I will create a list of Rangers who served with Evan and Floyd and are living in the LA area. I wonder how many of them will be involved in militias? How many of them will have communicated with General Ripper? Will any of them know why that collection of video games exists?

I pour myself a shot of Jamesons and chase it with a beer.

I set Faulkner's *Sound and the Fury* scrolling from the start of the second part, Q's consciousness at once considering death and his sister's purity. This is the voice of depression breaking free of grammar and punctuation and into a desperate song of the mind. To accompany this I start a Pedro Almodovar film in which a rape occurs in a dim garden where couples have slipped away from a party to find quick pleasure. And a bittersweet Laker's loss: Wilt plays a sublime game in the 65 division finals but Russell and the Celtics win.

I do another shot and another beer. See I can drink without getting drunk. See.

Chapter Thirty-Two

RANGERS

When I'm not driving to a destination, feet working the pedals, eyes watching the navigation screen, then I'm parked and turned toward my MacBook. The VA database gave me the names and LA addresses of Rangers Evan and Floyd served with. To learn about these men I query the big public databases for bankruptcies, civil judgments, criminal records, liens. I'm wearing the classic *Appetite for Destruction* cross: the skulls of the original GNR lineup framed by hair and headwear.

Josh Pulley is a prescription junkie. In a city like LA there are hundreds of open houses in the papers, all of them easily accessed with transit. Josh dresses up a little, walks in the door, nods to the real estate agent, then asks where the bathroom is? He closes the door, turns the water on, opens the medicine cabinet. OxyContin or Opana are the big scores for personal highs. Adderall, Xanax, and Seroquel can be sold for reliable prices to buy personal highs.

Josh has been pinched twice for this activity. This was before General Ripper started shipping packages to veterans. Maybe the combination of drugs and cash has been enough to stop his interest in LA real estate.

I find the Ranger living in his mother's house. He says his mother is sleeping. He offers to walk with me. Before we leave I see him pop a pill, dry swallow it, and then stuff a handgun into his waistband. We walk along the sidewalk.

"Evan and Floyd never tried to contact me. I didn't go to their funerals."

"You ever been tempted to join a militia?"

"I'm done with uniforms thanks."

"What are you going to do when you run out of pills Josh?"

"Buy more. I got cash too."

"Any trouble with people accepting that cash?"

"No. And I better not. For their sake."

"That's what the gun is for?" I ask.

"I'm a veteran. I fought for this country."

"The man who masterminded sending the drugs and cash to veterans—you think he's a patriot or a terrorist?"

"Patriot. He's done more for me than the government ever did."

"But don't you see what it is doing to the country?"

"This fucking country needs a wake-up call. The way veterans are treated." He spits.

"How do you feel about military video games?" I ask.

"Like you mean *Black Ops* and *Call of Duty*?"

"Yes."

"I play them sometimes."

"You think war is becoming a video game?"

"Never for the Rangers."

"Do you think modern weapons technology distances warriors from war?"

"No. A kill is a kill. You feel every one. What are you trying to convince me of?"

"Nothing. I just wanted to hear your thoughts."

Eddy came home from the war with head injuries. A month into his transition he started suspecting that his wife was an imposter and that his teenage son was a robot. When he fired through a barricaded basement door his wife called the police.

After observation at the mental unit he was judged to be suffering from Atypical Psychosis. Six months after that he was diagnosed with the exceedingly rare Capgras syndrome.

Eddy's wife tells me that they turned over all the drugs and cash that came in the mail to the FBI. I inform her that I'm a private investigator trying to find a son's father who was a Ranger. She grants me an audience in the back yard. I find Eddy in a lawn chair, fat and stoned.

"Sure. Evan wanted me to join Patriots in the Christ. Patriots in the Constitution with Christ. I forget what it was called. Just old warriors coming together. They weren't planning to over-throw the government or anything."

"Who said they were?"

"People get scared when veterans get together."

"Do they?"

"They like us to get dressed up for parades. But that's it."

"Authentic violence. Does that mean anything to you?"

"No."

"Have you seen Evan or Floyd recently?"

"They died in a fire," he tells me. "Long time ago now." He squints at me. "You think they're involved in the robberies and the packages being sent out?"

"I think they knew people who are," I say.

"I gave everything that came for me to the FBI." His wife has clearly coached him on this talking point. "I have legal prescriptions. I have an honest pension."

"How do you feel about military video games?"

"I don't feel nothing. Should I?"

"There are kids playing games where they play as you Eddy. In the same conflict you fought in. They kill and are killed thousands of times a day. They feel nothing. They know nothing. They play until mom and dad yell at them to get off."

"I don't care. They're just games."

"The graphics are so good you can't tell the difference between actors and animated digital puppets. The Army itself made a first person shooter."

"You think they're going to use video games to recruit? Like that Disney movie . . . what was it? . . . You remember it. . . . *The Last Starfighter*."

That makes us both laugh. I thank him.

Timothy Oliver is a corporate lobbyist working within the Military Industrial Complex. He's playing golf today. I turn off Sunset and onto Capri which curves into the Riveria Country Club. I negotiate parking and wait in the lobby. High ceilings, finished wooden beams, lots of light.

I watch the golfers come and go, so very pleased with themselves. I get the appeal of golf: a sport you can play as you get older and an excuse to build rich-guy only clubs that include dress-up games. Sounds fun. But what I hate is how it's become a required skill for executives in business and the public sector. Right before I was turfed out of the FBI a colleague I trusted advised me to buy some clubs if I wanted to be considered for promotion. Catching serial killers was helpful and everything but really my superiors wanted to see how well I hit a white ball while sharing clichéd jokes about wives.

When I see him I cut Timothy away from his foursome.

"Damn right I remember Evan and Floyd. Two of the bravest."

"Did you know anything about their militia?"

"I heard when they died."

I go right for the sale. "You know they are part of this ongoing terrorist action."

He tries a blank look. "I don't know that. Why would I know that?"

"Have either of them tried to contact you from beyond the grave?"

"Look. I spoke to them about . . . " he looks over to his colleagues and pulls me into a corner. "They took me for drinks a long time ago. Years."

"Before they died?" I cut in.

"Yes before . . . They asked me questions about how software companies get military contracts."

"How do they Tim?"

"Jets, tanks, drones, guns themselves require firmware and software. It's code. Just like code for smartphones."

"Or video games."

"Yes."

"Did they ask about video games?" I push.

"I don't remember. Honestly. It was a long time ago."

"But. You talked about code. About video games."

"I don't remember. We probably would have talked about video games . . . Because. I mean there's overlap between code for games and code for firmware that controls weapons. Increasingly it's the same companies generating the code."

"I'm going to ask you this straight a second time. I will know if you're lying. Have either Evan or Floyd contacted you since they died?"

"No." And I do know: he's not lying.

"Remember Kony?" The big man smacks the lectern with both hands. "The Ugandan-born warlord? Yes? Uh-huh. He led the Lord's Resistance Army across Central Africa. His soldiers were kidnapped children trained to kill. The army was fifty thousand strong when a viral video introduced him to the World."

The fourth Ranger on my list is standing at the public microphone for a Los Angeles Department of City Planning hearing. His clothes are pasty with sweat. Some have stopped listening to him. Some are frightened of him.

"Tens of millions viewers watched that video in a manner of weeks. Young people forwarded it to their friends. Legislators in the US and other countries responded with immediate sound bites for the news and a few paper resolutions. A year later the video had been watched almost a hundred million times and nothing had happened." The veteran shakes his head in operatic disbelief. "Nobody had been able to even muss the hair of this fucker who has been convicted in International Court."

The chair tries to speak. "While we value what you have to say sir—"

The Ranger just rants louder. "If that propaganda group had taken the ad revenue from the hundred million hits they could have hired an assassin who would have had no trouble ending Kony. Practicality is what's needed when facing evil. . . . And that is why I oppose this zoning change."

When the public hearing takes a break, I come up to Cameron. He smells. He smiles. I don't think he's a crazy like me. He just wants to warn everyone about the end of the world. And he's having fun doing it.

He doesn't need much prompting to start talking about Evan and Floyd.

"I knew they weren't dead at their funeral. And then all this time later the man himself came to see me. Floyd the Flood. Except Floyd was dead so he said he was John Harrod. He had new ID and everything. He showed me. He wasn't supposed to contact me but he needed a drink and so we went and fucking drank." He laughs. "Now who the fuck are you?"

"Chalk."

"Why should I help you find my comrade-in-arms?"

"Because you know they are involved in something big and bad."

"Yeah I do. Come on."

We find the nearest beer around the corner.

"Floyd told me they had to do some final recruiting work for the second army. And then he and Evan were switching to clean-up until the end."

"When was this conversation?"

"A few months ago."

"Who did Floyd say they are working for?"

"They call him General Ripper. Floyd said he's met him. But the General communicates with his forces remotely. Floyd told me he fought in the first Gulf War."

"Floyd wasn't trying to get you to join up?"

"If he was he never asked. Too late I think. We were just drinking and talking. He needed to do that. That's how he got his nickname. Floyd the Flood. Get him started and he'll drown you with a rush of confessions and jokes and stories. Not all the time. But when the weather is right." He chuckles.

"What did Evan and Floyd have to do to prove themselves and enlist in the first army?"

"Floyd said they had to work through a list of people."

"A kill list?"

"That's what I assumed. But he didn't say that specifically."

"Well you win. This has been the best interview of the day. Of the case."

"Floyd is a good guy. He's got himself involved in something big and bad. Just like you said."

"I'm trying to stop him Cameron. Not rescue him."

"I know. He's too far gone to be saved. I was talking to a dead man then and he's a dead man now. I get that."

"He talk to you about video games?"

"It came up here and there in the flood."

"You remember where in the conversation? Like after or before what?"

"He bitched about video games after he talked about the list of names that he and Evan had to work through. I remember that. Just about how . . . "

"Graphics have made warriors terrorists."

"Yes. I knew that was them when it was in the news."

I drop two bills to pay for the beers we've had and the next ten this guy is going to drink by himself. "And Floyd's resurrected name is John Harrod?" I ask.

"John Harrod," Cameron confirms.

I pat him on the back and am about to leave when the bartender stops me. "Is this veteran funny money?" He holds up the two hundreds that I dropped.

"That's real money," I answer.

"What the fuck is that supposed to mean asshole?" Cameron stands. "Veteran funny money?"

"They are old bills," the bartender comes back.

"Use your UV counterfeit detector," I say.

"It doesn't work on the veteran funny money."

Cameron reaches into his pocket. I didn't see the outline or weight of a gun while we were talking. But Cameron is a big man and he knows how to conceal a weapon. He draws it now, a snub-nosed revolver.

"Stop!" I command. "I've got newer bills."

I take out my roll and find two fresh hundreds. I take my old bills and replace them with the new ones. The bartender takes the money. He and I are both now still, waiting for the nickel plated revolver to go away.

Cameron speaks to me. "Give me them two old bills Chalk."

I hold them out. The Ranger takes them.

"You: asshole bartender. You're going to give me that almost full bottle of Cutty there behind you. I'm going to pay you with this veteran funny money. And then I'm going to go. Got it?"

The two fresh hundreds cover what we drank and easily extend to that bottle of Cutty as well. Two hundred more on top of that is a hell of a tip. So it's not a robbery. And yet Cameron is aiming a gun at the man.

The bartender moves slowly. He takes the old bills he refused before.

He gets the bottle and puts it on the bar. Cameron takes the bottle and returns his revolver to its concealed location. He walks out into the street. I watch him throw the top of the bottle away and move on.

Chapter Thirty-Three

CHASE

A John Harrod with a mug shot that looks like Floyd's VA picture was booked six weeks ago for DUI and assault on Santa Monica Boulevard. Whoever's life Floyd took over has a clean record. The Ranger was released when a bondsman posted his bail. He was supposed to show up for court yesterday but did not.

A bondsman is a gambler trying to make money betting on the fighters that always lose. He places a bet that this time the battered loser will show up for court. And when that battered loser does not show the bail bondsman calls or becomes a bounty hunter.

Floyd's arrest as Harrod seems wrong. The soldiers of Ripper's first army shoot their way out of problems and they leave quickly when the bodies have fallen. Why would Floyd allow himself to be arrested?

Because he was drunk? Is it that human? He's losing it? Drinking and talking?

But then why use a bondsman? Why not just pay the full bail?

Was this a massive fuck up Floyd was trying to hide from the boss?

And for the bonus marks: Was Evan the one who paid the bondsman?

In the act of signing the contract with the bondsman, an accused gives up his constitutional rights. That hasty signature authorizes the bounty hunter to enter his home without a warrant, search his private property, detain him with force and carry him across state lines. But an elite LA Bounty Hunter rarely needs to leave the city to capture his prey. He succeeds where the LAPD get frustrated because of his connections. He knows the streets, the families, and the grudges. It's not a high tech job. Fugitives running on a budget have to crash with family and friends. Neighbors see them. Neighbors don't like them. Neighbors talk. The fastest LA bounty hunter I know pays variety store clerks to tell him if any locals have made strange purchases: food that doesn't need to be prepared, batteries, flashlights, stacks of magazines.

I wouldn't rate Derek Matthews as an elite LA Bounty Hunter. He seems to mostly chase warrants issued for civil judgments. He works for Jailbreak Bail Bondsmen. They have small offices in Orange and Ventura Counties and on Astronaute ES Onizuka St.

Derek is on the hunt for the bail jumper John Harrod. I want to find Mr. Harrod's secret super solider identity Floyd. We should be able to work together for a short stretch. I call Jailbreak's office and tell them I have information on where Harrod is. They transfer me directly to Derek's cell. I say I'll drive to him.

I catch Derek eating Jack-in-the-box burgers in his truck. I park behind him and walk up.

"You Chalk?"

I hold up my iPhone. It has Evan's VA picture. "Is this the man who paid you to bail John Harrod out?"

"Yeah."

"What are you sitting on here?" I ask him.

"I'm having dinner."

"I see that. Why this street chief?"

"I took a picture of that guy's license plate when he came in to give us the cash. We do that."

"This guy?" I hold my iPhone up again. "You're tracking this guy's vehicle?"

"Yeah I am. It's two streets over."

So it's looking like Floyd just messed up. Evan helped him get free of the trouble with an amount of cash that they could raise themselves and not alarm the boss. Fake names, fake identities and no real LA addresses—they assumed the bounty hunter wouldn't be a problem.

But this bounty hunter got lucky.

His greasy lips chew. "I tracked the address down through DMV. I put a GPS tracker on his vehicle. I've been following him since. I'm waiting for a visual on my fugitive."

I look into the messy truck cab. There's a small nav screen for a cheap GPS tracker.

The hunter wipes his hands. "You said you had information that could help me?"

"Yes. It will save your life. Give me your GPS tracker and let this one go."

"That doesn't sound much like help to me."

"That is a dangerous man you are after."

"I'm a bounty hunter. That's how it works. Who the hell are you?"

I take out cash. "I'll give you a thousand for the GPS tracker."

"I'm going after a bigger bounty than that."

I see the dot on the nav screen beep and start moving. "Final offer. Two thousand. That's all the cash I have."

He takes the cash and hands me the tracker.

I run back to the 911 and clumsily mount the tracker as I start rolling.

The stupid bounty hunter is following me.

I follow a black Yukon in traffic until it has stopped outside the Southeast Community Police Station. I park a good distance away. Evan emerges from the street side back door of the Yukon. He's wearing a black hoodie over black combat fatigues. He has sunglasses on. He's carrying a brown paper parcel. He crosses the street and walks toward the station.

No one else comes out of the Yukon. The tinted windows make it impossible to tell how many others are inside. I can see the bounty hunter's truck ahead of me. But I can't worry about him right now.

I turn the volume up on my police scanner.

I get my Glock, check it, load it, ready it.

Evan is coming back to the Yukon already. He no longer has the package.

Thick grey smoke starts billowing out of the station. There's no flame, there was no thud. The package was a smoke bomb. People are running out. Chatter starts on the scanner: the station is being evacuated.

Three of the Yukon doors open when Evan returns to the vehicle and throws away his sunglasses. Three men get out. One of them is Floyd. They're dressed in the black combat fatigues and armor that have been seen over and over on the news. They're wearing gas masks. They are carrying assault rifles.

Evan lowers his hoodie and dons his armor and gas mask. He's handed his assault rifle.

The four men start dropping smoke grenades as they trot to the station.

The bounty hunter gets out of his truck and begins yelling after the attackers. One of the soldiers stops, pauses, and fires. The head-shot kills the idiot instantly. The soldier hurries to catch up with the others. And the four black figures disappear into the smoke.

There's only one reason that I can think of to attack a police station. They're going in there to visit the evidence locker. It's called the locker in every police station in the country, large or small. And it won't be evidence to do with Floyd/Harrod's DUI and assault.

I get out of the 911. It is just smoke not gas—for now. Muzzle flashes are blossoming orange and yellow in the swirling smoke ahead. There is yelling. There are screams. The gunfire is a dialogue: the scared single shots of police answered by precise bursts from the soldiers.

The Yukon explodes behind me.

The force pushes me down to the pavement. I get up, deafened.

The smoke is starting to dissipate. How long was I down for?

The LAPD have fallen back, they are attempting to surround their own police station. One of the soldiers stands sentry at the entrance. On one knee he scans. He sees me and his barrel stops. I roll to the ground as bullets fly through where I was.

Now comes the smoke of fire from within the police station. The soldiers found their evidence. They will be destroying everything in the locker—it's the fastest option and it camouflages the exact target.

There would have been a card controlled door. Fire proofing. Climate control.

They must have used contact explosives to blow the doors. They did it so fast.

Now the three are coming out. Now they are dropping tear gas grenades.

They pick up the soldier who stood sentry. And then they are gone like a magic trick.

The bomb squad arrives. EMS cares to the wounded. An LAPD mobile command center arrives. Barricades are erected. The news helicopters descend. The streets are blocked off and will be for hours.

I make it back to the 911. It's covered in dust and debris but there's no damage this time.

My MacBook reaches out to the court databases to see what I can learn. I want a query that returns a list of cases relying on evidence stored in the evidence locker just torched. But I can't get that to work. So I have to read.

An hour after the attackers have left, the bomb squad sends the robots in. And Rose opens my passenger door and drops into my German leather. He has food from one of the trucks, enough for us both: hotdogs and fries and cokes.

"Why am I not surprised to see you here?"

"I watched them go in."

"Thanks for the heads up."

"I had no idea what was happening until it happened. And it happened fast."

"And now here you are. Trying to figure out what evidence they burned."

"Do you know?"

"I do as it goes," Rose says proudly. "Let's share."

"I offered what I know to the FBI and they said I was lucky they didn't arrest me."

"I've always appreciated your talents more."

I tell Rose everything I've learned until he opened my door.

Predictably his response is: "Fuck."

"When this ends, when I've stopped them . . . You are going to have to take everything I just told you and whatever else I learn to the FBI."

"They don't listen to me either Chalk."

"When the time comes," I say again. "Now it's your turn. What evidence did they want to destroy?"

"Evidence that was transferred there today. As a way point. In a military trial. Treason."

"Treason?"

Rose opens the door and dumps our garbage out on the street. "Like you I knew right away they had to be destroying evidence. So I checked to see what was new in the records. All that shit is online now you know Chalk." He gives me a mocking smile. "If you have the right security clearance."

Rose explains that they were after evidence against an air force pilot.

After the bomb squad robots are done, the dogs go in. And then the chief makes a decision, a statement is released and the roads are re-opened. I drive home weary and turn the TV on expecting to see coverage of what I just escaped.

But again no. Again General Ripper has outdone himself.

A worm affecting the Xbox Live network is displaying video clips on televisions across the country. The clips begin with the flash of a name. And then words indicate which video game title that person worked on. After this information comes a loop of violence within the given game: bloody graphics, digital death. Then the video switches to reality: the producer, designer or coder, bound and begging before they are shot in the head. The results are messy.

There are thirty of these snuff clips randomized.

All the games are titles I found in that storage unit.

This is what Evan and Floyd did to prove themselves. This was their list.

The news is discovering that some of these game developers have been missing for years.

The murders are numbing.

The Narilam worm was the first of its kind to reach public awareness. It was malware that infected registry keys, spread through local and networked drives, searching for SQL databases that could be scanned for clear text words to be overwritten. Narilam was targeting corporations generally in the Middle East and specifically in Iran. It junked all the Persian content it could find. Iranian officials blamed the Israeli government but those of us in the IT Security Community knew that was laughable. Mossad Hackers are code assassins: unseen and unknown.

General Ripper's malware seems to be a variation on the idea of the Narilam worm targeted generally at Microsoft's Xbox Live gaming network and specifically at combat games like *Call of Duty*. But not just *Call of Duty*.

The second army coded this. Handpicked hackers that have proved themselves. Alexander.

The malware seems to be targeting not just titles but words in the meta information about titles. Clear text in a SQL table can be standardized data: words or phrases selected from dropdowns or indicated with radial buttons. But it can also be free form information: customer comments, additional information, feedback, communications.

About war.

I set up a dumb home network. I put ten virtual Xboxes on this, each with a slightly different hardware profile and level of firmware. I create a fresh-install Windows machine with no bloatware and no virus protection. On this I establish an enterprise server running IIS and a pirated copy of MS SQL and Xbox Live.

I connect the unreal consoles with real games. I start them all playing *Call of Duty.*

I run a routine that fills the SQL database with chunks of text pulled from the internet about war: millions of words with no meaningful organization. These will be the user profiles for my ghosts, the chat between them. I make an offline snapshot copy of everything. And then I push a copy of the worm to the dumbest Xbox.

I let it run.

My mind is racing. I won't sleep yet.

On the sports screen is a 1967 regular season game when Chamberlain shot a perfect 18 for 18 against Baltimore. Moving slower is Barbara Stanwyck desperate for romantic revenge in Preston Sturges' *The Lady Eve.* I love the surprise of the intimacy in this movie, the sensuality of simple touches. Scrolling on the book screen is Joyce's *Ulysses.* It's a tome I must have started twenty times before I stopped trying to understand everything and just let it happen. I have it run fast, making it impossible to read entire sentences and paragraphs even if it had my undivided attention which of course it does not. I just catch senses of where the narrative is.

This is how the case feels now.

I know more than anyone and yet I have no sense of General Ripper's overall plan.

I'm not keeping up.

CHAPTER THIRTY-FOUR

FIRE

Early morning I wake and pull on a Pearl Jam tour shirt from Berlin in which a suited man with conservative hair is wearing a strange mask over his mouth and nose. I sit down in my office and examine my Xbox Live petri dish.

I come to understand how the worm spreads. It's amazing programming. Smart. Elegant.

And there's really nothing more for me to discover. There's just that: its brilliance.

Nothing to investigate. Nothing to chase. Wasted time. Lost time in this race.

Microsoft will have a patch today. They will force it on every connected Xbox in the world. But the message has been delivered. Children, tweens, teens and young adults have seen the quickest view there is of real war: the shock and mess of sudden death.

I launch news windows on a monitor to hear what is being said about the worm: CNN, Fox, MSNBC. They are all covering an FBI press conference. The Director is explaining the broad outlines of the federal investigation into how the drugs and money were mailed to veterans. This becomes rhetoric to justify the new powers the President has just given the feds to intercept and stop packages whenever and however they want. As proof that this massive intrusion into our privacy is necessary, the Director smugly reveals that the FBI just intercepted the next wave of deliveries to go to vets: packages that contained ballistic armor—the exact kind worn for the assaults on the pharmaceutical warehouses.

Did General Ripper really expect these massive packages to reach veterans? Or did he calculate that the FBI would have figured out their tricks with the slightly wrong addresses and remailers by this point?

The Director says the investigation is ongoing. They're not ready to make any arrests.

That will have been the only entirely true statement uttered.

I turn my attention to the case for which the evidence was destroyed yesterday. There's little public information on it. An air force pilot working with a company that designs UI to control current and next generation drones was charged with treason. He is scheduled to undergo a military trial. His defense lawyer was trying to get a transfer of venue. And the federal judge going through the motions of shutting this request down asked for access to the evidence. The notebook computer was moved to the Southeast Community Police Station where Evan, Floyd and two other soldiers from the first army got to it.

General Ripper did not want that evidence to exist. He did not want the case in the news.

The company designing drone software is Ares. They are also working on a new generation of network-linked heads-up displays for American ground forces. They started out making first person shooters for the PS3 and combat flight simulators for the PC. Their two most popular shooters were *Headshot* and *Shrapnel.* Their legendary combat flight simulator was *Wings of Doom.* One of their developers was selected for General Ripper's Xbox Live snuff reel. I watched his brains splatter the shaky lens that was likely held by either Evan or Floyd.

The air force pilot is Major Daily. He lives in East LA. He's under house arrest.

I grab my coat.

As I drive into El Sereno I can see smoke. I flip the radio on and tune into the right band. Firefighters are responding to a house blaze on Amethyst Street—my destination. The Assistant Fire Chief is en route. I drop my window to get a sense of the winds outside. I hear sirens and see lights flashing up fast in my mirrors. I pull over for the roaring command SUV to scream by. A minute later I'm there too. The assembled fire trucks are red and still before the hot yellow flames engulfing all three stories of the home.

I park and wait. The LAFD will have everything under control within the half hour. Then the investigation will start. But Evan and Floyd don't care if the LAFD correctly determines this as arson. They wanted Major Daily dead and he's dead.

More clean-up done. How far was I behind them this time?

Why fire? Why not just shoot the air force pilot? . . . Fire scares. Fire terrifies. They are working to keep others quiet. People who know what the treason case is about. People who work for Ares. People who know about drone software.

I'm working this case with Rose now. We made it official last night with that silent ceremony of shared hotdogs. He's my partner whether he likes it or not. I hit his name on my iPhone. "Rose. We need to know everything we can about that treason case."

"It's a military trial. I don't have access—"

"Yes but the Major's lawyer was trying to get the venue changed. There has to be information."

"I'm not saying I can't get—"

"I'm at the Major's house now. It's a pile of ash. Find out what other suspicious fires there have been in the last few weeks."

"Can we slow down for—"

"No. We can't. Call me back when you have information."

I click off. I stand on the street. The fire is out. The home is smoking.

A Fire Investigation starts with the determination of which area suffered the most damage. Micro burn patterns then suggest the fire's possible points of origin. The usual suspects stand out: a frying pan, a tipped portable heater, a careless cigarette, frayed wiring and cords, candles forgotten, overloaded plugs, toasters. Fire Investigators say they don't just look for the lowest burn and the deepest char any more but they actually still do—they just disguise this with new academic phrases. Focusing in on a specific culprit, the spread of the flames must be traced and understood. Aside from how the blaze began, the most important part of the story has to be when the fire transitioned from being fuel-controlled to ventilation-controlled. Photos are taken and evidence is bagged. If arson is suspected the area becomes a crime scene but always a severely compromised one because of all the traffic coming and going.

I move behind a fire truck. There are two extra helmets sitting on a running board. I take one and put it on. There are no available jackets. I move with my head down into the steaming burnt ribs of the house. I see the body on the main floor. It's a gruesome doll but still discernible as human.

Major Daily was shot in the head first.

And then the house was set ablaze. To scare others.

I look around. This field trip can be over at any moment. I brush the ground with my feet. In the wet and black I feel and then see a melted cellphone. I crouch down and take it. I turn around slowly to see if anyone saw. No one did.

"Heh! Who the fuck are you? I'm talking to you buddy."

I turn for the man coming at me. I act like a bewildered civilian. "Yes?"

"What the hell do you think you're doing?"

"I'm Major Daily's neighbor. I wanted to make sure his dog is safe."

"This is a crime scene! You can't just take a helmet and go poking around!"

"I'm sorry." I start to cry and then I reach out and hug the fireman. "I'm so sorry. He was a beautiful man. And he loved that dog."

The sweaty and encumbered firefighter hugs me a little, pats my back. "It's okay. Just get out of here and return the fucking helmet."

I do. Rose calls me back. I tell him about Major Daily.

"I've got a fire you're going to want to check on. Glenda Baker. She works for Ares."

"When did her house burn down?"

"She lived in an apartment building."

"They burned the whole building?"

"No. They burned her in the elevator. There's video. And she's alive."

"Send me the video."

"Email coming your way."

"Where is she now Rose?"

"The Grossman Burn Center."

Back in the 911 I take the melted cellphone out of my pocket and look at it for a second.

The file comes into my email. It's security footage from a hallway in an apartment building. There's no audio. I watch the short film in episodes as I stop at lights en route to Van Nuys, hitting the spacebar on my MacBook to stop and to start each time.

Elevator doors in a hall open. Inside there is a man dressed in the black combat armor and mask now infamous. It could be Evan. It could be Floyd. The soldier is holding a large plastic jug of liquid in gloved hands.

The woman, Glenda, is standing in the hall. She was waiting for the elevator.

Shifting the jug, the man grabs for her with his right hand and pulls her into the elevator. He's so strong that the one tug yanks her in and against the elevator wall. Deftly, he stops the doors from closing with his back while simultaneously kicking her hard in the gut. She bucks forward and goes down to her knees.

He starts pouring the liquid from the plastic jug over her.

The smell, the sting, she realizes what's happening. She fights her way up and tries to get up and past him. He drops the container and uses both hands to hold her immobile. He beats her until she stays down. He picks the jug up again and empties the remainder of the liquid on her prone form as if it is all needed.

Still he's stopping the door from shutting. I can't hear but know it will be beeping at him.

He drops the empty container. I see the flame from the lighter before I see the lighter.

He throws it in and steps back. The doors shut.

Surely the doors will open. They have to open.

The man runs to the stairwell. The video keeps playing.

And then the elevator doors do open. Flaming and flailing Glenda bursts out and exits the shot as the sprinklers and fire alarm trigger. A neighbor enters the scene with a fire extinguisher and Glenda is transformed from human torch to black and smoking lump.

This horrible act of terror was lost in the media frenzy. It's worse than any of the murders and tactical kills I know Evan and Floyd have committed to this point. But was it enough to scare whoever else knows about the treason, about Ares, about drone software?

Do Evan and Floyd know that she isn't dead?

Chapter Thirty-Five

CONTACT

The Sherman Oaks Hospital on Van Nuys is home to a Grossman Burn Center. It has thirty dedicated beds. I grab a clipboard at a nurse's station and find Glenda's name. She's undergoing hyperbaric therapy.

I take a blue hairnet, blue gloves and blue over-the-shoe slippers from a cart.

I put them on in a handicapped bathroom.

I follow the signs and reach the right door. Glenda is alone in a Plexiglas tube. There is a television positioned above her, the images flashing on the surface of the expensive sarcophagus. This process is supposed to accelerate her healing.

She sees me. She doesn't know who I am. But she isn't alarmed by my presence.

She seems to have no friends or family here.

A nurse questions me. I say I'm here to see Glenda. He looks over to her and she nods that I'm okay. Instinctively she must know why I've come. A tech works the dials on the machine. And then slowly the nurse helps her out and back into the world of harsh air.

I follow behind her rolling bed, back to her room, where we are soon alone.

"Hi Glenda. I'm Chalk."

"Hi." Her eyes are wet. All else is dry and painful.

"You work at Ares?"

"I'm a programmer."

"What do you know about the treason case?"

"Major Daily was attached to work with us. From the Air force. He's a drone pilot. He copied our code base and sold it."

"This is the UI code for controlling drones? The remote flying software?"

"They told us he sold it to enemies of the state."

"But they didn't tell you who that was?"

"We assumed the Chinese. Or Russians. Why was this done to me?"

"To scare your colleagues at Ares."

"No one was talking," she whimpers. "To the media or anyone else."

"What could a terrorist do with that code?"

"Nothing without a lot of extra programming."

"Would it be possible to hijack drone flights?"

"Not realistically. You'd have to have—"

"An army of hackers," I answer.

"Good ones. And even then," she says doubtfully.

"Where are your family?" I ask her.

"They're coming. They live in Canada."

"You don't have anyone here?"

"I code twenty hours a day. And I play video games for two. That doesn't leave much time for dreaming about a boyfriend let alone finding one."

I look around the room: at the entrance, at the angles. "Are the military sending guards?"

"The LAPD said they were going to be in contact with them. I think. I pass out a lot."

"Did you know Major Daily personally?"

"He's dead?"

"Sorry. You couldn't know. Yes. His house was burned."

"By the same people that burned me?"

"I believe so."

"I worked with him. He seemed okay. Until he was arrested."

"Did he say anything about what's been happening in the news? Veterans getting drugs and money?"

"No."

"Did you hear about the Xbox worm?"

"No."

I tell her. And because she's a programmer I tell her how it works. It engages her mind before the pain overwhelms her again and she falls asleep. I step into the hall and call Rose. "She said the LAPD was working with the military to get guards here. But there are no guards. I just walked in off the street and talked to her for half-an-hour."

"Well you're really good at that."

"I feel like Al Pacino at the hospital in *The Godfather* Rose. You guys have to get someone here to guard her."

"I'll check what the holdup is."

I drift, always moving, always watching. I overhear a nurse talking about Glenda. She's had one surgery already and there will be more almost every day. They will use a whirlpool to scrub the dead skin from her burns and try to stop infection.

There's a waiting area for family down the hall from Glenda's room. It's not a perfect perch but I can keep an eye on most of the entering traffic without looking like a man standing around with a gun.

Evan and Floyd will find out Glenda is alive and they will be coming here.

I'm a little ahead of them this once. I have to make good use of that small advantage.

I get out my iPhone and call the Russian Pharmacist. He agrees to come to me at the Burn Center. I'm not going to win a gunfight with Evan and Floyd. But the right drug at the right time might be my ace.

I want to be ready if I get that chance.

Next I take out the melted cellphone. It's dead but the SIM behind the battery is fine. I pop it into my iPhone. There's an address book and a recently called list on the little chip. If the Major sold that code to General Ripper then he would have had a contact.

I start calling the numbers in memory. Friends and family that answer are understandably traumatized that I'm phoning from the dead Major's number. I just tell them it's part of an ongoing investigation.

I don't know what Evan or Floyd sound like.

But one call gets a strange and pensive silence. I say nothing.

"In wartime, truth is so precious that she should always be attended by a bodyguard of lies."

It's a code phrase. I'm supposed to know the response and I don't.

"Evan?" I ask.

The speaker hangs up right away.

Contact. Fleeting but contact.

Chapter Thirty-Six

PANIC

The Russian Pharmacist is an old man now. Another life ago, as a medical doctor in the KGB, he used vials and syringes to bring the tortured back to life so they could be tortured anew. He was in his early forties when communism fell and the Russian Mob took over the economy. Like many of his KGB compatriots he transitioned easily enough into doing the same work for different masters.

He bought his freedom from the Vory and made it to the US before he turned fifty with a collection of forged documents that established his medical education and his work experience as a medical researcher. He got a high paying job at a pharmaceutical company supervising drug trials.

It was his intention to stay legit. He learned to understand and even like American football and chicken wings. He couldn't come to like American or Canadian beer but he began making his own vodka in industrial quantities. He found an American woman and when she left him within two years he found another as easily and is happy to continue leasing them in that manner.

Two independent events set him up in the underworld again.

The first was a call from an old colleague from the KGB, a dangerous madman who he'd seen laugh and laugh while mutilated men were bound and bursting through their eyes. This man had pancreatic cancer and he'd heard that the pharmacist could procure drugs still in testing at his pharmaceutical company.

The pharmacist hadn't done anything like that yet but it proved almost trivial. He got the experimental drugs, gave them to the psychopath, and watched him die in a motel room where the TV was never off.

The Americans are amateurs when it comes to the black market. It's second nature to the Russians. The Russian Pharmacist was soon able to not only get drugs that his company was testing but drugs that other companies were testing as well. And customers found him.

The second event he initiated. Lonely and drunk, he wrote to a young man with one arm to whom he'd been a mentor when everything had been falling apart in the USSR. The pharmacist was embarrassed to write a letter asking the younger man how he was doing and did he remember the good times they'd had together? So he asked about business. The one armed man back in the motherland replied with the revelation that he had a contact who could reliably get stockpiled government drugs. When the variety on offer was described the Russian Pharmacist recognized it all as KGB inventory. The two men figured out a way to ship these drugs to the US.

And he was back working in the underworld.

The Russian Pharmacist finds me pacing in the waiting area. We walk to the cafeteria. There's an ATM there and I take out as much money as I can and add it to what I already have on me. I give the him a *War and Peace* stack of cash. He gives me back a syringe and three vials.

"It is of interest to me," he says with his thick accent. "That America, a country born once in revolution and then again in civil war . . . that she is unable to understand either when they are happening."

"Yeah isn't that just a head scratcher."

He looks hurt by my sarcasm. "You okay Chalk?"

"Fine. Why?"

"You're more wired than usual."

"Just on edge, you know? Just . . . just feeling fast."

We shake and the Russian Pharmacist leaves me with a farewell scowl.

I return to Glenda's room. She's still sleeping. There are still no guards.

Every time I look at this burnt young woman I get angrier. But she's proof they're not perfect. They wanted her dead but she's alive. They wanted her horrific burns to silence the story but she spoke to me.

Evan and Floyd will be coming here. I believe. But what if I taunted them?

Faster and faster yet my mind is racing through decisions. I'm acting before I've thought. This is panic. And knowing it's panic doesn't stop the panicking. My mental accelerator is jammed stuck.

Faster and faster yet. I could show them their failure. Yes.

Faster and faster yet. The SIM from the ashes is still in my iPhone. I take a picture of the sleeping Ares programmer, a picture of the screens charting her vitals and then a picture of the military police guards that have just arrived and question my presence and eager photography even as they take up sentry.

Faster and faster yet. I'm going to show Evan and Floyd their failure.

Faster and faster yet. I text the pictures to the number that hung up on me. And regret it right away. They were likely coming. But now I've summoned them here. I've put Glenda and everyone else in the hospital in extreme danger. . . . Faster and faster yet. Lashed with sweat I go into the bathroom and fill a syringe with my purchase from the Russian Pharmacist. It rests like a viper in my coat pocket. I return to the waiting area, brittle and nervous. All sound is a rush. . . . Faster and faster yet. I switch back to my SIM and call Rose. I try to tell him what I've done but I can't. I keep talking when he's talking and I know he's not hearing me. He says I sound like I'm on speed and I laugh inanely and then start to sob. I click off knowing that there's nothing he or anyone else can do. I can't even tell the people standing and sitting around me to run away. . . . Faster and faster yet. I made this situation. I have to figure it out. I have to try and slow down before the assassins come.

I pop a Seroquel. Everyone is looking at me. Am I still laughing? Are there tears?

Rose calls back. I don't answer.

I pop another Seroquel. And another.

Faster and faster yet. Which SIM should I have in the phone?

Faster and faster yet . . . and then everything slows. It's like jumping out of warp speed.

I've taken too much. I should have waited for the first pill to work. I feel sleepy and hungry. I sit. I nod off a little feeling so stupid so fucking stupid so very fucking stupid. I force myself up. What time is it? I get a chocolate bar. I drink a coke. I hate myself.

Rose keeps calling. I don't answer.

The panic fights back against the chemicals and starts to win again. I go from lethargic right back to wired but this time not quite as fast. This is a speed I can control—almost. This is a speed I can control—just.

Two more military guards arrive bringing the total to four.

Then I see Evan and with him Floyd. They are not wearing their armor. They've come dressed in street clothes and sunglasses, carrying gym bags. I watch them disappear into a patient's room and shut the door.

My heart thuds.

I reason that the two soldiers have decided to arm for the fight in there. They will come out and kill the guards, kill Glenda and then blast their way back out of the building and the chaos they have caused.

I run down the hall and to Glenda's room. The military guards raise their hands to stop me but then I see in their expressions that Floyd and Evan have already come out of the combat dressing room far behind my back. The guards hurry to ready their weapons and instantly forget me. I make it into the room where Glenda is awake.

The thunder of gunfire comes from the hall. The four guards fight back but not for long.

There's a crazy jazz beat of silence outside.

And then nurses and doctors and family are screaming and running about the hospital.

I position myself just behind the open door to Glenda's room.

Evan or Floyd will be advancing to this room while the other remains in the hall watching their flank. Whoever enters this space will check my position. It's standard urban combat training. I need a quick second of distraction.

Glenda's eyes are on me. She's scared.

I step to her bed and hand her my Glock. I return to my hiding spot and ready the needle.

Floyd enters the room and is surprised for the single instance I need as Glenda points the Glock at him. I jab the needle into his neck. I jam the plunger. The drug delivers cold. Floyd tries to move and nothing happens. The chemical has cut the wires between his nerves and muscles. I stop him from falling. He's standing trapped. And will be like this for seven or eight dangerous minutes.

I push his assault rifle out of his hands as if he were a mannequin. I kick the weapon away on the floor. I take my Glock from Glenda and press it to the side of my captive's head. I position myself behind him and behind his armor.

"Evan," I yell into the hall. "Get in here."

I wait five seconds and call again. Evan appears at the door, gun lowered, curious.

"The diaphragm is a muscle. There is a good chance Floyd here could stop breathing. But it's a certainty that I'm going to blow his head off if you don't answer some questions."

An alarm is sounding in the hospital.

"You'd better hurry," Evan says. It was his voice on the phone.

"You needed hackers to hijack drones. That's the big attack, isn't it?"

"The General is waking this nation."

"General Ripper."

"That's right. General Ripper."

The commotion in the hall and the hospital beyond is organizing. There is a voice of leadership. Evan can hear it as well. Are my words keeping him here? No. It's Floyd. He's deciding what to do about Floyd.

"Did he pick his own nickname? Or was it given to him?"

"It started off as a joke. And I'm not giving you the punch line."

"You're going to hijack drones," I state it this time. "When? What are you going to attack?"

"We don't allow hostages to be taken."

The decision made, Evan raises his assault rifle and shoots Floyd in the head. I lose my balance in the sudden splitting of meat. I fall back. I see Evan turning slightly to aim at the recumbent Glenda. I get a shot off. The bullet hits Evan's gun, jerking it out of his hands. My second shot gets him in the chest of his armor. He was reaching for his .500 caliber handgun but winded he now turns and retreats to the hall.

Through echoes and gunshots I hear Evan start fighting his way out.

I search Floyd's pockets but there's nothing of value. I sit in a chair by Glenda and hold her hand gently. The LAPD shows up. Patrol first and then detectives including Rose. My partner helps explain my presence here. He gets my statement taken and gets me away before the FBI show up.

I shower at the hospital and Rose and I go for a beer.

"General Ripper."

"Your brain is on tilt Chalk. You need to go home and sleep."

"They're not doing this for a uniform or a flag or a medal or a badge. They're doing it for a man. A personality."

"You're a cult expert. You think he's a cult leader. I get it. Everything is a nail to a man with a hammer."

"I'm ignoring that. The name and the movie mean something more."

"You still have blood in your hair dude." Rose drinks.

"What are you working on tomorrow partner?"

"I'll see if I can find more on Ares," he says. "You know: in and around my day job."

"You have to start convincing the FBI that they are going to hijack drones."

"I think they're on that. Especially after what just happened."

"Except the FBI have no idea how or where or when and I'll bet they still don't really believe it's possible."

"And I'm going to change their mind? A lowly LAPD detective running their errands?"

"Eventually we'll have the right evidence."

"That's nice to know. I find that comforting."

"You work Ares and the drones. I'm going to find out who General Ripper is."

"Oh you've penciled that in your planner for tomorrow have you?"

"Heh fuck you."

"How Chalk?"

"I don't know yet. It will come to me."

I drive home and I watch *Dr. Strangelove.*

As I absorb the cinematic masterpiece, a notion of how to find out more about General Ripper comes to me. It's an approach the FBI would never try. It's almost silly. But I bet that it's going to work. I just don't know if it will work in time. It's going to be connection to connection to connection through Hollywood.

CHAPTER THIRTY-SEVEN

RECALL

Carl Jung wrote about the collective unconscious: a mighty dream ocean containing the images, symbols and icons that humans have used for stories since we first slept under the stars. This ocean is why we understand the recurring myths that are the same in cultures separated from one another by deserts and jungles and the wasteland expanses of time.

The leader of the terrorist group I'm trying to stop has allowed his public name to be that of a film character. I've seen that the soldiers of General Ripper's first army are loyal to the death. I understand the handpicked hackers of the second army are hidden for their work. But I know there are men who were approached to enlist and chose not to. I know there will be men who left over the many years it has taken for the plans of this national terrorist campaign to develop.

These men didn't go to the news.

They didn't go to the police or the FBI.

But Hollywood has far more reporters and many more agents. Mighty brokers like the Hyena, desperate producers, lost directors, hungry screenwriters, and aspirants to all of these levels in the business listen for character ideas, plot hooks, magic loglines. They steal life story elements when they can. They pay for them when they absolutely must. And they visit the same dream ocean we all do when their eyes close on the hustle for a few hours. A warrior, strange militias, diamond heists, complicated plans to manipulate the mail system . . . there are people in Hollywood who will have knowledge even more valuable than their wildest hopes for sales.

I start in Hollywood's dumpster: the hundreds of websites tracking the business of rumors. I read about scripts commissioned, scripts optioned, scripts in turn-around, scripts killed, scripts re-assigned, directors and actors attached, production, post-production, premieres. Following the deceased Hyena's lead many studios have projects about General Ripper's ongoing attacks already in development.

I don't care about those. I want to find movies in development before this all started.

I print out a good list. I put on a Blondie *No Exit* shirt and head down to the 911.

I call Rose while shifting to make sure he's on Ares. He assures me he is.

My first stop is a production company called Dream Recall.

Lucid dreaming is when you wake up in your dream. You become aware that you're dreaming and you can even try to control what happens. It's a drug free trip. Most people never achieve escape velocity from the pillow. But a few of those that do try to control the experience. They explore the dream landscape and interact with the characters conjured therein. Neurological researchers have theorized that these spirits are dramatic creations of the mind: fears with faces, longed for lovers, the dead not done with us—all costumed by the vast wardrobe of the subconscious. The possibility of dialogue and action have made these scenes ideal for new age therapists to promote personal development, problem solving, quitting smoking, sexual understanding, fantastical escape for the physically disabled.

Dream Recall Productions has office space with beds instead of desks in the cubicles. The company hires people who represent the demographic of the target market for a given movie, induce them to dream lucidly and then collect their ideas.

Eight years ago the first script Dream Recall Productions created was called *Shine On Crazy Diamonds*. It was about old army buddies all horribly injured on tours of duty in the middle east. One is missing an arm, another a leg, a third both his hands, and a fourth his face. They come together to form a Pink Floyd cover band and then plan a diamond heist in Surat. The leader of the group, the singer without a face, is called General Ripper.

The script was purchased but never produced.

I stalk past the cubicle field of lucid dreamers, brainwave scanners, pleased attendants, and aim for the biggest office. The name on the door says Scott Mann. He's the President. The door is closed. I can see through the window inset that he's in there on the phone.

I open the door, move in, and hang the phone up with my finger.

"Who the fuck do—"

"*Shine On.* General Ripper. How did you come up with the character?"

"It's from *Dr. Strangelove.* General Jack Ripper. He's the commanding officer of the air wing who . . . he goes insane. He thinks the communists are coming after his precious bodily fluids. And he orders his air wing to drop nukes in Russia and start world war three."

"Thanks for the synopsis. That's the allusion. Tell me about the character in your movie. Start with him not having a face."

"It was all dreamed." He waves his hands in a mystic gesture.

"I'm more likely to believe that than most. But someone had to connect it all. Your name is on the script but that doesn't mean you necessarily wrote a word. Who created the character?"

"It was a team effort."

"Don't bullshit me. Who wrote the character?"

"Matthew Jenkins. He was an assistant at the time. He teaches screenwriting now."

"Where?"

"Loyola Marymount University."

I call while driving and type while sitting at lights. I discover that Dr. Jenkins is teaching a doctoral level screenwriting seminar. I make it to the School of Film and Television, park illegally and go into the building.

I find the classroom and listen from the hallway. I can hear a young woman discussing which stars would represent the best casting decisions for her lesbian coming of age techno thriller set in an alternate future past. This must be a regular part of the class because there are no nervous laughs at the idiocy of it. The students are actually debating the pros and cons of Jodie Foster for the role.

I'm not waiting for the end of the class. For all I know these students have ascended to an ethereal academic plane where the start and end times of classes are meaningless. Plus I can't listen any longer.

I move in. I stop. The conversation sputters as everyone looks at me.

"Can I help you?" Dr. Jenkin asks.

"I need to talk to you."

"We're in the middle of a class. Can you wait outside please?"

"I cannot. My time is more valuable than yours."

"Is that so?"

"I am from the government." I hesitate until Dr. Jenkins tries to speak again. "Department of Education," I talk over him. "Value Enforcement Division. This class has been deemed to be worthless in both design and delivery."

"What?"

"Kids. Adults. Whatever you are. A screenwriting class is fun. But a doctoral degree in screenwriting is what we in the Value

Enforcement Division refer to as a WEMT: a Waste of Everyone's Motherfucking Time. You are encouraged to visit the Registrar and see how much of a refund you can get. Spend forty dollars of whatever money that is on Lew Hunter's book and use the rest to start paying your loans back."

Dr. Jenkins fights back with pissy. "Every student in my class has Lew Hunter's *Screenwriting 434* book," he says. "It's a part of the curriculum."

"You think that somehow makes what you do less of a motherfucking waste of time? Because you tell people to buy the right book? Amazon does a great job of telling everyone what books to buy—they don't charge tuition. This class is over."

No one moves.

"Class is over! Go now or I'm calling your parents with new career ideas!"

Now they leave.

"I have to tell you that I feel like I'm being threatened here."

"Not yet," I say. "*Shine On*. You came up with the character of General Ripper."

"Scott Mann actually admitted to that? You must have put a gun to his head."

"Your General Ripper character had no face. And his crew pulled off a diamond heist. Where did that come from?"

"Not that lucid dreaming crap. Okay one person dreamed about a person without a face but I'd already come up with the character."

"Did you talk to soldiers? Vets?"

"I'm a writer. I talk to, of course, I mean of course I talk to everyone. I catalogue it all."

"You know what I'm asking you. Was there a specific soldier you talked to when you came up with the faceless General Ripper character?"

"Norton. His name is Jenson Norton. He was hanging around parties playing Russian Roulette by the pool. It got him talked about and invited to other parties. That got him a gig as a paid expert for a sitcom pilot that takes place in a combat hospital in the middle east. It's like *M.A.S.H.* It's like a new *M.A.S.H.* I think they're calling it . . . *The New M.A.S.H*," he says weakly. "It's totally outside of the normal production schedule."

"What network?"

"Fox."

Back to the 911.

I call Rose. Ares' next generation software for drone control has been developed for domestic missions. The company's design challenge was to create software that will allow any military or law enforcement personnel to fly a strike from a regular PC.

War becoming a video game.

General Ripper has been planning his terrorist attacks for more than a decade. Drones weren't so omnipresent that many years ago. How did he plan the timing of his coming attack so perfectly? Is he that prescient?

Or are drones just the latest manifestation of what he's fighting?

Graphics have made warriors terrorists.

Chapter Thirty-Eight

SHOW

More than a hundred TV dramas and comedies make pilots each season.

Pilots may be aired, they are usually included in the DVD set, but they are a specialized creation. Pilots are scripted, cast, performed, filmed and edited to be shown to focus groups that are brought together to generate research reports.

The first fight is over the demographics. Up to fifty people are selected. These are the people the show is supposed to be for—the group that the network will offer up to the advertisers as a marketing sacrifice. Each of them is placed before a dial they use to indicate their moment by moment enjoyment of the pilot they're watching. Often they have a button to indicate that they would, at this point, were this real, change the channel to another show. These people watch the pilot and the producers watch them and the real time fluctuations of metrics while behind one-way glass.

When the pilot is done playing the facilitators break the people into different groups that go into different rooms to discuss the show. It's not an open forum. There are prescribed topics and carefully considered questions. All of the rooms being used again have one-way mirrors. Producers often have an earpiece connection to the facilitators. The stakes are very high. Millions of dollars and hundreds of jobs are on the line.

The same pilot can be focus-grouped many times with every step of the process contested and challenged by those invested in the results. All of the data generated is fought over. The demographics were wrong. The room was too hot. That woman was drunk. That man was an intimidating racist. . . . Savvy producers pay their own cheerleaders: TV historians, sociologists, psychologists and content experts.

Norton is a military expert involved in the production and selling of *The New M.A.S.H.* He advised on the creation of characters. And now he is involved in hyping the pilot, convincing the suits that the hundreds of thousands of soldiers who have fought in the middle east and come back to normal life in the US are really going to laugh at this shit.

I learned this from phoning his agent.

The corporate skyscrapers of Century City stand like mighty crystal steeples to the gods of entertainment unknown but seemingly appeased for the moment. The 911 reflects in the shiny office windows as I pass. Everywhere are fountains. I pull into open parking for the Fox Plaza and walk out to wait in the green space behind the right building.

I got Norton's picture from his agent's website. I catch him coming out to his car.

"You still play Russian Roulette, Norton?" I ask his back.

He comes around and sees me. "Wild rumors," he says.

"Enough to get you over as a wildman soldier. To earn that expert fee."

"So I palmed a bullet and fooled a few executive assholes. Good story."

"You know who General Ripper is."

This was the end of the day for him. Now he has to deal with me, with this.

"I'm Chalk," I tell him.

"And who is Chalk?"

"The man who is going to find General Ripper."

"He's a movie character buddy."

"You told Matthew Jenkins about a faceless soldier and he had his character idea stolen by a producer for a film that didn't get made."

"Welcome to Hollywood. Stay for a bit and you'll get paid for doing something."

"Thanks but I'm a disdainful lifelong resident."

Norton gives this a flash of teeth that isn't exactly a smile. "Sterling Hayden played General Ripper in *Dr. Strangelove*. He's been dead a long time. Maybe his grave is on one of those maps you can buy."

"Who is the real General Ripper, Norton?"

"A soldier who has decided to start his own war. He's terrifyingly insane."

"Good nickname then."

"You haven't the slightest idea."

"So tell me."

"He served as a solider in the first Gulf War. He was badly disfigured. His face. Maybe his genitals too. It was said . . . I heard it said that he couldn't have kids. He came back from the war and his wife was with another guy. The army wouldn't take him again so he became a mercenary. Different names, different companies. He made a lot of money and fixed his face. And then changed his face. And kept changing it. Always different faces and always different names. Don't ask because I don't know any of them."

"That's how the Ripper nickname started?"

"Yes."

"Talk to me about now. There are two armies," I start him off.

"He tried to recruit me for the first one. To steal weapons and technology and diamonds and pills. To kill people on lists. He's done it all very slowly over many years."

"Why? What's the advantage of drawing it out?"

"He was waiting for the second army to be ready."

"Why?"

"I don't know."

"How were you contacted?"

"There was a hidden message in a digital picture. It told me where to go. I was blindfolded. Driven for hours. Even then he was just on a screen. I said no. They dumped me home."

"Was there an Evan and Floyd?"

"I didn't talk to anyone except him. My chaperones were wearing masks. Ripper wanted someone to take over recruiting. He said I could do that after we'd got underway with the robberies."

"Evan got that job after you turned it down."

"Lucky him."

"How many veterans are there in the first army?"

"Less than you think. We probably saw all of them on that coordinated takedown of the three drug warehouses."

"Do you know what the second army is going to do?"

He shakes his head. "No, I don't. I have no idea."

"You didn't know General Ripper before you were contacted."

"I didn't serve with him."

"Do you know any of the units he was in?"

"I know he fought with Eagle Guard. Mercenaries," he clarifies.

"You didn't go to the FBI with this information."

"It would have fucked up my gig here. They're paying me a lot of money to be an expert."

"And just fuck the country then?"

"No. Fuck you. But. I will tell you this. There's a script . . ." he sighs. "A horror script. It's about a postal worker who mails . . . things all over the country."

"Things?"

"It's a famous floater script. Trust me: I'm not a player. I just want enough to keep making my condo and Mercedes payments. But I've read a draft of this infamous script. And when the drugs started getting mailed around the country . . . ? It was the second thing I thought of. . . . Right after Ripper."

"What's this script called and where can I find it?"

"It's called *Dear America.* Talk to the producer with control of it. His name is Rolando Lingk. If I was looking for him I wouldn't drive to his office. I'd go to the Hideous Hunger."

"The Opium Den."

Chapter Thirty-Nine

SCREENPLAY

Opium is not heroin, it's not oxycodone, and it's not fentanyl. Opium dens were disappearing from the Chinese enclaves of major cities after Jack the Ripper brought in a new century with blood. Now they are historical curiosities, thick smoke in classic fiction. But there is one in LA today.

The Hideous Hunger is a new hip way to spend money being bad. The name comes from a description in *The Picture of Dorian Gray*. From what I can gather the den started like an exclusive wine tasting club.

Creating quality opium begins with the soaking and boiling of raw leaves. Only the finest pure water is used for this. Filtering is done with oriental silk many times over and lastly with cotton. This takes weeks. The drug is mixed with brandy and boiled a last time to create the paste, the chandoo. It is then ready to be smoked. But for further perfection it is aged in ceramic jars sealed tight and embossed with the date of sleep. Opium aged ten and twenty years is expensive. But for the studio executive eager to spend the most money and attain the rarest experience ancient jars from special collections around the world can be ordered. It's all so very cool: a hidden club, an expensively exclusive high.

Except that opium is still pretty addictive.

The den is located in the basement of a small office building on San Vincente Blvd. The first floor houses a health club. The second and third floors are home to an insurance company, two production companies and a social media advertising agency. The fourth and fifth floors are currently vacant. There is excellent parking out front.

Beyond the muted reception where I offered my ID as Benjamin Franklin, the den is a single large room of pillows and recumbent humans. The sense of heavy smoke is everywhere. There are five men and a woman lying around with dark full eyes.

Pulled back to the den again and again to satisfy their hunger, these heavy lidded addicts have learned of the noble oriental philosophy within opium. Vaporizing the drug through smoking is the key. Imbibed like this it does not just sedate like other opiate experiences. It energizes the user in a peaceful calm manner that allows inward reflection and wild dreaming.

I find Rolando Lingk sleeping on silk pillows. I sit at his feet and wait for him to pass through this world for a moment. While I wait I search for what I can find on the *Dear America* script with my iPhone. It does have quite the reputation.

Floater scripts are screenplays that have been drifting around Hollywood for years and even decades. They sit dog-eared on desks in production companies. They get copied from flash drives to cloud storage to the temporal interest lobe of studio executive brains. They were and still are faxed a single page at a time to old school directors. They are emailed to agents and actors. New stars are attached and then new writers are brought in for rewrites. Harry told me about one script that started as a biopic about Caligula to star Charlton Heston and became a science fiction epic before turning into a historical romantic comedy. He may have been exaggerating. But well paid writers for that script included Harold Pinter, David Mamet and Tom Stoppard. *Dear America* has been floating for thirteen years. Twenty one different writers have turned in more than fifty different drafts.

Impatient, I leave the den and take the elevator up to the contemporary world. I saunter around until I find a vending machine. I buy a bottle of water and go back down. I twist the top on the plastic bottle, take a sip and pour the rest on Rolando Lingk's face. He wakes up with a gasp.

"Rolando. I'm from *Variety*. I want to talk to you about Dear America."

"You're not from *Variety*," he moans.

"The script for *Dear America*."

"Is shit," he admits.

"Which version?" I ask.

"Some are all shit and some are mostly shit. But I always said it was a strong concept. And you see I was right. Just look at what's happening now. Now everyone else is going to make money off of it."

"I assume you believe the 'strong concept' is the deranged mailman sending mysterious packages around the country. So tell me who came up with that."

"I came up with that. It was totally my idea. My idea, my vision."

I slap him across the face. "Who did you steal it from?"

He's shocked. I slap him again.

"I read it in a spec script I got a long time ago! Written by this vet mailman."

"What are in the packages the mailman sends around the country?"

"Well it changes in the different drafts. It's a horror script so they're all, you know, scary."

"Tell me about the packages in the first draft."

"Blood. Vials of blood. Spooky. Blood. See: this vet mailman sends samples of his blood across the country to like teenagers. And the teenagers believe that if they inject the blood they'll get super high. Right. See. But the mailman is actually a demon and it's demon blood. And his blood makes them become like his unholy army. . . . That's what it was in the first draft. But that changed many times over the years. One draft had poisoned money in the packages. Another had body parts that re-animated. Another had murder weapons that possessed the teenagers. In one version it was magical video game cartridges. But the DNA of the idea is there in every script."

"Blood," I say. "Precious bodily fluids."

"I don't follow."

"That's from *Dr. Strangelove*."

"I wrote an essay on Kubrick in film school. But I've never seen it."

There's something here but I'm not making the connection. Is it possible that General Ripper was the original screenwriter? No. He was a soldier and then a mercenary. Not a fucking mailman. Did Ripper steal some of the described mail tricks from the hopeful screenwriter? Possibly. But if it was just that then why does the horror element of mailing demon blood bother me so much? Did the original screenwriter know General Ripper and know something not yet revealed?

"Did you pay the original scriptwriter?" I ask.

"The mailman who sent his script in without an agent? Uh, no. I was inspired by it."

"I need his name." I slap Rolando again so he knows we're not done with that. "What's his name?"

"Alfred Connor."

"Where can I find his original script?"

"I keep every script I've ever read, written, consulted on or been . . . inspired by . . . on my notebook. Because. See. The creative process is complicated and challenging."

I see his computer bag. I take it.

"Heh. You can't—"

I slap him again. "What's your password?"

"Money. With a capital M."

"Go back to sleep." I feint slapping him a last time. He reacts and dodges—slowly but fast enough to confirm that he's finally awake. "If I can't find the script I will be right back."

Sitting in the parking lot, I power up the producer's notebook. I find Alfred Connor's original script and I read it. It's terrible. The story is unclear and incoherent. The dialogue is chewy. But the author's knowledge of how packages are routed around the country is interesting and detailed. Much would have changed since he wrote this abomination but likely the main distribution rules and policies are still the same.

I turn to my MacBook and start researching Alfred Connor. He left his job with the US Postal Service to serve in Desert Storm. And then he returned to the same job in the same small town on the east coast. If he wrote any other scripts they didn't leave an impression on the internet. He died of lung cancer. And this death I believe. His daughter is a photographer. She took hundreds of black and white photos of his final moments. They are all online. I don't know why anyone would do that but the still and sad face matches his picture in the VA database.

There's still something about the horrifically laughable demon blood plot I'm not getting.

But I have to leave it for now.

My big takeaway from today is this: faceless veteran, Eagle Guard mercenaries.

I call Rose on the dusk ride home. "I spent the day looking for an original idea in Hollywood."

"How'd that go?"

"The creative process is complicated and challenging. Talk to me about drones."

"The FBI are telling everyone involved in this cluster fuck that there's no credible risk of drone takeovers. And the military needs their flying robot kill machines to hunt for wherever Ripper and his soldiers might be hiding. So the drones are staying in the air."

"Their IT guys don't know the quality of hackers General Ripper has working for him. The only thing he has clearly communicated to the country is his disdain for how video games are changing war. Drones are the ultimate expression of that."

"I believe you Chalk. And when you get me the evidence—"

"I'm working on it. I learned a lot today but nothing that is a straight line to Ripper. I'm going to work the mercenary angle tomorrow. I need sleep. I need to keep my brain fresh. There are connections I'm missing."

"Talk tomorrow. You call when you need to."

I don't put the news on even for a second when I get home. I watch *Dr. Strangelove* again. Once without my meds. And the second time after I've taken my pills, as the chemicals are bringing me down and I'm ready to leave this world for a few hours of swimming in the dream ocean.

Chapter Forty

EAGLES

Mercenaries are big business.

Blackwater is still the largest. They keep changing their name but they can't escape their legacy. They have billed the US government billions. Most politicians consider it money well spent. Blackwater's missions don't have to suffer the scrutiny of any real government oversight. Their deaths don't show up in the loss column on the news. And they are not bound by the silly rules of war made up by international whiners like the UN. Their founder famously said he wanted to become the Military FedEx and now their most lucrative business is a Worldwide Personal Protective Service contract to ensure the delivery and return of US dignitaries in conflict zones.

I know a little about the Danish SIRAS Group. I've heard of the French Secopex and the Canadian Tundra. I've read about South Korea's Bullet-K and the UK's Aeghis, Gurkha Security and Tecnodef. But Eagle Guard is new to me.

They do not present themselves to the world. They seem to have no corporate network to be scouted and assaulted, no phone number to be socially engineered, no servers and databases to be raided—all of which can't be true except that it is.

But the mercenary group isn't suppressing discussion of their existence online. Soldiers tired of saluting the flag and ready to earn some money, untrained psychos deluded into thinking they've found a gig where they will be paid to kill, potential investors, civilians that have interacted with the corporation on a business level, the chosen who have fought for them, family members of those mercenaries and angry hippies have all posted thoughts about Eagle Guard in different online forums.

I send hundreds of emails to the usernames I scrape. I identify myself as a journalist willing to pay for short phone interviews. A young mother whose husband is deployed with the Army in the middle east writes back to me with questions. I email her money and she replies with a phone number.

I call and talk her through how to deposit the e-transfer. This takes twenty minutes of patience and she still doesn't entirely trust it when we're done. I ask her if there is an ATM on the base? She says there is. I tell her to call me back after she's gone to it and taken out the money.

Ten minutes later she calls me back. She must have run to the mess hall and back. She's desperately short of breath. Did she take the baby I can hear with her? Did she get a neighbor wife to watch the child for a moment? Did she just leave it at home?

Even after this she's nervous that she's doing something wrong—not that Eagle Guard is going to come after her but just that this situation is too good to be true. She's so desperate for money and I've just made money materialize. She feels that there has to be a catch.

But she does talk. Her husband is in the Rangers. Eagle Guard approached him at the end of his last tour. The interview went well but her husband decided to sign up for another hitch with Uncle Sam.

I ask her if she knows what kind of work Eagle Guard would have wanted him for?

"When he was going to take the job and the big pay increase we really needed he said it was mostly guard work. When he decided he was going to stay with the army and the nothing they pay us then all of a sudden Eagle Guard was super dangerous. We had this big argument right before he left again. He said he'd lied. He said Eagle Guard actually wanted him to go around the world starting fights."

By the end of our conversation this abandoned wife has gone from nervous to greedy. Now she wants to know if there's any other information I would be willing to pay for? She tells me she's heard a lot living on the base. That's how easy it would be for me to get all of her secrets. I feel sad for her. I can hear the close walls of her small little house, the baby screaming, no money ever and only other military wives to talk to. But I can't do anything for her except say thanks.

Next I start calling journalists that write about mercenaries. Samson Aldo has had pieces in *The New Republic*, *The Atlantic* and *Vanity Fair*. He's working on a book. I won't be able to buy information off of him. But I might be able to barter.

We connect. Samson tells me that Eagle Guard are the first Private Security Company to create Combat Profile Reports. They covertly send teams to areas of potential conflict—Iran, Egypt, Syria, North Korea—and attack carefully selected targets. These could be barracks, airports, fuel depots, border defenses. While the attack is happening a second unit records everything that is happening. How quickly does the enemy respond? How well trained are they? What signals make it out? How do they utilize their technology?

Bold almost beyond belief.

But if they use non-US weapons, non-US vehicles for insertion and extraction . . . no uniforms, no flags . . . no contract even with the US government. If they do it all on supposed speculation . . .

My immediate thought is that they risk starting a war. But they don't. Because war is never declared anymore. Warlords, criminal enterprises, paramilitary police forces—they start firefights in conflict zones all the time. They're just not recording the battles. They're just not treating it like a . . . game.

"You've had contacts within Eagle Guard. I'm looking for a man who served with them."

"I can't reveal my sources."

I laugh at this.

"You think journalistic ethics are funny?"

"I do yes. I mean they're just so darn cute."

"Goodnight Mr. Chaucer."

"It's Chalk. Shut up. Listen. I am chasing down the madman behind the pharmaceutical robberies and the mailings of counterfeit currency to veterans and the Xbox worm with the snuff reel and a coming domestic terrorist drone attack. I have broken enough laws in my chase to be locked up for centuries. You're going to give me names. Or I can use this phone number to track down your identity and go after your computers and then come after you. It's not a question of if. Just a question of how long it will take me. My guess is just long enough for me to be good and fucking pissed when I get to you."

"I'm recording this."

"That's great because you can play it back later and know you made the right choice."

"I could go to the police."

"That's not going to help you. But if you help me."

"Will you . . ." His throat is dry. "Will you give me the story? If you . . ."

"If I'm still alive. Yes. I'll give you the story as long as my name is kept out of it."

"So now you want the protection of the ethics you laugh at?"

"I wouldn't call it ethics. I'd call it a deal."

"Kian Knowles."

"He's your main source?"

"No. He's the Eagle Guard mercenary all my sources talk about. I've never been able to find out who he is or how to contact him. He supposedly lives in the Mojave desert. Everyone who did any time with Eagle Guard talks about Kian. My sources won't give you any more than you can get from reading my articles. You want to talk to Kian. But. You're going to think I'm crazy."

"What?"

"He's . . . he's listed as dead. But I don't think he is."

"I don't think you're crazy Samson. Coming back from the dead is really hip right now."

"You're mocking me."

"No. I'm truly encouraged." I get the exact spelling of the name. "Last question for now. Did anyone describe Kian as . . . faceless?"

"What do you mean by that?"

"That he'd suffered facial injuries in combat. Had his face blown off. And then rebuilt. Replaced."

"No."

"Did you hear that about any Eagle Guard mercenary?"

"No."

"Okay. Thanks for making me feel stupid." I hang up.

I run the name through the VA database. Kian is indeed listed there as dead. And in the big public databases. But I'm getting a good feel for this. Even before I saw the photos of Alfred Connor dying he felt deceased. Evan and Floyd and now Kian just don't feel dead in the data. They just feel suspended.

The cemetery Kian is supposedly buried in has a website that can be searched by name. The site has a professional photo of the grave, the bracketing information of birth and death, and what plot to look in if I want to come and visit.

The inscription on Kian's grave is: Still Watching You All.

That seems intriguing enough to buy flowers.

I put on a Rolling Stone's shirt with the *Goat's Head Soup* in yellow.

Chapter Forty-One

GRAVE

I pull into the Calvary Cemetery gates and find the parking. The cemetery dates back to 1896 but it's the same as all the rest: peaceful rolling greens, quiet, and all the thoughts about the end that waits for you.

I walk on the paths and follow the signs to the lot that lists Kian's name on the website. There is a plastic covered pedestal that directs me to the exact row. I shuffle to the grave. And there is the tombstone exactly the same as it is presented in the online picture.

Just a regular grave.

Until I see it: a pinhole camera recessed in the stone, a small dark glass eye in the "o" of the inscription. I drop to my knees and claw at it with my pen knife. The eye comes out a few inches and I can see the wire behind it.

I hug the stone rectangle like a surviving lover and rock it with my body. A fraction of movement is enough for me to sense that the inside of the tombstone is hollow. I stand up and look around, the world spinning faster than I can turn or think.

I swallow and stumble back to the 911. I pop the frunk and start going through my bags of tools. I'd need a sledgehammer to bring down a real tombstone. But for this one a crowbar should do it. I carry it back tucked into my jacket like a criminal.

There's a family visiting a grave in the same lot now. They will see this.

I swing the crowbar downward. The black metal bounces back off of the surface. A second swing gets the same result but there is progress. I swing again and again. I stand straight. I push the tombstone back with my heel. It leans back but doesn't go over. I get on my knees and put my shoulder into it. It goes over slowly and then all at once. I go around and wrench the bottom out of the dirt. There are lights flashing inside. There are two components that can be pulled out. I yank them both. One is a high capacity battery. The other houses a flash storage device and a Bluetooth transmitter.

No cell phone. So my image was not immediately transmitted.

Kian likely works these like I work my ghost transmitters—he comes by to get the latest pictures. He could do that weekly or monthly. When he comes this time he's going to see his final resting place desecrated.

Shaking dirt off and sweating I carry all the electronics back to the Porsche.

The family that saw me are shocked and outraged. I look past them and see a woman who has been tending graves. She's standing watching me. She's wearing a golf shirt branded with the cemetery's logo and font. She's not sure what to do with this situation.

Maybe I can help her. I close the distance between us.

"Are you on drugs?" she asks me.

"Yes," I answer honestly. "And they work quite well for me. Most of the time."

"You destroyed a grave."

"Well I've got you on a technicality there. A grave has to have a dead person buried in it. And he's not dead."

"You've terrified that family."

"That wasn't my intention. And I feel bad about it. Not bad enough to go over there and apologize. But still vaguely shitty. . . . Can you tell you me who visits that grave?"

"The one you just ruined?"

"That would be the one yes."

"Men in uniform visit that grave."

"Veterans?"

"I think so."

"Have you ever seen these men looking closely at the inscription? Maybe talking to it? Pleading?"

"It's called praying."

"Alright."

"It's one grave of thousands. My job takes me all over the cemetery."

"So you would remember if you saw something peculiar or strange."

"I saw this. I don't know how long ago. A middle aged man in uniform sat cross-legged before the tombstone. He'd brought a bag full of Halloween masks: monsters and celebrities. He was putting the masks on one after the other and then peeking out from behind them and laughing."

"Strange prayer."

"Yes."

"If that family bitches to head office about their emotional trauma you should give them a discount on their next burial."

"Thanks for the input. I think I'm going to call the police now."

I make it home and plug the graveyard flash storage in. It's a visual registry of veterans who came to pay their respects to Kian Knowles in the last month. The veteran playing peek-a-boo isn't here. I capture faces from the continuous shots that were triggered by a motion sensor I didn't see. I run these forlorn guises through the VA database's facial recognition tool.

Carmine Toscano interests me right away. He came to see Knowles' grave several times.

Carmine was a drone weapons expert.

Chapter Forty-Two

PTSD

The VA database shows that Carmine was part of a research study administered out of the West Los Angeles VA Medical Center. Veterans suffering from Post-Traumatic Stress Disorder were given pure MDMA in conjunction with active psychotherapy. The findings of this study were published. The conclusion is the standard scientific one: we were right and if someone gives us more money we will consider saving society with our big brains. The researchers all have websites, Linked-in accounts, and public email addresses at the universities they are affiliated with. The most junior member of the research team, a PhD candidate at UCLA, believes I'm an HR scout from Pfizer and sends me files that include the raw study data and contact information for all of the participants.

PTSD is a dark odyssey. There are the sweats and terrors: flashbacks to the screams and explosions. There are the constant thoughts about how this calm facade of civilization will be shattered any second now. There's the electrical overload in the brain of being always on, always ready. There's the anger at those that don't see the dangers. I understand how MDMA helps with this. Half an hour after ingestion a user feels happy, confident, at peace, and emotionally extroverted.

I did it once. I felt warmly in love with the entire world. I shudder to remember.

All the addresses and numbers I have for Carmine are old and wrong. I phone his fellow study participants with different lies until a corporal who talks slowly tells me he sees Carmine in MacArthur park. He says Carmine lives there sometimes.

The homeless in MacArthur Park are less desperate than those on Skid Row. They stake out little camps on the grass. Because so many of them are veterans there is a relaxed military order to the divisions of sleeping bags, tents, shopping carts, plastic wrapped possessions and damp clothes flowering in the different degrees of stink.

Standing by the statue of General Harrison Gray Otis I ask passers-by if they're selling X. It's a stupid way to buy drugs. But I know someone will pass on the news of my presence to a dealer long before anyone thinks of tipping off a cop.

Within the hour a kid comes up to me. "How much X you want man?"

I show him two bills curled around my index finger. "I need the good stuff. Pure Molly."

"My shit is pharmaceutical grade."

"And how do you know that?"

"I know because I know."

"Have you ever had a customer who got the pharmaceutical grade stuff come back to you and say your shit compared?"

"You a cop or a fag dude?"

"Why are those mutually exclusive categories?"

"I'm outta here."

"You want the money?" I extend it. "Money for information. Here."

He takes it. He hangs around.

"I'm looking for a veteran by the name of Carmine Toscana."

"I don't know names. What business you think I'm in?"

I show him the VA profile picture on my iPhone.

"Yeah. He buys from me. When he's here."

"Is he here now?"

"No they picked him up. Took him to his nice rubber room."

"When?"

"Who knows? He's in and out that guy."

"They are the cops?"

"You know anyone else who chauffeurs to the crazy house? . . . We done?"

"Yeah. Okay. Fuck off now kid."

Sounds like I need to talk to a man about a 5150.

CHAPTER FORTY-THREE

5150

Section 5150 of the California Welfare and Institutions Code empowers police officers and paramedics to involuntarily confine an individual that appears to have a dangerous mental disorder. An MH 302 allows for a 72 Hour Detention of that person for Evaluation and Treatment. It's a simple form. There are a few basic definitions and instructions. There are slots for badge and ID numbers, addresses, names, signatures. There are check boxes to pick the established reasons. It can be filled out in under five minutes. It's supposed to be shown and explained to the person being detained. Which is a sick joke. Then the christened crazy is taken to a mental health facility to be observed for three complete days.

That is time enough for street drugs to wear off and hospital meds to kick in.

After the 72 hours in the zoo a psychiatrist can either rescind the 5150 and allow the exhausted individual to walk. Or sell the patient on voluntary psychiatric admission. Because they're in such a great state to be making decisions.

If the psychiatrist can't sell voluntary admission, he or she can invoke a 5250 which specifies another 14 days of observation. 5250s require more than a few quick signatures. A full Certification Review Hearing is specified within the first four days. The detainee can also request to see a judge. But it's so easy to say a mental health patient wasn't clear, didn't say that, isn't remembering it correctly. Doctors can't be reached, the review board takes time to co-ordinate, paperwork is misrouted, lost, needs to be redone. And orderlies can be bribed to administer the wrong drugs, to incite altercations, to give bad information to the psychiatrists, even to smear feces on the walls and stage attempted suicides.

People are buried in LA's psych industry all the time.

Carmine likes burying himself.

Finding the freshest 5150 for the veteran, Rose informs me that Carmine is currently a resident at the Gateways Hospital and Mental Health Center. It's in Echo Park. I eat quickly and then drive there.

The day room is large and bright. The windows are covered with wire grates but there are no curtains and the sun comes through strong. Along the walls are couches and bookcases. In the center of the space are tables and chairs. There are about a dozen patients in the room. There is a thin man in worn children's pajamas moving about and mumbling. Three women are standing talking as if they just happened to meet here on their way somewhere else and yes they have time to talk for a little. An old man is on a couch reading in French and dying in Russian. The man I've come to see is at a table doing a puzzle. The box says there are 500 pieces but it looks like he only has about a 100.

That pisses me off. So much has gone wrong in this man's life and they can't even provide him with all the pieces to a puzzle? They can't give him a chance at putting something, however trivial, together? I stop for a moment before I approach him. I bring Amazon up on my iPhone, find a puzzle, order it gift wrapped and delivered to the hospital under his name.

I approach him. "Carmine?"

He looks at me and through me at once.

"I'm Chalk."

"I was General Ripper." He smirks at my reaction. "He is why you're here."

"You were Ripper?"

"Well really he was me."

"He used your identity."

"He took good care of it. I didn't mind."

"When did you fight with him?"

"Many thousands of pills ago for me. Many faces ago for him."

"You were a weapons expert."

"I still am. The drugs haven't been able to wash that away. . . . Ripper consulted me about the attack. I've told the police and the shrinks and the judges. But it's just further evidence that I'm crazy, isn't it? . . . I think he has maybe six drones and a good assortment of armaments. All stolen from the middle east over the years he's been waiting. The military doesn't care. There are still tens of thousands over there and soon tens of thousands over here."

"Wait. Ripper has drones. . . . You're telling me Ripper has his own drones."

"Ready to fly."

"It's not going to be a hijack," I grasp.

"Kind of it is," Carmine says. "He's going to hijack the pilots. The pilots are going to think they're attacking targets in the middle east when really they're striking here in the US."

My mind accelerates through what this means. "The modified drone software is to pull off a switch. Same drones, same graphics . . . but it's domestic terrorism instead of colonial war. That's the hack. And the targets don't matter."

"The targets never matter."

"Ripper has to get the modified flight software onto the computers the drone pilots are using. Onto their screens. . . . " I reach the conclusion: "To do that they have to get onto an air force base."

Carmine plays with a puzzle piece.

"Will Kian lead me to General Ripper?"

"He might be able to. If there even is a General Ripper anymore. . . . Real identities, fake identities, new flesh masks. How would you know it was the real him if he didn't tell you? And why would you believe him if he did? What proof could he give you that would be enough? You're not going to find him sitting next to a button Chalk. Trying to stop the attack and finding General Ripper are two different jobs. Stick with the first. Forget the second."

"I'm going to do both."

"I've told you he has his own drones. I've told you he has the armaments. I've told you that he's going to get US pilots to pull the triggers. I know you believe me. Kian doesn't know more than that."

"But Kian is my best chance of getting to Ripper."

"Which still isn't much of a chance. Forget Ripper. Stop the attack."

"Kian lives in the desert. Do you know where?"

"No."

"Did Ripper ever use Kian's identity?"

"I'm sure I don't know."

"Why do you visit his gravesite?"

"For him to see me."

"Why?"

"I don't know. It's just a compulsion."

"I've got to go."

I get up to leave but Carmine grabs my arm. "Do you know what face Ripper had on when he came to consult me about the attack?"

" . . . no, how could I . . . "

"Sterling Hayden's face. The actor Sterling Hayden's face."

"How is that even possible?"

"He's had so many facelifts it's like his head has hinges. He goes to his black clinic in Germany, pays the money and they give him a new flesh mask as close to his specifications as possible. . . . Listen. You won't know it's him even if you talk to him. Just stop the attack."

"Thank you."

"You're not listening."

"I appreciate what you're—"

"Listen! General Ripper is a megalomaniac with a messiah complex. Don't try and find him. Just stop the attack."

"Input received."

I make it out of the dayroom and then out of the hospital. I sit in the 911 and breathe.

A buzz tells me I've got an email. It's from Amazon to say the puzzle has shipped.

I phone Rose while driving. "Ripper has his own drones. The software trick is to get US pilots to unknowingly attack America."

"What's your source on this Chalk?"

"I trust the information."

"Then tell me the source. Better yet give me the evidence so I can start shouting."

"I trust the information."

"Because it was hard to get?"

Rose knows only too well that this is the trap for investigators. But I know what I've heard is right. That's not stubbornness and it's not just gut. I trust it because it's the perfect statement: Graphics making warriors terrorists.

"Do you have any evidence?" Rose presses.

"I'm working on that."

Rose talks to someone off and then returns to me. "I've got some news for you. One of those three brothers you were investigating. Harlan. He turned up dead in a motel room in Bunker Hill yesterday. It was a suicide."

"Is the FBI there?"

"No, right now it's just the suicide of a kid. I can keep it like that for a little while."

"Harlan was a part of the second army."

"That's what *we* believe."

"What's the address?"

Chapter Forty-Four

CLEANER

There have been times when I can't remember how many sedatives I've taken and I'm drinking endlessly and I think I might have done it this time I might have ingested enough to end it all tonight. It's always a peaceful thought. As I feel myself slipping below the surface of consciousness, drifting under, surrendering to merciful oblivion that could be sleep but might be death, my thoughts are never angry. I silently forgive and hope for forgiveness. When I wake up alive, head pounding, mouth dry and stomach volatile, I'm never relieved to have survived . . . just surprised in a silly way.

I have a suicide box now. It's a large black metal rectangle that takes a simple key. In it are two bottles of Ambien and a bottle of Silent Sam: the easiest vodka to drink quickly. I don't sit with it. I don't open it and brood. I just know it's there, under the bed, ready if I need it. Knowing this makes me think about suicide less. Because I know I can do it whenever I need to. Which makes the assertion that I do not want to right now a positive one.

I know most of the reasons I would do it. If my son died. If I was facing jail. If I killed a kid driving drunk. If I was losing my mind and institutionalization was unavoidable. If I lost control of my body.

I wouldn't write a note.

I have never been with a woman I could explain this to.

I'll have to tell my son if he's inherited my head.

I wonder if Harlan had a head like mine.

I'm standing in the motel parking lot. The yellow tape is still up but the motel room is no longer really a crime scene. Whatever evidence there might have been to explain how the violent act happened has been bagged, numbered and removed. The search for hairs and fluids is over. The pictures have been taken. The surfaces have been sprayed. And the body has been removed.

Suicide. Simple, sad. Move on.

Now the room is being restored to functional use by a death cleaner. They also call them 'trauma cleaners' and 'CTS Decon' but death cleaner pretty much says it all. While the medical examiner makes the final determination of how the individual died, the death cleaner can learn about how the deceased lived those last hours.

Leaning against the 911 I see the assigned death cleaner come out to her van to get a clipboard. She's wearing a blue biohazard suit. She doesn't see me. I watch her go back into the splatter diorama. I don't know when she started on this scene but I know the stages of the job.

First she will remove the biohazards. Tissue, brains, and bone fragments scatter. Blood pools, especially under carpets. It will all have to go in that special vacuum to be later burned in a medical waste incinerator. She will have to assess decontamination. She will have to document her actions and their perceived results. She will recommend that furniture and carpets which can't be salvaged should be disposed of but she will not dispose of them herself. Last of all will come the scrubbing: of walls, of floors, of ceiling.

I wait for her to take a break. I only have to wait ten minutes. It's hot work. She takes off the mask, pulls back the head covering. Her forehead is sweaty. She lights a cigarette. She sees me and understands that I've been waiting for her.

"Hi. I'm Chalk."

"Pavlina."

"I knew the young man that killed himself."

"I'm sorry for your loss." It sounds like she might even mean it.

"I couldn't have stopped him," I say. "We weren't in touch. He disappeared on me."

"I'm not supposed to let anyone into the room while I'm cleaning it."

"I assumed as much. I won't ask you. Have you been doing this work long?"

"Three years."

"Do you like it?"

"There's a lot of classroom time. The actual work in the suit is tiring but it's not bad. It pays well. Yes I like it."

"Do you think about the people who died in the rooms you're cleaning?"

"Every second."

"I don't expect Harlan lived long in there."

"His name was Harlan?" She draws on her cigarette. "No. He didn't. Five days," she confides.

"What have you seen?"

She finishes her cigarette early. But then lights another and stays. "I don't think he entered the room planning to kill himself. I think the gun was originally for protection. He kept it in the bed with him. There are oil stains on the sheets. He sweated right through those sheets. He pulled and twisted at them. But they were never changed and the bed was never made."

"He had the privacy sign out so the maid would leave him alone."

"He had a notebook computer. There is a brick for the charger but not the cord part that plugs into the wall. The police must have taken it for evidence. But they left a small case of DVDs."

"Japanese wrestling?"

"Yes. I guess he watched them on the notebook. But not at the little desk."

"Because that would have put his back to the door."

"Yes," she says.

"Food was delivered," I reason. "And likely booze. He must have been drinking."

"You say that because you would have been drinking?"

"I guess," I admit.

"No. He was doing Ecstasy."

"Why do you think that?"

"There are water bottles everywhere. It's not a big room. He chewed through two baby pacifiers. I found them under the mattress."

"And you found pills," I venture.

She sparkles to admit. "I found a small mint case of E hidden in the vent."

"You did a much better job than the police."

"They don't like to hang around on obvious suicides."

"Ecstasy is not a good drug to do when you're alone and already paranoid."

"Did he have a problem with it?" she asks me.

"Some vets like Ecstasy. He's been hanging around vets."

"I'm done my second cigarette now. I should go back in."

"Two questions before you do. No three. Four." I smile.

She laughs a little. "Okay."

"The notebook computer is for sure not in there?"

"No. That's one."

"You saw the cord for the charger. What make was it?"

"It says Sony. That's two."

"Are you in a committed relationship?"

She wasn't expecting that. "No."

"Can I pick you up when you're done your shift?"

"That will be late."

"That's okay."

"Alright Chalk. Give me your number and I will call you."

I give her my number. She puts her suit back on and goes back into the motel room.

I walk down to the motel's main office calling Rose on the way. I ask him to check if a Sony notebook was taken as evidence from the crime scene. He puts me on hold to check and comes back with a definitive no.

I step up to the motel front desk. There's a greasy middle aged man with glasses.

"Who found the suicide?" I demand of him.

"The maid."

"Try again. The maids weren't cleaning the room."

"Who are you?"

"I'm the guy looking for a Sony notebook computer."

He swallows. "I found one. In the dumpster out back."

"That's a really shitty story. Did you wipe it down? When you stole it from near his corpse?"

"Look:"

"No. Fuck you. Get it. Now."

He comes back with the Sony notebook and the charger cord he took in his hurried theft.

I take it and say nothing more. Let him worry.

CHAPTER FORTY-FIVE

MESSENGER

On the way home I stop at a Best Buy and purchase a new Sony charger.

In my office, the lock screen reveals that the running OS is Whonix. Harlan didn't log off or shut the machine down before he killed himself. That means the operating system is in suspend. I dig through my drawer of USB jackers. I usually use these to defeat the laughable security on Windows machines. But I have one for Linux too. The stick has backtrack, steelboot, potofgold and coma installed on it.

I push it in.

Coma allows me to wake the OS from suspend without bringing it fully back to life. In this twilight state I can see recent activity in all of the system's buffers. I can't learn Harlan's password. But I am able to convince the system that his password has been entered. This in turn allows me to zero all passwords, expose the encrypted hard disk and change the bios to permit a direct boot from my jacker.

I use steelboot to start up and explore the system before I bring it back up normally.

Whonix is an operating system that runs two virtual machines at once. The first acts solely as a gateway to the Tor Project: an anonymous onion network that utilizes randomized relays and protective layers of encryption to be invisible to surveillance and traffic analysis. The second virtual machine is the workstation client that only ever connects to the gateway—essentially acting as an isolated private network of one machine. The OS is brilliant because it has to be: the stakes are torture and death for the dissidents who use it throughout the world.

I could never have intercepted Harlan's Whonix messaging with Alexander on the open internet. It would have been almost impossible even if I had one or the other under close watch. But the deceased wrestler left it in suspend and I had the right tools. And I can see his last exchange with his brother.

Alexander: *He wnts u to be a ppart of this.*

Harlan: *I can't do it. I'm srry. I'm sory. I'm sorry.*

Alexander: *People die as flashes of ligt on a screeen all over the world every day.*

Harlan: *I know yes I know. I listend to all of his sermons. But I can't DO IT! I've failed u and I've failed him. I'm sorry Let me go brother. Pleaz..*

And then Harlan shut the lid, put the notebook in suspend and blew his own head off.

Alexander doesn't know that Harlan is dead. The hacker will try to communicate with his brother again. I'll be ready to drop a few smilies, maybe ask how that terrorist attack we were planning together is going?

I start researching bases from which UAVs and drones are flown in California.

Pavlina calls me. I answer planning to say that I have to work after all. But I don't. She tells me where to pick her up and I drive there. She's showered and fresh even though it's 2AM. I bring her back to my condo.

I talk about my time in the FBI. She talks about when she was a literature student at UCLA. We bitch about exes. We order Chinese. We drink cold beer. We share our excitement about books and music and film. We kiss and have sex in the bedroom—desperate at first and then slow and wonderful the second time.

Rose texts me but has nothing new on his end.

Samson Aldo calls and leaves messages reminding me about my scoop promise. Jerk.

I think about Carmine and his puzzle and his advice. I think about Kian in the desert.

I check on the Whonix machine but not obsessively. No Alexander yet.

I need a down night, a few hours. I put *Dr. Strangelove* on while we lounge naked in bed.

We drink a little more and laugh at Peter Sellers' brilliance. Pavlina says to me: "General Ripper's actions are the only sane ones in the movie. He believes his sacrifice is saving the American way of life. Everyone else is just doing their insane jobs in an insane cold war."

I don't disagree with her.

I take my pills when she's asleep so she doesn't see.

Pavlina is gone when I open my eyes. I slept harder than she did. It was my intention to drive her home. But I guess she got a cab. She left a note in the kitchen saying she'd like to get together again.

Dr. Strangelove looped and looped while we dreamt and is still playing silently.

I shower and pull on a shirt with the Weezer logo-sketch of an Apple II computer.

I make coffee and carry it into my office.

Alexander is back on the Whonix instant messenger client.

Alexander: *Harlan?. . . Harlan? . . . You there?*

I start typing as Harlan. I consciously make typos.

Harlan: *I'm stil here. I dunno why.*

Alexander: *The General isnt mad at u. He'll take u bac. You can come bck.*

Harlan: *Is he sending Evan to kill me?*

Alexander: *No.*

Harlan: *I sleep with a gun Alex.*

Alexander: *R you still doing E? U know how u get when u cme down.*

Harlan: *R you still gambling?*

Alexander: *No. because my life has meaning now. Im a part of sometrhng important.*

Harlan: *If I'm going to come back . . .*

Alexander: *What?*

Alexander may have decided I'm not Harlan. Everything from here on could be misinformation. So there's no point in not taking the risk—no point in not asking for information. But I'll only get the one shot. Do I try to elicit information that will help me stop the attack? Or do I ask about Kian and try to get to Ripper?

I can hear Carmine's advice in my head. But fuck him: he's in an asylum.

I am not. Right at the moment.

Harlan: *If you tell me how I can get in contact with Kian then I might come back.*

Alexander: *What are yu going to ask Kian that The General can't answr?*

Harlan: *i want to ask Kian ABOUT The General.*

Alexander: *Kian had a chance to be a part of this. He made his choice. You herd that.*

Harlan: *That's WHY I want to tak to Kian. He's outside but inside. The General respects him but he dosnt control him.. And AND Idont want to talk to him remotely like we do fucking everythinng.*

I flinch even as I hit send. I've assumed too much.

But he comes back.

Alexander: *You know why The General has to communicate with us remotely.*

Harlan: *You get me in contct with Kian. And I will come back. Or just kill myself. And then the drama with me isdone.*

Alexander: *Hang on a sec.*

I'm buzzing. I watch the screen until my eyes hurt from not blinking.

Alexander: *Kian is not The General Harlan. Don't fuck your-self up wieth that idea.*

Harlan: *But Kian knws him beter than any of us. I havequestions to ask him.*

Alexander: *Alright. The General says you can see him. Here's the GPS:*

And there are the co-ordinates.

A trick to kill Harlan?

A trick to kill me?

I log off and hurry down to the 911. I fill the tank for the long drive.

I call Rose from the road. "Look into security breaches at air force bases in California. Attempted break-ins. Trespasses. Anything like that."

"That's a little broad."

"Good thing you're a smart guy."

"Strange to have you off the grid last night. What are you working on partner?"

"Chasing down someone. I can't tell you right now but I will. Trust me."

If I made the right choice.

CHAPTER FORTY-SIX

MOJAVE

Where there are Joshua trees in central and southeastern California there is the Mojave Desert. It reaches into Nevada, Utah and Arizona. It's California's geographic dreamscape. Storms bring powerful winds, terrifying thunder, rain and even snow. Beneath the hard surface are the bones of animals that can poke through the surface bright white.

The state road, a throbbing but pocked vein, takes me most of the way. But for the last stretch I have to turn my tires off the tarmac and onto the desert flat. The GPS is a little panicked without a road but it continues guiding me.

The ghost towns throughout the Mojave are almost all old mining settlements. The companies that erected these wooden skeletons had a hopeful expectation of the future. The survivalist tribes that make camp in the Mojave now all believe that an end is coming soon. The final possibilities include: big rocks hurtling from outer space, AIDS going airborne, volcano PMS, a global economic collapse that starts a nuclear war.

There's also the cult of climate doom. They first named their prophecy Global Warming and then changed it to Climate Change and I think are now just calling it Weather Bad. It's a fun delusion because whatever weather happens exactly supports what their priests have foretold.

I arrive at Kian's camp. There is an old streamline trailer covered in antennas and dishes. There is a diesel truck with extra capacity tanks in the bed. There is a closed military tent blowing wildly in the wind. There is a large metal trunk locked with chains. There is a BBQ with extra propane tanks.

I stop the 911, get my Glock and slide it into my coat. I get out. I clear my throat and call his name. No sound, no movement comes. There is just the blowing. I move closer to the edges of the settlement.

I call his name again. This time an answer comes from behind me. I turn.

Kian is pointing an AK-47 at me.

"You're not a young wrestler."

"Who told you he was coming? Alexander? The Great and Powerful Ripper himself?"

"If I shot you right now I could have your body and possessions dissolved within hours."

"What would you do with my 911?"

"Leave it somewhere out in the desert and walk back. I've done it before."

"Do you know Ripper's real name Kian?" I challenge him.

"He has no real name anymore. Just like he has no real face."

"Yes. I wouldn't know him if I found him. I've been told that. But you have a real name. Alexander knows that name. I guessed Harlan knew that name and I guessed right."

"Ripper wanted me to be a part of his show. I turned him down. More than once. I prefer my desert solitude. I don't know who Alexander or Harlan are."

"Why has Ripper mentioned you to them?"

"I couldn't tell you."

"Enough of this. My name is Chalk. Kill me or offer me a drink."

"Beers it is." Kian lowers his assault rifle. He points to an open lawn chair.

I sit. Kian goes into the streamline with the AK and comes out with two cold cans of beer. He gives one to me and gets a second lawn chair for himself. We sit almost side by side, as if we were watching dogs or children play in the dust.

"He has military drones," I say. "He's going to trick US pilots into pulling the trigger on US targets."

Kian spits and opens his can. "You figured this out yourself?"

"Did you know?" I ask. I open my can.

"No. But it sounds like his kind of crazy." Kian leans back and the cheap chair flexes under his weight. "He's always contacted me. Remotely. On a screen. Always with a different face. For years."

"Why you?"

"Because I fought with him in Eagle Guard."

"Lots of soldiers fought with him there and in the Gulf."

"Maybe he likes my sense of humor."

"He was sending the wrestler out here. To meet you. To talk to you."

"If you were pretending to be the wrestler then I believe that was your idea."

"Why would Ripper even entertain it though? Were you going to tell Harlan what a great guy he is? Or were you going to kill him and dissolve the problem?"

"I wasn't going to kill him."

"You were ready with an AK when I arrived."

"That's the welcome everyone gets out here mister."

"Sending the lost kid into the Mojave for a chat though Kian—it sounds to me like you're involved."

"And yet here we are talking all neighborly like. Drinking beer like buds."

"What would you have done if I was Harlan?"

"I don't know. I've never met any of them. I was just told he was coming."

"You're acting like Ripper's older brother. Like Uncle Kian."

"I've never met any of the kids," he insists.

I slow the rhythm of the back and forth. "Did any of the kids, the second army hopefuls, ever visit your grave?"

He fixes me with a stare. "You're the asshole that knocked over my tombstone."

"Why do that Kian? Why watch who is coming to your fake grave?"

"So I know who might be coming out here."

"Even though you're not a part of Ripper's video game revenge fantasy?"

"I've got my own past. I want to be left alone. I'm willing to kill to be left alone."

"You haven't killed me," I push.

"I still might. I'm not done finding out what you know."

Neither of us laughs at this.

Kian gets up and goes back into the trailer. He comes out with two more cold beers.

We sit in the heat, silent and unsure of each other.

"Do you know Carmine the weapons expert?"

"No."

"Did you know Floyd?"

"No."

"What about Evan?"

"No."

"I think you're lying."

Kian shrugs. "Think what you want. What happened to the wrestler?"

"He killed himself."

"That's sad," he says and looks down.

"How does Ripper know how to reach you remotely? What technology does he use?"

Kian drinks. "I think it's my turn to ask a few."

"Alright."

"Where did you learn to hunt?"

"The FBI."

"But you don't work for them anymore."

"I hunted serial killers and cult leaders."

"You think General Ripper is a cult leader?"

"Sure. But that label doesn't really help me."

"Tell me who you think General Ripper is."

"I know the psychology. I read it and I wrote it. I used it to help catch monsters and then explain them away with insights about child abuse, head injuries, chemical dependencies. But I know there is evil in this world. And I believe there is a Dark Pantheon in America. Serial killers that are never caught, never even known. Cult leaders who secretly access ancient rites to further modern madness. Technological shamans conjuring chaos. I am confident that General Ripper is a member of this Dark Pantheon. These dark figures know of each other and likely even communicate. It sounds like a myth in the dismissive way sociology uses that word. But it is mythic in the real and powerful sense that literature reveres it."

"General Ripper. Member of the League of Ultimate Evil. Wow. He will be honored."

"Scoff if you want. I've seen one of them," I snap. "Twice. A serial killer that will never be noticed by the Behavioral Analysis Unit. And who will never be fucking caught with profiles and silly psych games."

"I'll be right back to listen to that."

Kian goes into the trailer and gets our third beers. And I tell him about the Bacchus Killer. I'm astounded to hear myself doing this. But true to his word Kian listens. He asks smart questions. And he clearly believes me. It's cathartic.

We haven't become friends. But we've related on a strange and dangerous level.

When it feels to us both like the conversation is winding down, my host carries the last two empties back into the trailer.

I'm thinking about how I will ask to check out the computer used for the remote video connections with Ripper when Kian comes out of the streamline with the AK-47 and fires on me.

The first bullets impact short of where I'm sitting. They punch into the desert floor.

I roll out of my chair and to the ground.

I come up with my Glock ready but I don't see Kian.

Then I see the barrel of the assault rifle angled behind the back of the trailer. He steps out and fires. I feel the rush of air as he misses again but misses closer this time. I run in a crouch for the 911 shooting back toward the BBQ and the propane tanks as I do.

My fifth shot hits a tank. It's not a massive explosion but it buys me dear seconds. I am able to get into the 911, start it up and pull away, tires digging for traction in the dry. I see Kian in my rear view mirror but he's not firing after me.

On the drive back to LA, I question everything I did and said. How pathetic and lonely am I? He didn't torture me. He didn't even threaten me. He shared a few beers and listened. And I told him almost everything. Carmine warned me to forget finding Ripper and focus on stopping the attack. I didn't listen. Now my enemies know who I am.

And Evan will be coming for me.

I can't fight him.

I have to stop the attack and bring the FBI down on Ripper. And I have to do it fast.

"Where have you been?" Rose asks me when a call connects us.

"Out of range. Making a massive mistake."

"I'm too tired to pretend to be surprised at that."

"Do you have anything for me?"

"I have El Segund Air force Base for you."

"They've had perimeter break-ins?"

"Not that anyone knows."

"A suspected cyber-attack then?"

"They lost the military satellite network for an hour today."

"And?"

"Are you fucking kidding me? The military satellite network they use to fly drones."

"Right but how did it happen?"

"That's where you do your IT magic thing and figure it all out."

"Did you talk to a special agent? This is something tangible connecting to drones."

"The FBI have gone in an entirely different direction Chalk. I need evidence to turn them around."

"I should have got it today. I could have figured El Segund out myself. If we're even an hour late on this it's my fucking fault. I will get the evidence tomorrow."

"How fast are you driving? I can hear the—"

"I have to move to a motel until we end this."

"You want me to take some sick days and be your bodyguard?"

"No. Thanks. Just be ready when I need you."

"I always am."

The grand trick could be staged from any Combat Air Patrol base in the US but so much of Ripper's activity has been based in Southern California and El Segund sounds right—especially with this strange news about the military satellite network going down.

I need to survive long enough to find a pilot and get on the base.

I enter my condo Glock drawn. I grab my meds and clothes and Harlan's notebook and a few jumpers and an external hard drive and some external chargers and a slim case of PC tools and a camera. I put everything into a bag.

I exit the condo Glock drawn. I drive to a motel. I check in under a different name.

Just like Harlan.

Chapter Forty-Seven

FLIGHT

I wake in the motel after a few hours of tossing.

I pull on a Megadeth shirt of Rattlehead in a General's uniform with mirror shades.

I arrange all my electronics, turn everything on and focus my intellect on the task.

Predators and Reapers are the two main offensive UAVs used in the middle east. Combat Air Patrols consist of four Predators. The big launch sites are in Afghanistan, Pakistan and North Africa.

There are Predators and Reapers here in the US. They are owned by both the military and law enforcement agencies. They fly far fewer missions than their forwardly deployed siblings. They don't need dedicated launch sites. They can be launched from almost anywhere there is digital sky.

Predators carry Hellfire missiles. Reapers carry Hellfire missiles and laser guided bombs.

I don't know which drones Ripper has, where they will launch or how they will be armed.

But I think I know the pilots he has chosen for his unique false flag mission.

Crews at the 61st Air Force Support base in El Segund fly sorties all over the world.

A standard UAV flight crew has a pilot and a sensor operator. Because the endurance of the drones outlasts that of the humans flying it, flight crews often switch out on a schedule of eight hour shifts. The burnout rate is much higher than that for pilots engaged in the traditional folksy American way of delivering doom from above. UAV pilots kill on almost every shift and they kill in great numbers.

The pilots at El Segund don't live on the base. They come into work like they're headed for a normal corporate cubicle. They sit down in front of an array of flat panel screens that display present satellite images, choppy video, status metrics, chat windows. They have keyboards, mugs of coffee.

Finished their shift of remote killing these pilots go home to suburbia. To beer and football. To Xbox games where the controls are just a little simpler and the kills just a little quicker. And to their home computers which they use to reach out on Facebook and Instagram and YouTube.

To their unsecured home computers.

To their unsecured home computers slowed by spyware, bloated with adware.

Yes. That's how.

Illegal botnets are connected clusters of compromised computers that can be tasked with performing distributed crimes. The Russian syndicates have the biggest and best. Their botnets can be hired to run denial of service attacks, to execute scripted exploits, to scout good targets for ransomware or phishing, even to force browsing that will inflate ad numbers. The most popular service is still sending spam. For twenty dollars a Russian syndicate will allow anyone to spam a million addresses. On most spam scams a single bite makes that a profitable exchange.

I am buying botnet power for a brute force spyware attack to learn about UAV pilots at El Segund. The cost is ten thousand dollars to search a hundred thousand computers with IP addresses near the base and as many as three hundred thousand computers that communicate with those machines. The results are almost immediate upon payment. I am slammed with a digital tsunami of private information about the pilots and people who know and communicate with the pilots. I see address books, emails sent and received, drafted and deleted. I get credit card numbers, passwords, scanned documents that include driver's licenses, college transcripts, deeds, legal letters. I receive browsing history, purchase receipts, insurance documents, health questionnaires. There is the artwork of children, digitally converted photos of dead grandparents, recipes, shopping lists, homework.

From this mighty hurricane of data I select Major Erick Mueller.

It's one thirty in the afternoon. Major Mueller has a flight shift at 1400.

I drive to Major Mueller's house and block the end of his driveway with the 911.

"Would you mind moving your car?" Mueller is dressed in his uniform.

"Major Mueller. You've lived at this address for two years. Your best friend is a guy called Mike who lives in Vegas. He just left the air force and I think you're wondering if you want to make that transition as well. You were married for three years and have been divorced for two. No kids. Your ex blames you for that. Or did. She's moved on and gotten remarried and you want to find out when she gets pregnant but she hasn't yet. You have a younger girlfriend. Nancy. She's a legal aid here in town. You had a fight with her two days ago and you haven't spoken since. You like to drink Black Tower wine but you only ever buy two bottles at a time presumably because then you don't have a problem. You've gone up a pant size in the last four months. This is since you quit jogging. You're favorite porn videos are threesomes. Usually two women and one man but lately two men and one woman. You have no savings to speak of and a line of credit that you're not paying off. You spend a lot of time online on the Ford website customizing a fast Mustang that you can't afford."

"What the fuck do you want?"

"My name is Chalk. I'd like to drive you to work. And then come in as your guest. I believe the domestic terrorist group in the news has patched the software you use to fly UAVs. They're going to have you unknowingly attack an American target."

He goes to speak but there's nothing there. He tries again but just gets out a squeak: "Call the FBI."

"They won't listen to me until I have proof. Get me in the fly room and I'll get that proof."

"We just had techs in the other . . ."

"To upgrade the flight software. Am I right?"

"Yes. But that doesn't . . ."

"Get me in the fly room. I'll give the proof to the FBI. Hopefully in time."

"And until then we what we just keep flying missions?" he asks hysterically.

"You believe me. Don't you?"

"I . . . no."

"You saw the techs that came in recently." I bring up a picture of Jason on my iPhone. "Was he one of them?"

"I don't know. I don't remember. No. He wasn't."

I bring up a picture of Alexander. "How about him?"

"Yes. Jesus." Major Mueller staggers and steadies himself on his vehicle. "I . . . I've always feared . . . always . . . what if . . . what if what's on the monitors is not what is really over there . . ."

"Will you get me on the base and into the fly room?"

"Yes."

He's white on the drive to the base. We don't talk. At the perimeter check-point he leans over and is recognized by the MP working the gate. I'm explained and we're waved in with instructions to go and get a visitor's pass.

Mueller points where to park.

I grab my tools and follow him in. When he gives salutes, I just stand mute.

The fly room is clean and sterile but the focus on screens and arcade joysticks makes it feel like an expensive Chuckee Cheese for tweens. I expect to see pepperoni pizza and sugared drinks.

Mueller shows me to the rig he'll be flying when his sortie starts. It's not in use.

So far we have not been challenged even though I don't have a guest ID.

"Listen," I say to him. "I'm going to bring down this computer. You explain that somehow. I'll do the copying as fast as I can."

And that's how it mostly happens. Until a commanding officer shows up to inquire why drones have not yet launched a world away. Mueller melts down and starts shrieking about Ripper's threat.

It's enough of a workplace freak-out for them to stop drone flights for now.

I take my external drive back to the 911 and race off the base and to the motel. I need to pull apart the software to find what has been modified. This is not my best kind of work. But after several hours I think I've got it. I've rolled back through the versioning and have been able to extract the changes in the last patch.

The dissected code shows how the hijack was going to work. It will help the FBI locate where the armed drones are. And it should help them determine where the hackers are hiding. Because Alexander and Jason and the other kids were planning to record everything live—likely to release the coverage to the media.

I call Rose.

My East Hollywood destination is The 3 Clubs Cocktail Lounge. They do live bands, dance music, burlesque and sometimes comedy. They're doing comedy tonight. I park, go in and right to the back for the bar. It's been redone recently but it's still got that plush LA noir feel.

Rose is waiting for me. We order beer. I give him the external drive with the copy of the code and the evidence I've extracted from the cryptic dialect we humans use to talk to computers. I talk him through a passable explanation of how he could have got it.

Rose sighs. "They're going to know this came from you."

"They might. I don't care."

"I'm sorry it can't be you that presents it."

"I don't like the limelight anyway. You know that Rose."

"I know but."

"Just go. Forget it. Seriously. Fuck it. Just go and end this."

Rose pats me on the back and runs out. I pay for the beers and drive to the motel.

Microsoft regularly makes the decision to stop supporting a game on the Xbox Live Servers. The reasoning is predictable enough: MS wants the passionately dedicated players to buy and play the new version of that game. Every now and then these players will show their dedication by keeping their favorite game alive. If they don't turn their consoles off, don't lose their internet connection and don't lag out then their shared reality survives. The world is doomed but alive as long as they keep playing. It's unlike any human situation before and yet just like trying to hang onto childhood, faith, love.

I'm ready for this game to end. I'm happy to log off and be done with this case.

It's early but so what. I'm done. I take my meds.

No *Dr. Strangelove* tonight.

Just the sound of my thoughts in this cheap motel.

Ripper is crazy. But I've decided he's not wrong about war becoming a video game.

It's not just war over there. It's not just war with bombs and missiles.

Drones of all sizes will soon fill the dark digital sky over the US. There will be more and more law enforcement drones patrolling rural airspace watching for meth labs, hidden marijuana patches, cattle rustlers. The same machines will fly and flit in the city gathering intelligence. There will be a hovering congestion of corporate logoed drones: FedEx, Amazon, Apple, Garmin, Verizon, Google—all of which will of course share their information with the government.

You remember the first time you saw a domestic drone? Not yet? Well you will.

You remember the first time you saw a domestic drone crash? Not yet. Well you will.

These are not thoughts conducive to sleep.

I get up and go out and get beer and Jamesons and I drink until I'm done.

And I do put *Dr. Strangelove* on my Mac after all.

Chapter Forty-Eight

FATHER

The terrorist threat has been defeated when I wake the next day.

It all happened while I slept.

I put on the Soul Asylum *Grave Dancer's Union* logo shirt. I walk down the street to get coffee and an Egg McMuffin from McDonalds. I sit on the motel bed with the greasy wrapper and watch the TV news as my mind wakes and my body complains.

There's released video of three night raids.

The first raid took place against a new office building recently built in San Diego. It presented itself to the world as the development studio for Strangelove Games. This is where the first army were hiding with all of their armaments—in plain view among companies like Rockstar, Sony Online Entertainment, Zynga. The veterans fought back. Tracers streaked through the dark. Missiles shrieked. Explosions illuminated the progress of destruction until all the vets were dead and the building was desiccated.

ATF drones won the battle.

The second raid was an attack on a barn on a farm in Northern California where Ripper's stolen Reapers were armed with Hellfire missiles and fueled ready for their launch. The barn was undefended. But the FBI went in ready for tripwire bombs, biological weapons, radiation.

Small helicopter drones were used as scouts.

The third raid was an uncontested assault on a buried bunker in the Sequoia and King Canyon National Park. This is where the second army was operating: inside an underground tin cave with computers, freezers of frozen food, cases of pop, microwaves, cables running to satellite dishes and antennas at the very tops of the mighty trees above them. There were a dozen of them, all young men about the same age. They were arrested as FBI drones hovered with cameras.

The FBI Director is getting ready to hold a press conference.

Rose is already being mentioned specifically as the man who broke the case.

General Ripper is known as the architect but he hasn't been identified or captured.

I organize my stuff and drive home to my now safe condo. I go right to sleep again.

I wake in the afternoon and shuffle into the kitchen. I see what's in the fridge. I throw the leftover Chinese out and it makes me think of calling Pavlina. I get some bacon out, fry it up, and make myself a BLT with an unhealthy amount of mayonnaise.

That reporter is trying to get a hold of me. I will call him back but not now.

I turn the news on again. They're now admitting that General Ripper is a fugitive.

The FBI have begun to release the names of the killed veterans in the first army and the arrested young men in the second army. The media doesn't know what to do with the veterans yet: American Heroes Become Villains is a powerful headline but the story will have to be told carefully. In contrast the talking heads are finding it quite easy to attack the young men of the second army. Because they're young. Because apart from Jason and Harlan they're all hackers and everyone is scared of hackers.

CNN is interviewing the mother of an arrested young man identified as Riley. She's sobbing. Anderson Cooper is being nice to her now so he can set her up for the challenge in a minute.

Blubbering she says that Riley didn't ever have a father figure in his life.

Sure. Tell us something we don't know lady.

"I went to a sperm bank. Because I wanted a child so bad. I didn't understand how important a father was."

All my other senses shut down. I scrabble for the remote and roll back the CNN broadcast to hear the woman say it again. I play it once more but now I'm not actually listening. She went to a sperm bank. . . .

In my office I bring up the records I have for California Cryo Futures. I scrape the major news sites for the released names of the hackers in the second army and their families. And I reference public California birth and death records.

The mother of every young man in the second army was a customer of California Cryo Futures in the same year. It seems that General Ripper broke into Cryo Futures two decades ago and started himself a very big family.

He watched his kids grow up.

He tried to influence them all to become hackers.

When the time was right he contacted those boys that had become the young men he needed and he gave them challenges to prove their worth. He recruited Alexander that way. He took Harlan and Jason because I had brought them together and they were a team.

I am alive with possibility. I can still do this. I can still find Ripper.

I go through all of the California Cryo Futures pregnancies from that year. The total number is four hundred and fifty six. That's how many it took Ripper to get the dozen hackers he needed.

One record stands out as strange. There's no indication of a miscarriage and no record of a birth. The mother is listed in

California as dead. But she didn't die while pregnant. She died months after she would have given birth. More accurately: she was murdered months after she would have given birth.

She has a twin sister still alive. I grab my 911 keys.

Mar Vista is a large housing project in Del Rey. It's home to the Culver City gang, Santa Monica 13, the Venice Shoreline Crips. It's a place where a car moving without a booming stereo should be watched. The Housing Authority of the City of Los Angeles has mounted anti-graffiti programs but the tags always come back. The city has started anti-drug programs but the clockers and runners are out under both sun and moon. The city has launched anti-gang programs but the colors can't be missed.

I knock on the twin sister's door. An old man answers. I tell him I'd like to talk to Astrid.

She comes next.

"I'm here about your sister."

"Every three or four years you guys come around. Different guys but the same dumb damn questions."

"Detectives working cold cases," I say. "Trying to get their homicide percentages up."

"You're not a cop though."

"I'm a private investigator. I was hired by a man who donated to California Cryo Futures. Your sister used his sperm to get pregnant. My client wants to meet his child."

"My sister didn't give birth to that child. You wasted your time coming here."

"What happened?"

She steps out of the doorway. "I don't have to tell you what happened."

"I know that. I think you want to. Because you've told the cops before and they didn't really listen. They didn't hear what you were saying about your sister's killer."

Astrid starts us walking around the housing project. I sense that she does this often. We are never more than ten feet away from children creating games and revising the rules as they go, tweens bursting with energy that is becoming sexual even as their bodies bud, teenagers surly and stoned and suspicious.

"My sister was engaged to a rich man. They had an argument about having kids. She wanted them right away. He didn't. They broke up. She sold his ring and went to California Cryo Futures."

"Not the first time someone has gotten pregnant out of spite."

"Then as soon as she was pregnant the rich man wanted her back. He said he wasn't going to raise another man's baby. My sister had the abortion. He paid for everything."

"They didn't get married?"

"They got married. Then she got murdered."

"You think it was her husband?"

"I tell the detectives that every time they come to ask the same dumb damn questions. They say he's been fully investigated. But that's just it. Of course he has an alibi. He paid someone to do it."

"How did the hit happen?"

"My sister was in front of their massive new house planting flowers. A van pulled up and the door opened. A killer dressed all in black like military clothes fired an automatic weapon at her. He fired twenty rounds and not one missed. I've lived in this hood my entire life. I've seen and heard drivebys. Lord yes I have. Bullets go everywhere. Not with this guy. All of them were right on target. . . . My sister's asshole husband was married again in a year."

"The husband didn't hire a hitman," I say to her. "I'm going to tell you what happened. And you can believe me now or believe me later. But I don't have the time to try and convince you."

She stops walking.

"A soldier replaced the banked sperm at California Cryo Futures with his own genetic material. He wanted to raise a special army of young men loyal to him. When your sister had an abortion she killed one of his sons. He took revenge on her. The police would never have figured that out."

"You're working for this psycho?

"No that was a lie. I'm trying to find this psycho."

"I don't believe you."

"A lot of people don't. I have to go. I'm sorry."

This story of vengeance convinces me I'm on the right chase. It shows me how actively Ripper must have been watching the women carrying his children. And that in turn convinces me of how actively Ripper must have tried to influence the development of his sons.

If I'm going to get him that's how I'm going to get him.

His attempts at influence.

Chapter Forty-Nine

RIPPER

The seized social media presences of the young men in the second army are being picked over just as always happens with school shooters. People who knew them then and now, teachers, priests, coaches—they are all being interviewed. I have nine different news feeds open on various screens around me.

The young men themselves are locked away like seized alien weapons.

I have made three big discoveries in my hours at the keyboard.

The first is a company called American Veterans Home Security. They have a slogan: "We fought for your freedoms overseas. We will protect your home on American soil." Their logo is the silhouette of an armed soldier standing sentry in front of a suburban home. The company only hires veterans of the American Armed Forces.

Beyond this unique HR practice the packages AVHS sells are fairly standard.

The entry level system has contact alarms for doors and windows with motion detectors inside the house. A tripped alarm will trigger a call from the command center and the dispatch of a patrol car.

Their top level system installs interior cameras that can be remotely accessed by the home owner and the company. A tripped alarm in this setup initiates immediate voice connection with the command center.

AVHS was a real business run by the veterans in the General's first army when they weren't planning international diamond heists. All but one of the hackers in the second army and it seems like over a hundred of their half-siblings grew up in homes secured by AVHS's top level system.

Ripper watched his children through the cameras.

My second discovery is a charity called Veterans and the Digital Front. With very little pretense this charity sent free computers, free computer books, free computer DVDs and free computer peripherals to the many children the General was watching. This jump start of knowledge and tech didn't work with Harlan and Jason and hundreds of their half-siblings. But it did work with Alexander and the young hackers who almost pulled off the drone trick.

The third discovery is a hybrid of a business and a charity.

This isn't even debatable: *Teen Wolf* is the best teen movie ever made. Because lycanthropy is the perfect metaphor for the teen experience. Michael J. Fox is a normal kid in high school. The girl he wants is with another guy, he's not one of the cool kids and he's small. Then his body starts to change. He becomes The Wolf: strong, fast and hairy. His entire life changes. But he can't control it.

The Troubled Teen Industry provides solutions for parents scared of the monsters their angelic children have transformed into. These parents call the right number and shake the fallen tears from their ready credit cards. Their kids are extracted in the middle of the night and taken away.

The destinations are called boot camps, natural lockdown facilities, wilderness retreats. The setting is always bucolic. There's something about turning your life around that requires woods and water. The costs can run into the thousands per week but the food is plain and the rooms are small. The miracle cure is tough love. This brand of compassion is best administered through yells. It is best felt through shoves and pushes. It is best accepted through the physical weariness of work.

There aren't many standards regulating the Troubled Teen industry. The word "expert" is used on websites shamelessly. And the list of wild werewolf sicknesses that can be cured ranges from Severe Entitlement Issues to Heterosexual Aversion to Autism to Atheism.

The Christian Military Camp for Troubled Teens was run by the veterans of Ripper's first army when they weren't stealing hellfire missiles for drones hidden on a farm. More than half of the sons that enlisted with the second army and dozens of their half-siblings that did not become hackers spent time with the CMCTT.

I have so many companies, so many records, so much data.

The name that will lead me to Ripper is somewhere in the midst of all this.

Another botnet attack won't do it this time.

But Non-Obvious Relationship Awareness software   might.

The video surveillance technology in Vegas Casinos is even more amazing than you think it is. Thousands of cameras and thousands of terabytes of storage index everyone and everything everyone does while worshipping in the grand desert cathedrals of money and chance. Big wins are reviewed frame by frame from all angles.

Because every big win is suspicious. Those prayers aren't supposed to work.

Card counters are the glamor cheaters. Brains that can do the counting are rare but it is even rarer for them to be anatomically accompanied by the proper sized balls. The house is more likely to be hit by card players working together at a blackjack table: duos that can expertly palm cards under the nose of a busy dealer.

Yet still and always the best way to win is to have a man or woman on the inside.

To combat this the Casinos have invested millions in Non-Obvious Relationship Awareness software for more than a decade now. Did a newly hired dealer go to the same high school as a regular gambler who has started to win? Does a dealer who just moved now live in the same apartment complex as a gambler under scrutiny? Did a long tenured casino employee just open a new account at the same bank a flagged card counter manages? Fascinating connections are found and investigated to pre-emptively defend against cheating.

Starbucks Socialists will no doubt ask how this is legal?

To which the only response is two letters: "H" and "A."

It doesn't matter how you arrange them. Or how often.

The most advanced Non-Obvious Relationship Awareness software currently available is called Janus. I get a pirated copy from Bobba's Wake, install it, set it up, fuck it up, uninstall it, install it again. I feed it everything I have: the names from the news and all that I can scrape on them, California Cryo Futures, the VA data, all the other information I've raided and stolen. Janus connects itself to public databases. I manually enter fields on the information I've gathered from humans.

When I'm done I'm able to see connections between all the people I've investigated.

I drag lines and work through the list of the identities I know Ripper used.

The strongest name connection comes back as: Kian Knowles.

Again and again: Kian Knowles.

The desert survivalist waiting for the end of the world. The only man I spoke to willing to open up about the General. Because he was the General. I sat down and drank beer with the madman and did not know it was him.

His first army was in San Diego. His second army was in the woods. His drones were in a barn on a farm. He controlled everything remotely from that streamline trailer. It's not even that strange really. Many cult leaders only appear to their followers on occasion to maintain their mystique.

Kian is General Ripper.

Is there any chance he's still out there?

Chapter Fifty

BOOTLEG

Driving fast to the Mojave I'm alive and alert and thinking about Ted Kaczynski.

The Unabomber was a poor bomb maker. His first pipe bomb used wood on the ends and that's weak even for an anarcho-primitivist. When he did start to get the hang of the explosive craft, he still just used whatever parts he could find. Cuts and burns, shrapnel wounds, hearing loss—these were the majority of the injuries he caused. He didn't kill anywhere near as many as the Columbine shooters did in a single day. No it wasn't the Unabomber's acts of terrorism themselves that scared the country. It was his commitment to his terrorist campaign.

The Unabomber promised the authorities that he would stop bombing if his manifesto was printed. *The Washington Post* and the *NY Times* gave him their ink in September 1995. His rambling explanation for his actions quoted Eric Hoffer, the author of *The True Believer: Thoughts on The Nature of Mass Movements*. It's a book I read once disinterestedly when I was forced to for a class and then with intense interest years later when I was drunk. Hoffer rants that when people become convinced of the inescapable truth that their personal lives have been made worthless then their only hope is to sign away their individuality and become part of a radical group. And he points out that the pseudo-intellectual costumes of these groups—Nazi, Communist—can easily be exchanged for one another.

Three brothers who a Hyena thought were his sons wanted to be a part of a radical group.

They wanted to be Ripper's soldiers. And that's what they became.

They wanted him to be their father. And he was.

How easily he convinced them to kill for him.

What I'll call "pure" psychopaths are still rare—killers who demonstrate all or almost all of the characteristics associated with the disorder. But I believe more and more normal people in our society exhibit psychopathic traits.

We're supposed to be a more enlightened and tolerant society yet the only evidence to support this is the facade of perfect cosmetic beauty we project. Read the comment threads on YouTube and you will be exposed to vile racism and homophobia instantly. Play an online game for more than a minute and you will be threatened with rape and murder and worse. The barrage of sensationalist media, the loss of religion, and the suicide of the family have left so many of us with no empathy for others. Citizens who have some vestige of impulse control take street drugs to fix that problem and experience the release of temporary psychosis recreationally. How easy it becomes to cut that car off, steal that computer, rape that woman, kill that kike, fulfill the doom prophecy of a faceless remote master revealed as your father who preaches about how we have lost our way in war.

What did Jason and Harlan and Alexander care about war?

I come upon Kian's camp just as I left it. I roll to a stop.

I take the Glock, make sure I have an extra clip and step out into the wind. I call his name, this one name by which I know him. There is no answer. I take the safety off my weapon. I approach the trailer.

I yell my attention, open the door and jump back.

I cover the entrance and wait. Nothing comes and nothing happens.

Leading with my gun I enter the trailer.

Inside are guns, ammunition and army technology for field communication between units. And just in case there was any question Ripper is insane there are partially dried faces in lucite frames. Faces he wore before the one he had on when he spoke to me.

There is an Android phone with a hardware encryption dongle attached to it. It's connected to a charger. I pick it up. It's not locked. It is displaying a contact card for General Ripper. I touch the number and it dials.

Kian answers. "Chalk?"

"You got away."

"That was never in doubt."

"I stopped your attack. Was that ever in doubt?"

"It's almost as powerful for the country to know how close I came."

"Almost," I spit back.

"I enjoyed our chat before."

"I know about your children. How you tried to influence them into becoming hackers."

"I knew I would need them however I decided to attack. I was right."

"Why did you make Alexander and Jason and Harlan go after that samurai sword?"

"I gave all my aspirant hackers challenges."

"It wasn't much of a hacking challenge though was it?"

"Alexander was the only recruit bringing non-hackers with him. The three were a team. I knew Jason liked samurai movies. I knew the sword was in LA. I wanted it."

"Did you have time to take it with you? You left some of your faces."

"I enjoyed our chat before," he tries again.

"Yeah you said that."

"Your theory about the Dark Pantheon. That is what you called it?"

"Yes."

"You're somewhat right. We don't go bowling together or anything like that. But we are aware of each other's work. We do communicate."

"Who is we Ripper?"

"Who you said Chalk. The great serial killers that are never known or feared. The madmen that control what seems like chaos. The cult leaders that preach apocalypse. . . . That's close to the cadence with which you say it, is it not? I liked listening to how you talk. Your rhythms."

"Which do you see yourself as? A madman or cult leader?"

"Oh I'm a patriotic father."

"That's a laugh."

"I didn't have a cult. I had two families. My military and mercenary brothers. And my children raised to play a computer game. . . . I have to go in a minute."

"I'm not trying to trace the call."

"I know. But I'm a busy man. And you have guests coming."

"Have a new face yet?"

"Soon. Soon."

"Go for George Clooney this time."

"I'd like to give you a gift Chalk. Before I go. You are still in my trailer?"

"Yes."

"Do you see the stereo on the small kitchen table?"

I turn and see it. "Yes."

"There's a CD case on one of the speakers. Go and take it."

I holster my Glock, keep the phone to my ear and reach for the CD case. It's a cheap generic plastic square. It has been labeled by hand: Alice in Chains, Rocklahoma, May 25th 2013. I hold it.

"You've found it?"

"This is from the Bacchus Killer?"

"It was interesting to hear you describe him. To name him. He sends myself and others music occasionally. . . . It adds so much to the listening experience. When you know that one of the screams is real. That someone's life is ending."

"He's still doing this?"

"He never stopped. His boxed set would be massive. I just have the one in that trailer. And I gift it to you Chalk. Thanks for the talk. Good luck explaining your presence alone in General Ripper's command center in the desert."

He clicks off. I put the phone down.

I hear a roaring and a rumbling outside. Instinctively I hide the CD case within my jacket.

I step out of the trailer to the simultaneous arrival of three apache helicopters, three battle tanks, an armored personnel carrier loaded with soldiers, hovering drones and black SUVs flashing red and blue lights.

I show my hands and don't move.

I hear Paula's voice over a bullhorn. She tells me to lower myself to the ground and put my hands behind my back. I do this. I'm roughly cuffed and searched. My gun is taken. The CD is looked at but not questioned.

"What the fuck are you doing here?" This is everyone's greeting to me over the course of the next hours. I tell them everything I know about Kian. They're not grateful. They stopped the attacks but they haven't put it all together. And I really can't be bothered to persuade them.

Paula drives my 911 back to LA.

My condo is searched and my meds are brought to me. I sleep on a cot in an interrogation room. When they've run out of questions and have figured out a way to fuck me out of any accidental credit, I get my CD case back and I head home.

Rose has left messages. I will call him back. But not now.

The CD case is my first proof of the Bacchus Killer and the reality of the Dark Pantheon.

I don't own a CD player. So I put it in a drive and hit play in iTunes.

Alice in Chains starts into "Them Bones" at Rocklahoma.

THE END

Caracallison.com